Crazy In Love

Crazy In Love

Yoshe

www.urbanbooks.net

Urban Books, LLC
97 N18th Street
Wyandanch, NY 11798

Crazy In Love Copyright © 2010 Yoshe

ISBN 13: 978-1-60162-597-7
ISBN 10: 1-60162-597-9

First Mass Market Printing May 2014
First Trade Paperback Printing March 2010
Printed in the United States of America

10 9 8 7 6 5 4 3 2 1

This is a work of fiction. Any references or similarities to actual events, real people, living, or dead, or to real locales are intended to give the novel a sense of reality. Any similarity in other names, characters, places, and incidents is entirely coincidental.

Distributed by Kensington Publishing Corp.
Submit Wholesale Orders to:
Kensington Publishing Corp.
C/O Penguin Group (USA) Inc.
Attention: Order Processing
405 Murray Hill Parkway
East Rutherford, NJ 07073-2316
Phone: 1-800-526-0275
Fax: 1-800-227-9604

Dedication

This book is dedicated to my friend, Shomari Hill, and to my aunt, Barbara Thomas. May your souls find eternal peace.

Acknowledgments

First, and foremost, I would like to thank my father, God, for giving me life. I am humbled . . . . I would like to give thanks to:

My son, Pauly, keep making Mommy proud, my sister, Monica, for being my rock, my mother, Mary A. Thomas, for your support, my niece, Taya Dickinson and my nephew, Anthony Turner, Jr., my big baby brother, CO J. Dickinson, my Daddy, Jimmie Dickinson and stepmother, Ada, my stepsister, Dawana and my niece, Yanni, my Auntie Delois and Uncle Robert, my cousins, Curtis, Keith, Candice, Mark Anthony, cu-zo, who inspired me to do this and I thank you sooooo much, Uncle Clarence, my cousins, Keisha, CJ, Brandon, Kenya, A. Turner, my "Bruh-in law", Big Pauly, Mr. and Mrs. George Miller, Uncle Mike, Aunt Nay, cousins Nate and Mike, Captain J. Shipman, my BFFs, Brigitte and Raquel, my goddaughter, Bria, T. Majors, my sister for life, my BMF, Poo-kah, my homie, S. Wilmer, for makin' moves @ Ol' Boy for me, sister-in-law, Marilyn, and my niece, Johanna, T. Speights, who gave me the strength to hold my head during that rough time in my life, H. Ford, keep that white shirt clean, Ma, Shawn Hill, my first love, my partners, Lashina and Tannile, my Charlotte, NC amigos, Tasha Boyd, DeMarcus "Wink" Miller, Erick S. Gray aka Mr. Prolifick, K'Wan, Charlotte Young, Sistar Tea and the Arc Book Club, Brandon McCalla, Divine of Books in the Hood, A. Whyte, Aretha Temple, Nakea Murray, thanks to the Urban Books staff for all of their support, Carl Weber, Natalie Weber, Brenda Owen, Deshawn Taylor, Al-Saadiq Banks, J. Benjamin, Adrian "Ox" Mendez, Sexy, Donald Peebles, Shaifire, T. Harvey of Urban Written, Brook Lynn. My D.O.C. family: N. McFadden-Garlington, B. Salmon, C. Council, T, Washington, L. Black, R. Cunningham, T. Hope, M. Pollard, R. Howard, T. Traylor, K. Washington, O. Bunmi, B. Feaster, L. Hicks, Y. Green, L. Yearwood, B. Pope, W. Credle, V. Capers, L. Garrett, L. Douglas (MsDee), S. Buckhalter, L. Monroe, J. Clark, I. Irizarry, and a host of others that I had the pleasure of knowing . . . Thanks for your support.

The Pink Lip Gloss Vintage Boutique, Platinum Skills Hair Salon, The Bus Stop BarberShop, my Starrett City peeps, East New York, Georgia

Avenue, my old school crew since the late '80s, early '90s . . . Arif, Blunt, Corrin, Nigel, Tammy, Du, Chuck, DeeDee, Rocky, Powerful, Hoz, and the list goes on.

For those I did not mention on paper, it doesn't mean that you aren't in my heart . . . .

LOVE IS LOVE . . . YOSHE

Prologue

It was a cold, wintry Friday morning and it was also a visit day for the inmates at the Rikers Island correctional facility. Although the area was bustling with activity, the visit area was a place that was filled with joy and pain. The joy came from the visitors happy to see their incarcerated loved ones. The pain came at the end of the visit when it was time to leave.

The visit area was nothing more than a large, open area furnished with plastic chairs and small tables, used to separate the visitor and the inmates from having close contact with each other. Inmates shuffled into the visit area with grey jumpsuits and jail-issued slippers. Depending on who was visiting them, they seemed excited to see the person and what packages they had to bring. It was the survival of the fittest, and some inmates were like scavengers to a degree. No matter how well they were taken care of while behind those walls, they would still do whatever they had to do to get what they wanted, even if it meant breaking the rules.

Women, men, and children sat outside of the control room in a stuffy waiting area that consisted of plastic chairs neatly lined up next each other. After being registered, visitors were to put their belongings in a small locker that cost fifty cents that was returned upon the retrieval of their items. At the visit magnometer, the visitor was searched. A correction officer would put them through a procedural search without physically putting their hands on them. A strip search was only permissible if there was reason to believe someone had contraband on their person. The visitors would walk through the magnometer that was designed to beep if there was any metal on the person.

The visitor would have to take off their shoes, of course, and once the magnometer was cleared, they would run their hands through the waistband of their pants, open their mouth, and pull the pockets of their pants inside out. The only items that were allowed on a visit with an inmate were a locker key, a commissary slip, and the registration card that was time stamped by the visit officers at the desk on the visit floor.

Sometimes, pictures were allowed as well, but only with the permission of a supervisor. With babies, the CO would have to look inside of a baby's diaper. Many people have gotten desperate enough to put weapons, drugs, or other contraband inside of their babies' pampers, too. They were also allowed to bring in one bottle for the child; with most women allowing their children to cry at the top of their lungs for another if the visit surpassed the contents of the bottle. It was a sad sight to behold.

The correction officers who worked in the visit area were another story. They were there to provide a service and that was the care, the custody, and the control of the inmates who were waiting for their trial dates or to be sentenced. They didn't care one way or another about inmates, afraid to "humanize" themselves by showing any type of compassion to the criminals and their families. Rightfully so, they had to desensitize themselves; for fear that they would become the unfortunate prey of the inmate population. If they didn't, it could cost them their jobs, their freedom, and sometimes their lives.

On the other side of things, the correction officers had their own personal dramas. In the course of the correction officers doing their jobs, such as dealing with irate visitors and inmates, they had to deal with each other. Personality clashes, troubled relationships, and psychological issues were the icing on the cake of a highly stressed work environment. No correction officer was a stranger to harassment of any kind, and no man or woman was safe from it. Working in close confines with someone who is a nuisance sometimes puts a damper on one's job performance and personal life. Unfortunately, many officers did not realize that mixing business with pleasure was a no-no until it was too late.

Chapter 1

Correction Officer Sean Daniels scanned the visit area with the eye of a hawk. His job was to make sure that no smuggled goods of any kind were passed to an inmate from a visitor. He knew that he was unable to catch every time this was done, but as long as they knew better than to pass it in front of his face, then it was fine with him. Working in visits, he saw attractive female visitors everyday. He even, on occassion, goofed off with them in order to break the monotony of the tedious work he was paid handsomely to do. He also got offers from the women, who were attracted to his rugged good looks and, of course, his uniform.

He was single and available, with limitations, of course. He had to be careful, though, because he knew that he could have easily been swayed, which sometimes got him into trouble. He had caught himself checking out a few of the women who came to visit their inmate boyfriends. It was unauthorized for female visitors to wear revealing clothing but the women would dress in the skimpiest clothing they could get away with. Sean was a man first before he was a correction officer, and he loved the opposite sex. On the other hand, he didn't take his profession with a grain of salt, because, after all, his paycheck did pay the bills.

As Sean walked around the visit floor, talking to various people and making sure that everything was going okay, he looked up at the female CO who was banging on the glass that encased the visit control room. Sean smiled and walked over to the window. The CO smiled back.

"Hey, Cruz," he beamed. "You just got to work, didn't you?"

She sighed. "Yeah, Devin was usin' my car," replied Cruz, referring to her boyfriend of seven years. "I will be so glad when he gets his truck out of the shop."

Sean frowned. "What happened to it? I mean, damn, his truck has been in the shop for weeks now. He needs to go get it if using your car is makin' you late for work."

Cruz rolled her eyes. "I dunno, Daniels." She quickly changed the subject. "Well, I just wanted to let you know that I was here, just in case you were lookin' for me," she said with a flirtatious smile.

Sean looked Cruz up and down. It was no secret that they were attracted to each other. "Oh, yeah? Well, you better stop flirtin' with me, girl. You ain't ready for Sean Daniels!"

Sean secretly fantasized about getting Yadira Cruz into his bedroom. He chuckled to himself as he imagined her long, wavy hair lying across her mocha-colored 34Ds, while he had his face submerged in her garden of love. Sean stood by the window for another moment and watched Cruz's silhouette shuffle around the visit control room, even though it was dark inside. It was dark in the control room, thereby preventing the visitors and inmates from looking inside to see if someone was in there watching them. For the times that Sean may have his back turned and there were culprits who thought they were being slick, the control room staff would serve as a back up.

Yadira Cruz was the only daughter and the youngest of three children born to a Dominican father and an African-American mother. Sean thought that Yadira, or Yadi, as everyone called her, was drop-dead gorgeous. With her five feet five inch hourglass frame and her flawless cocoa complexion, she made heads turn, women and men. Her killer body and face had men wishing that her boyfriend, Devin, would drop off the face of the earth so that they could have a chance with her. Men never tried to pressure her, though; for fear that she would only push away. Therefore, they just settled for being a confidante or acquaintance, whatever it took to be near her.

There were many women jealous of Yadi, and upon meeting her, it wasn't hard to understand why. Yadi seemed modest about her looks, as if she was no threat to any woman, and with her overt kindness, she seemed like a great person to have around. Unfortunately, her warm and inviting outer personality was only a diversion from her underlying problems. Yadi was a woman whose insecurities had her on the verge of obsessive behavior and it was almost uncontrollable, targeting the men with whom she was romantically involved. She painted a rosy picture, but once men got to know her, the rose petals quickly withered away.

Yadi walked into the small room and placed her lunch into the refrigerator in the back. She hugged her partner and her best friend, Vanita Garrett. Vanita was a patient and understanding woman, who reluctantly stood by as she watched Yadi go through her difficulties with Devin. Understandably, Vanita wanted her friend to be happy but she concluded that Yadi had to want what was best for her.

"Look at how Sean looks at you, Yadi," Vanita announced, with a smirk on her face. "Looks like he wanna take a dip in the puddin', girlfriend!"

Yadi laughed. "Oh, please," she replied. "That man isn't thinkin' about me. Sean looks like he likes those spontaneous, wild women. He knows that I am the complete opposite, and of course, he knows I have a man."

Vanita rolled her eyes up in her head. She had grown weary of hearing about Yadi's no-good man. Devin was a correction officer with the Emergency Service Unit. They had one daughter, Jada, who was four years old. After witnessing the drama unfold between the two, Vanita told Yadi many times that she needed to move on from Devin. Of course, her suggestions were ignored. It was then Vanita figured out that Yadi was weak when it came to a man.

"Yadi, Sean likes you and he is fine as hell, too," Vanita insisted. They both watched Sean patrol the visit floor. "I mean, look at his sexy, caramel ass. I'm not one for the men with braids but he keeps them neat. They look good on him. And that body is built like steel and his back . . . mmm, what a back!" Vanita said, secretly fantasizing about having Sean in her own bed.

Yadi laughed. "Yes, he is some eye candy, I can't deny. But, Nita, I can't, with anyone that works for the Correction Department. My man is on the job, too . . . remember?"

Vanita waved her hand and returned to her duties. "Yadi, I'm not even gonna entertain that bullshit right there. You can do whatever you want. Personally, I am sick of you stressin' Devin's tired-ass. I don't think that he's worth the damn pussy he came out of. Then again, I don't have to deal with his sorry-ass. That is your problem, child," Vanita said, all while operating the gates on both sides of the control station.

Yadi didn't know whether to cuss her friend out or cry, but she knew Vanita was right. It did seem as if she was invisible to Devin. They barely talked anymore. This had been going on for quite some time. Devin would make her feel like she was walking on eggshells with him, so Yadi didn't know if she was coming or going most of the time.

Therefore, Yadi worked overtime to try to recapture Devin's interest and worked even harder to hold his attention. Whether it was good or bad attention, she didn't care, as long as she got some type of reaction from him. She couldn't deny that she was partly, if not fully, responsible for his change of behavior. She was afraid to question Devin's actions, for fear that she would have to take responsibility for some of the things she had done to him, and even worse, he would walk out on her for good. In addition, as bad as she thought he treated her, the reality that he was no longer in love with her would push her over the edge.

After some deep thought about the present state of her chaotic relationship, Yadi finally regained her senses. She gathered the visit registration cards that sat in a pile on top of the desk. She then walked out of the control room to call out the names of the inmates waiting for a visit.

Yadi carefully scanned the room of visitors. The waiting area was filled with mostly downtrodden women, whose main goal in life was to ride or die with their incarcerated boyfriends. A lot of the female visitors couldn't stand female officers, especially good-looking ones like Yadira. She ignored the women's dirty looks and got down to her business.

"People, please make sure that before you step onto that visit floor you have permissible items only! Now, listen up for the name of the inmate that you're visitin' today," Yadi began. The room was silent while everyone anticipated hearing their inmates' names being called.

"Fowler, Ramirez, Epstein, Shelton, and Wallace! Please line up over here and walk through the double gates! Put your right hand under the light and proceed to the visit desk where your card will be time stamped and you will be seated!"

The visitors walked through the metal sliding doors into a sallyport area. They put their hands under a light to display their stamped hands. Once that was done, a second gate opened. As the visitors filed through the open gate to the visit area, Yadi's voice was drowned out by the loudness of the people already on the visit floor.

Meanwhile, on the visit floor, Sean made sure everyone was seated in their proper places. Some of the things that he observed on a day-to-day basis, people would have to see to believe.

While walking around, Sean zeroed in on a couple in the corner of the large room. The female visitor had her hand in the grey jumper of the inmate that she was visiting. Sean could tell by the inmate's face that she was jerking him off. They thought no one was looking. He sighed as he tried to figure out why the women who came to visit degraded themselves for the incarcerated losers.

Sean walked over to their table. The female pulled her hand back when she saw him. The inmate sat there with a hard penis and a dumb look on his face.

Sean pointed at the young woman. "Get up, say your good-byes and get out," he said calmly.

They said good-bye to each other. The inmate began to say something, as he watched his girl-friend leave. "Yo, c'mon, Dee," he began. "Why you kicked my chick out?"

Sean frowned. "Man, get your ass off this floor! Say somethin' else and you will be in no contact visits for a month!" Sean replied.

The inmate walked off the floor and through the metal door that was opened for him. Sean shook his head and continued to patrol the floor.

"These chicks will do anything for love," Sean said to himself. Little did Sean know that he had sealed his own fate. He was going to find out just how far women will go for love in the weeks to come.

Chapter 2

Sean Daniels stood at the visit desk, conversing with a few of his coworkers. When he looked up, one visitor in particular instantly caught his attention. Sean normally kept his libido under control when he saw an attractive female visitor, but this one was different. He could tell that she wasn't the normal, run-of-the-mill, ghetto chickenhead who frequented Rikers Island's visit areas. The woman was dressed in what looked like an expensive business suit, which was tailored to fit every curve of her voluptuous body to a tee. Her hair was stylishly cut very short at the nape of her neck and her lips were shined up with lip gloss. Sean was mesmerized as he watched her sweep her extra-long bang out of her face to reveal the most beautiful eyes he had ever seen.

Wanting to be respectful, Sean didn't let his thoughts get out of control. The woman looked like a fish out of water, which was a surefire sign that she wasn't a regular. She stood there looking

like she was unsure of what to do next, making
Sean conclude that it was her first time there.
He wondered who she had come to visit. Sean
crossed his fingers, hoping that she wasn't there
to see a boyfriend, husband, or a baby daddy.

Sean continued to watch the woman while she
got her registration card time stamped. She cau-
tiously wavered over to the table that was marked
with a number sixteen on it in permanent magic
marker, and slowly lowered her rear end onto the
seat. Seemingly upset, she impatiently squirmed
in her seat while waiting for her inmate.

Sean wanted to talk to her but he knew that
wasn't going to happen. Talking to her was
something that couldn't be done without inmates and officers zeroing in on his every move.
Sean had no other choice but to keep his cool. He
couldn't let that woman leave the facility without
him getting to know her. Sean walked to the
other side of the visit area, positioning himself so
that he could keep her within his eyesight.

"Damn, I hope the dude she's comin' to visit is
her cousin, her brother, anybody but her man,"
he said to himself.

When the heavy metal door slid open, Sean
held his breath for a moment, as some inmates
filed to their respective tables with their visitors.
This was when he observed a lanky young man

about six feet tall walking over to the table where the woman was sitting. She instantly stood up to greet him with a smile and a warm hug.

The young man looked much younger than her, but these days, a person could never tell what floats someone's boat. Sean encountered some older professional women who were definitely into young thugs nowadays, thanks to the rapper 50 Cent dating Vivica Fox. They both sat in the chairs and began chatting with each other. Figuring that that was the time to make his move, Sean worked his way toward their table. He walked around for a brief moment, trying to play it off by talking to the other visitors. No one knew that he had an ulterior motive.

When Sean arrived at their table, he noticed that the young man, who was looking dead at him, had a scowl on his face. Sean ignored the nasty look and greeted him anyway.

"Hey, what's up, youngblood?" Sean stated. "Everything is a'ight over here, right?"

"Yeah, we're straight, old head, we're good over," the young man replied, looking at Sean, up and down, with a suspicious look on his face.

Sean looked at the woman, who smiled at him. "Oh, yes, officer, we're fine. I'm just here visiting my son. You have to excuse his attitude. He's a little overwhelmed by all of this," she added, giving the young man a dirty look. She looked at Sean's nametag. "Um, Officer Daniels."

Sean extended his hand to the mother and to the def-iant son, who looked at Sean up and down but ended up reluctantly giving him a pound anyway.

"Ma'am, not to worry, he's in good hands. I'll make sure I look out for him while he's here." Sean looked at the young man. "What housing area you in?"

The young man sucked his teeth. "I'm in Five North." Sean nodded his head.

"Oh, yeah, yeah, you good then. That's my old steady housin' area right there. I'll put the word out and tell the officers up there to hold you down."

The young man impatiently shifted in the chair. "Look, CO, you ain't gotta do for me! I don't fool with too many of these cats in here anyway, so trust me, I'm gonna be okay. Oh, and I damn sure don't fuck with the police!"

The woman had a sour look on her face. "Shut the hell up, Shamari!" she said loudly. "That's why your ass is in the trouble you're in now," She looked at Sean apologetically.

"Officer Daniels, I apologize for my son's ignorance. He always had a problem with au-thority and now this is where he ends up. He's only nineteen years old and he doesn't belong here because I didn't raise him like this. On the other hand, this is just a pit stop before death. I don't know what it's going to take for him to get it right!" Her eyes began to get watery.

Sean felt uncomfortable, dying to comfort the distressed mother, but he had to remain professional. He reassured the woman by telling her that everything was going to be okay. Sean glanced at the teen, wanting to whip his ass for making his mother cry and wondered if the boy's father was still around. It was then he figured that it was time to walk away, half hoping that he would have an opportunity to talk to the woman before she left the facility.

"Well, I'm sorry for interruptin', so I'm goin' to do what I get paid to do. Enjoy the rest of the visit," Sean stated before quickly walking off. After the brief interaction, he spent the next twenty minutes pretending to be busy. He still was unable to keep his eyes off the woman. Sean laughed to himself and figured that if anyone was going to pass some drugs, the time to do it would be while the mystery woman was there keeping his eyes and thoughts preoccupied. Sean sat in a seat alongside the desk, leering at her from afar. Suddenly, the inmate's mother got up from the seat and was about to walk out. Sean immediately walked over to the table to stop her.

"Um, ma'am, is there a problem here?" he asked, as he summoned her to sit back down.

"Yes, it is!" she replied angrily. "I'm leaving! I have to go to work this morning and my son obviously does not appreciate me coming up to this disgusting place to visit his ungrateful ass!"

Shamari sucked his teeth. "Ma, c'mon, cut it out, you—" he said.

She gave him a stern look and pointed a well manicured finger in his peach-fuzzed face.

"Shamari, I'm gonna tell you this and I'm not gonna tell you anymore. I gave you the best years of my life so that you wouldn't have to go through this. I was sixteen years old when I gave birth to you. I made all kinds of sacrifices trying to provide you with everything that you needed so that you would not be out in these streets trying to steal, cheat, and rob, and this is how you repay me? Then when I come up here to see you, you talk to me like I'm one of those hoochies you like to run around with. Remember I'm your fucking mother! When all the smoke clears, who do you come running to? Me! Not your friends, not your uncles, not your grandmother, nobody else but me! So don't ever disrespect me like that again!"

Shamari wore a smug expression on his face while some nearby visitors and inmates stared at him. Shamari sat there with his arms folded, never answering his mother. She almost walked out at first but Sean explained to her that the inmate had to leave the visit area before she did and that it was procedure. Shamari stomped out of the visit area like the spoiled brat he was and walked through the metal door with an attitude without so much as a good-bye to his flustered mother.

It took everything in Sean's power not to snatch Shamari out of his jail-issued jumpsuit for being insolent to the one woman who loved him so much. He was going to be handled, but right then, Sean was more concerned about the mother, who was very upset. When she finally was able to leave, Sean took the time to walk her to the visit registration area. He waited patiently while she removed her personal items from the locker and took a seat.

There were a few visitors in the area waiting for the visit bus. It was the bus that transported visitors back to the main registration building. It was there the visitors would catch the Q-101 bus to the parking lot on the other side of the Riker's bridge or Queens Plaza for the subway.

"Thank you, officer, for everything. I want to apologize again for my son's behavior," she said with a forced smile.

Sean could tell that she was still upset about her son's behavior. "Oh, it was no problem, sweetheart," Sean replied. "I'm still gonna look

out for him, though. Don't be too upset, Ma.
He was just tryin' to be hard. I been doin' this
for a while now and he's probably just scared to
death." He paused. "Oh, by the way, what's your
name, Miss?"

She giggled. "Oh, shoot, forgive me. All of this
newness and I forgot to introduce myself. I'm
Brandi Wallace. That's 'Miss' Brandi Wallace."
She made sure she stressed the fact that she
wasn't married.

"Brandi. What a beautiful name."

Brandi quickly placed a business card in his
hand with her information on it. She walked
briskly to the other side to line up for the bus. As
she walked away, she put an imaginary phone
to her ear and mouthed the words, "Call me" to
Sean and put on a megawatt smile. Sean stood in
that one spot and watched Brandi until she was
out of his sight.

Sean looked around for any nosey officers
who may have been watching him talk to Brandi.
Lucky for him, everyone seemed to be too busy
working to notice him. Sean knew that fraterniz-
ing with visitors who came to see inmates was
against the rules, but looking at Brandi's sexy
ass, he knew that his mind was made up. He
was about to break that rule and he didn't need
anyone to remind him of that.

Chapter 3

Approximately an hour later, Brandi was driving her champagne colored Lexus IS 300 on the FDR Drive and singing along to a Keyshia Cole CD. Even though she was excited about meeting Sean Daniels, she felt emptiness. Her only child was locked up in a jail cell on Rikers and there wasn't anything that she could do about it. She desperately missed Shamari but she also realized that it was time for him to grow up. Brandi knew that Shamari didn't have the type of street smarts that she had growing up. In those days, they were called survival skills. Fortunate enough to have never done any jail time, Brandi had been careful to hide her own criminal past from Shamari.

Brandi was the so-called "gangster bitch," the ride or die chick every thug needed and wanted in their lives. With the exception of drinking and drugging, there was nothing that Brandi had not done on a street level. Never knowing what it felt like to actually struggle, Shamari was sheltered.

He was protected from the mean streets by his mother; she knew that the streets would only swallow him up and spit him out.

When Shamari's father, Maleek, was murdered in 1993, Brandi decided that it was time to finally straighten up her act. She thanked God for her mother, who looked after five-year-old Shamari while Brandi went back to school and got her GED. She eventually went to college and succeeded in getting her master's degree in sociology, although now it seemed ironic that she chose the major when she couldn't even understand her own child's problems.

Brandi remembered the day she first met Maleek. It was 1986 and she was attending Boys and Girls High School at the time. A rebellious teenager at fifteen, Brandi stood in front of the school on Fulton Street, cutting last period, accompanied by her best friend, Sheba. They were standing around talking shit with a few other girls and chain-smoking Newport 100s when she noticed Maleek. He was leaning against his black Saab convertible, with Rakim's lyrics coming through his booming system. He was with three other guys, Dollar, Gator, and Peeto, who were all just as fly as him. They were sporting expensive truck jewelry and velour FILA sweat suits with the sneakers to match. Brandi used to see Maleek around the way all the time, but he was always on the move and Brandi never had a chance to catch him alone. This was probably her one opportunity to get with him and she was not going to miss it for the world.

As Brandi and Sheba stood nearby, they watched closely as Maleek talked to one of their female schoolmates. Brandi and Sheba were extremely popular with the student body at Boys and Girls. They were known for being unruly and disobedient to most of the administrative staff and whomever else they didn't like. They were boosting at the time, so sporting the latest gear was nothing for the duo, who thought that the world revolved around them. Brandi, being the tough girl that she was, finally grew impatient with Maleek talking to the girl and slowly approached the two.

"Um, excuse you!" the girl exclaimed, looking at Brandi as if she had lost her mind. "Don't you see me talkin' to him?"

Brandi turned around and faced the girl. "No, you was talkin' to him, bitch! Now step off!" she yelled.

When the female looked as if she wanted to jump, Brandi spit a single edge Gem Star razor out of her mouth and into her right hand. "Now, what was you about to do?" The girl froze in her tracks. "'Cause I'll carve my fuckin' name in your face, ho!" Brandi said, as she raised the hand with the razor over her head, waiting to attack.

The girl shook her head and backed away with a look of defeat on her face. Shamari's future dad seemed impressed with this display of aggression, a move that he would have never expected from a girl with such a pretty face and feminine appeal. Maleek and his boy, Dollar, began laughing hysterically.

"Yo, shorty, why did you do that shit to home-girl?" Maleek asked with a big grin on his face. He was kind of flattered by the violent gesture. "You ain't right!"

"I ain't gon' lie," added Dollar. "That was some sexy shit right there. We love a chick that could hold her own!" Gator and Peeto slapped each other five in agreement with what Dollar said.

Brandi smiled at Dollar then looked at Maleek with a smirk on her face. "Maybe I did it because I wanted you for myself, that's why. I always get what I want," Brandi replied. "Anyway, my name is Brandi, and yours?"

He held out his hand to shake hers. Maleek looked Brandi up and down, surprised by her straight forwardness. "My name is Maleek, shorty. You're real sexy, you know that?"

She blushed a little. "Yeah, you too, boo. You're the reason I walked my ass over here and spit my razor out on a bitch in the first place. I just hope that I'm not wastin' my time."

Maleek blushed. He liked Brandi's approach and he was more than happy to accommodate her. He could see that she had been around the block and back; Brandi was no amateur in the game. Brandi had no idea that Maleek was familiar with her and Sheba. He also knew that they stayed fresh to death. They rocked all kinds of colorful Ralph Lauren and Guess? gear, along with the multiple pairs of dooky earrings in their ears and four-finger name rings on their fingers.

"Nah, shorty," Maleek replied, licking his smooth lips. He paused for a moment and looked back at his friends, who nodded their heads in approval.

"You know what, Brandi? I like you. I'm gonna give you my house number and my beeper number, okay? Hit me on my hip later on tonight." After that day, they were like Bonnie and Clyde, inseperable and joined at the hip.

Having grown up as the only girl with three older brothers, Brandi held herself down like one of the guys in the streets. Alongside Maleek, while she was six months pregnant, she trans-

ported kilos of crack along 95 South. They hustled in cities like Washington, D.C. and Norfolk, Virginia. They were young and disobedient with no respect for the law, growing up in an era when drug crews policed their hoods.

Meanwhile, Brandi and Maleek stood by each other, through good and bad times, with Brandi sometimes bringing that heat to a motherfucker, if she had to. She had killed at least two or three men in those days, and lucky for her, the cases went cold and unsolved. Sad to say, no one was concerned about young black men being murdered during that time there were crack wars going on. But one day everything stopped for Brandi when Maleek was found dead on the side of Interstate 64 in Norfolk, Virginia in his Range Rover SUV.

Brandi was then left to raise her son—alone. Although she knew that he was in a better place, she missed Maleek. These days, she hadn't been with a decent man in years, focusing on her career and raising Shamari by herself, trying to keep him out of trouble. It was ironic because no one would have ever suspected that Brandi was a reformed bad girl, and she wanted it to stay that way.

While Brandi steered her car over the Queensboro Bridge toward Manhattan, she shed a few tears. She prided herself in coming a long way from being the 'hood chick she once was to becoming a director for the Administration of Children Services. With her professionalism and new attitude about life in general, Brandi had managed to redeem herself of all the negative connotations that came with the mere mention of her name. She knew that it was no use trying to beat herself up about the things she had done in the past. Brandi found herself wondering where she went wrong with Shamari and feeling like God was punishing him for all of the sins that she and his father committed.

Brandi shook her head, waking up from the recurring nightmare that haunted her almost every day of her life. The only thing she needed to do now was concentrate on trying to bring her son home, and getting him on the right track so he could also experience the joys and success that she had worked so hard to achieve.

Chapter 4

Back at the jail, Yadi and Vanita exited the control room, preparing to go home. Sean gathered his belongings and walked out too.

"Where are you goin', Mr. Daniels?" Yadi asked in her usual flirtatious manner. She looked up at him and was suddenly tempted to kiss his soft lips, but decided to keep her cool for now.

"To my second post. I have North on overtime," he said.

"Dag, Sean, you stay workin' overtime in that rat hole!" Yadi replied with her nose turned up. "I couldn't stand workin' up there with those ignorant asses! Ever since Captain Phillips allegedly got caught up with that inmate, females don't even wanna work on that post anymore!"

Vanita frowned at Sean. "Yeah, Daniels, you don't get tired of those Five North assholes?" Vanita asked.

Sean laughed and waved the two women off. "Those crooks! I'm here to make my dollars. They serve their time and I get paid. Fair exchange, no robbery."

"Well, okay, CO, since you put it like that."

"So, Yadi, are we goin' to, Roosevelt Field? I need to pick up a few things for this weekend getaway," Vanita asked.

Yadi cut her friend off. "Look, Vanita, I'm just gonna pick up Jada and head on home."

"But I thought you said that you was going with me to Roosevelt Field? Now all of a sudden, you're goin' home?" she asked.

Yadi held her down. "I gotta pick up Jada from her school because Devin—"

Vanita put her hand on her forehead. "Yadi, when are you gonna let that lame-ass dude do what he's supposed to do as a father? Damn, Jada is his child too! You can't even enjoy yourself because you always gotta worry about his dumb ass messin' up!" she said.

Yadi sighed. She knew that Vanita was right. Yadi also knew that it was time to leave Devin alone. The fear of being alone and without a man ravaged her body like the bubonic plague.

Vanita rolled her eyes at her friend and walked toward the locker room. Vanita was sick of Yadi making excuses for Devin.

Sean shook his head as he watched Yadi walk briskly in order to catch up to the disgusted Vanita.

Roll call had just been dismissed and officers were everywhere. Vanita walked through the sea of blue, with Yadi on her heels. When Vanita finally arrived in the locker room, she walked directly to the aisle where her locker was located. Yadi walked into the aisle behind her to try to explain.

"Nita, I know you're mad at me for not wantin' to go with you, but—" Yadi began.

Vanita snatched the locker door open and looked at her gorgeous friend. "Yadi, you don't have to explain anything to me from this point on. I'm tired of askin' you when are you goin' to stop allowin' yourself to go through these trials and tribulations," Vanita said without giving Yadi any eye contact.

"What are you talkin' about, Nita? I said I had to pick up Jada and I just didn't want to drag her with us bein' that Devin wasn't able to pick her up."

"You're the one always talkin' about how Devin doesn't make an effort to be a family. He has two other daughters by two different women, the child support drama and blah, blah, blah, but you don't even love yourself enough to leave him. It's called emotional abuse, Yadi. It's only a matter of time before he gets physically abusive."

Yadi chuckled nervously. "Well, it's been seven years and he hasn't hit me yet, so I don't see us goin' through all of that. He knows better than to hit me."

"So, if you're so tough, Yadi, why do you have to stick around and wait for the situation to get to that point? Why would you want to wait until he puts his hands on you to leave? Okay, so you'll fight back, sweetie, Devin is a man. There is no way that you can fight him without him tryin' to half kill you first."

Vanita sighed as she changed out of her uniform and into her street clothes. She knew that all of her points had fallen on deaf ears.

"Look, I'm goin' to the mall by myself. You can go home with your slavemaster."

Yadi had a look of defeat on her face. She didn't want to lose her friendship over her fixation with having a man in her life.

"That was fucked up, Nita! I hope you know that you hurt my feelings!" Yadi exclaimed as she walked away.

Vanita shrugged her shoulders. "Well, that doesn't matter. You should be used to gettin' your feelings hurt, Yadira!" Nita shouted.

Vanita's words stung Yadi, but she knew that everything that her friend had said to her was the truth.

Chapter 5

The windows facing the still waters surrounding Rikers Island were anything but serene. Across the polluted water was freedom, something that almost everyone in there yearned for but could only dream about having once again.

Anyone familiar with the three to eleven shift on Rikers Island knew what time it was. This was the tour that inmates were off the hook. The inmates residing in the area were locked in for the three to eleven p.m. count. Most duty posts were closed at approximately six p.m. Working inmates were returned to their respective housing areas before the seven p.m. count.

After the institutional search, Sean walked into Five North at 3:40 p.m. and relieved the seven to three officer. The young male officer seemed more than happy to be going home. Shortly after assuming the post, Sean toured the top and bottom tiers, taking a count of the inmates presently in the housing area.

"Um, you have forty-five inmates in here, right?" Sean asked the CO that he was relieving.

"Yeah, it's forty-five in here now and I got two out to the clinic, two's workin' in the clothesbox and one should be comin' from the law library after the count. Total count is fifty."

Sean signed the count slip and handed it to the officer. He gave Sean a pound, relinquished his equipment, and happily walked out of the housing area.

Sean missed working his old shift in his former housing area. Half of Five North consisted of new inmates. After working in the visit area for the past six months, he was not surprised that most of the inmates who were there when he was steady had been moved to other facilities.

Sean looked around at the nasty-looking salmon color that was painted on the walls, an effortless attempt by the Department of Correction to try to "soothe" the notorious criminals locked up inside of Five North. The area reeked of mildew and Sean casually removed incense from his carry bag and lit it up.

When the inmates had the opportunity to come out of their locked cells, a few gathered around the nineteen inch color television, watching The Maury Show. Simultaneously, they began shouting out, "You are not the father," at the disgruntled guests on the show. Other men did their daily calisthenics by pulling up on the staircase rails. Some inmates talked on the phone to their loved ones.

Many COs did not like working in Five North because they thought that the inmates housed there were knuckleheads. Sean had no problem being on the post and the Five North inmates respected him. Jail was jail to him and Five North was no exception.

After completing his paperwork, Sean stood up from his chair and stretched. He walked around the housing area, chatting with a few of the inmates here and there about some of the mishaps that occurred throughout the facility.

While conversing, Sean noticed Shamari Wallace sitting at a table playing cards with a few of the older inmates. He seemed very talkative and appeared to be eager to fit in. Sean knew that Shamari wasn't built for jail and he was wearing it like an old shirt. Shamari could play the extra tough role with Sean if he wanted to, but his fear was so transparent that it was almost comical for Sean to watch him.

"What's up, Born?" Sean said, greeting a man with a bald head and an inviting smile. No stranger to incarceration, Born had been back and forth to prison since adolescence and Five North in particular was his second home.

Born gave Sean a pound. "What's up, Dee?" Born replied. "Surprised to see you up here, man."

Sean shook his head. "Yeah, I'm tryin' to make me extra money. Plus I gotta keep an eye on somebody in here for a friend of mine."

Born frowned. "Who? Maybe I can help you out."

Sean nodded his head in Shamari's direction. "I'm talkin' about Shorty Wop over there. You know anything about him?"

Born was commonly referred to as the "ghetto almanac." He knew dates, names, and places of any information about the hood and its residents. He looked at Shamari through his expensive Gucci spectacles, while rubbing his bald head.

"Oh, yeah, I was just tellin' my man about this dude. I knew Shorty's pops."

Sean was curious. "Word? You knew his pops? His father is dead, huh?"

"His pop's name was Maleek. He was a get money nigga from East New York; a real stand-up dude. Didn't fuck with nobody unless they fucked with him. He was into his money. Had cars, jewelry, you know, the usual shit that comes with that territory, and a crib in Queens and one in, um, East New York, somewhere."

"Hmm. When did he get killed?" Sean asked.

"Oh, that nigga been dead and gone for a minute. He got killed in the early 90's. His son musta been like four or five years old at the time. Found Maleek on the side of some interstate, man. Somebody shot up his truck with him in it."

"Damn. That's fucked up," Sean replied, looking at Shamari and shaking his head. "What about Shorty's mother? You know her?"

"Well, homie did have two other baby mamas from what I heard. I think those kids were younger than this dude. If I'm not mistaken, this kid's moms was off the chain back in the days. Finer than a motherfucker, though. Bad bitch with a nice, fat ass and a pretty face but you couldn't let that shit fool you. She was layin' a nigga down in the streets and the broad kept some heat on her at all times. Funny shit was this chick was gettin' just as much money as her baby daddy was."

"Are you sure we talkin' about this dude's mother, Born? I saw his mother when she came up here to visit him and I didn't get gangsta bitch from her," Sean said, glancing at Shamari.

"Yeah, Dee. That's her. I think his mom's name is, um, um, oh yeah, Brandi. That's her name, Brandi. I didn't know her personally, but we have mutual people that we're cool with."

Sean was surprised. The woman he had seen earlier that day in a business suit couldn't have been the same person Born was talking about. She seemed well spoken and extremely professional.

"Man, are you sure his moms was that type of chick? I still find that shit hard to believe," Sean asked in amazement.

Born looked at Sean strangely. "Damn, nigga! You soundin' like you wanna holler at homegirl."

"Nah," Sean stated. "I just find it kinda crazy that the same woman I saw on the visit today a reformed hood chick. She came to see him all decked out in a business suit and shit. Her son is an asshole, though."

"Well, Brandi ain't your average sister. She was a certified dimepiece and all, but she will put a bullet in a nigga's ass if she had to. I haven't seen her in years, so I dunno what she's doin' now. After Maleek got killed, she kinda fell back from hustlin' and fell off the face of the earth." Born paused and looked at Shamari. "What's up with this dude? He ain't givin' you problems, is he?"

Sean laughed at the thought. "Heelll no!" He held up his scraped-up hands. "You know these things are registered. I woulda slapped the dog shit outta that nigga if it was that serious." They gave each other a pound. Born knew that Sean was telling the truth and chuckled.

They conversed for a few moments more and then Sean walked back toward his desk to use the phone. He noticed Shamari's eyes following his every move, but he ignored him for the time being.

When Sean got to the phone, he pulled Brandi Wallace's card out of his pocket and proceeded to dial her number. Sean noticed Shamari staring at him again, with a look of contempt on his face. It was as if he knew that Sean was calling his mother. He ignored Shamari's dirty look and continued to do what he was doing. To his surprise, Brandi picked up on the first ring.

"Hello, Brandi? How are you? This is Daniels," he replied.

"Hey, Officer Daniels," she exclaimed. "How are you? How's Sha—"

Sean cut her off before she could mention Shamari's name over the phone.

"Hey, Look, I'm still at work so, you know," he warned. He didn't know who could be listening to their conversation.

Brandi caught on quick. "Oh. Okay, no problem. How are you?"

"I'm good, ma. And yourself?"

"I'm fine, considering everything that's going on."

Sean sighed. "I know. I know. By the way, you can call me Sean."

"Well, Sean, I've been waiting for your call."

Sean was still finding it hard to believe that the Brandi he was talking to was the same person who Born described to him earlier.

"And you know what? I've been wantin' to call you. I know that you hear this a lot, but I think that you are a very beautiful woman."

She giggled. "And I must say that you are extremely attractive yourself. Do you work out?"

"Yeah, I do. I train sometimes, you know, I was a boxer. The workout regimen is excellent and I still use it."

Brandi seemed impressed. "It's working, so keep up the good work. When I first lay eyes on you, I was instantly attracted to you, do you know that?"

She's good with her game, Sean thought. He couldn't help but wonder what kind of panties she was wearing. He laughed at the thought.

"Well, I feel the same way about you, sweetheart. You seem like you're in good shape, too. Do you work out?" he asked.

"As a matter of fact, I do. I live in Starrett City and we have a gym in the recreation center. You know where Starrett City is, don't you?"

"Yeah, I do. Right on Pennsylvania Avenue, exit 14, off the Belt Parkway. What about workin' out together one day? Do you think that that would be a problem?"

"That would be great." There was a brief silence. "So, um, where do you live, Sean?"

"I was born and bred in Bed-Stuy. I still live there in a brownstone on Hancock and Stuyvesant. Why? Are you comin' by?"

Brandi laughed. "I might. You never know. But then again, your girlfriend might want to beat me up," replied Brandi.

Sean chuckled. "Nah, sweetheart. I'm a single man in every sense of the word. The only person that lives in my house is a tenant of mine. She lives on the top floor and she's gay. Now she's the one with the girlfriend, not me."

"Oh, okay. I guess you told me, huh? Well, with that being said, I suppose I will come to your humble abode one day. You never know. It might be real soon."

"And I will be waitin' for that day," Sean replied.

As they continued their conversation, Sean realized that he wouldn't mind seeing what Brandi was about. She sounded so confident over the phone and he couldn't wait to see her for a face-to-face tête-à-tête. Sean gave her his contact information and hung up shortly after, so that he could concentrate on Five North. Brandi was so easy to talk to that he almost forgot that he was at work. Sean remembered that he had to make a tour around the housing area again but he couldn't get up from his seat just yet. He had to sit down for a while so that his erection could go down.

Shamari glared at Sean. He didn't want CO Daniels to say a damn thing to him and clearly didn't want to have anything to do with the man. Shamari rubbed his smooth skin as he continued to play the card game with some of his cronies, taking the opportunity to get some feedback on Sean Daniels.

"Yo, Ant, what's up with CO Daniels?" he asked.

Ant looked in Daniels's direction. "Man, Daniels is a'ight. Why?"

Shamari sneered at Ant's comment. "I think that nigga is a real bird. When I was on the visit with my moms earlier, he tried to holler at her, yo."

"Man, that's grimy! You not suppose to holler at a nigga's moms, even though she is fine as fuck, no disrespect, son," Ant laughed.

Shamari was unmoved. "Yeah, I know my moms look good, nigga, but damn, this Daniels was on her shit today. Ain't that shit against the rules?"

"Hell yeah, it's against the rules but these CO cats don't care. They're mad thirsty when it comes to female visitors. Shit, my girl came to see me the other day and these COs was on her, too," Ant exclaimed.

Shamari laughed because he saw Ant's girl before. She was not attractive, to say the least. She reminded him of a pit bull in the face.

"Yeah, you right, man. They are thirsty!" The sarcastic comment went over Ant's head. "Anyway, I ain't feelin' that nigga not one bit."

Ant attempted to change the subject. He was not one for gossip. He was just waiting to be sent upstate to do his time. He couldn't careless about some police dude flirting with Shamari's mother.

"Look, man, let's play cards. Daniels ain't no threat to nobody. That nigga is cooler than a fan and your moms is a grown-ass woman. I'm sure if she didn't want to be bothered with that dude, she could get him off her back. It ain't that serious, son."

Shamari waved Ant off. "Man, you don't even talk to that nigga."

Ant smirked. "That's why I say he's cool. He no fucka with me, I no fucka with him. Now deal the cards, nigga. Damn!"

Shamari laughed and picked up his cards when Sean finally made his way over to the table. Ant and Sean greeted each other, but Shamari ignored him.

"What's up, Wallace?" asked Sean. Shamari nodded his head. "You a'ight?"

Shamari was annoyed. "Yeah, man, I'm straight," he retorted without giving the officer any eye contact.

"Good, good. Anyway, just checkin' on you." Shamari continued to play cards. "Just hold your head, Wallace. You'll be outta here in a minute."

"Man, don't you got work to do? Why the fuck is you worried about me? Ever since the visit, it's like you been stalkin' me."

Sean snatched the cards out of Shamari's hand. Everyone looked at the two men, anticipating some drama.

"Yo, what the fuck is your problem?" Sean asked. He was beginning to wonder why he had taken a sudden interest in the slender teen with the bad attitude.

Shamari stood up and looked Sean up and down. "You just met me today on the visit and you was busy tryin' be in my mom's face. So stop actin' like you checkin' for me, nigga! You ain't my god-damn daddy!" Shamari announced.

Sean smirked. He really wanted to slap the shit out of Shamari. Sean had already checked Shamari Tashaki Wallace's rap sheet and saw that he was in jail for robbery in the second degree and assault with a deadly weapon. He had been held on Rikers for the last couple of months and was immediately moved from the adolescent facility after his birthday last month.

Sean looked at Shamari, who was a clean-cut and good-looking young man, with a light moustache over his top lip. He saw himself being Shamari at that age, but he thanked God for the positive male influences in his family who kept their feet in his ass every time he got into some trouble. He sincerely wanted to help the wayward adolescent get it together.

Sean stepped up to Shamari's face. "Nigga, I ain't tryin be your damn daddy, I'm just tryin' save your ass from gettin' fucked up in here. Remember, I'm the one that's in the middle of keepin' these niggas in here off ass!" A few inmates in the background began to snicker.

"What the fuck do you want from me, CO? Huh?" Shamari asked after backing down a bit. "You tryin' to win some brownie points with my moms or somethin', nigga?" Sean looked at Shamari with his nose flared. "Well, if that's what you tryin' to do, it ain't gonna happen, pa, so fall back!"

Shamari pulled his chair out and sat back down to continue his card game. Sean looked around at the small crowd that gathered around to watch the drama between the officer and inmate.

Born shook his head as Sean walked away from Shamari without putting his hands on him, and smiled. He knew that Sean was a real man for doing what he did, but Born was determined to teach Shamari a lesson. A lesson that every young man who comes through the jail system should learn so they won't ever want to come back.

Chapter 6

Later that evening, Yadi opened the door to her apartment and watched her rambunctious, four-year-old daughter, Jada, run inside first. She put her shopping bags in the kitchen and stripped down to her bra and panties in the middle of the spacious living room. She took off Jada's clothes, as well, and smiled as the adorable little girl ran into her pink-colored bedroom to play with her toys. Yadi ran some water in the large bathtub, deciding that Jada could take a bubblebath with her. She was just relieved that Devin was not home yet, hopefully giving her a few hours to unwind.

As Yadi sat on the edge of her king-sized bed, Jada came into the bedroom and gave her mother a big hug and a kiss. She beamed because she couldn't think of anyone she loved more than her daughter. At one time, she wanted to have more children with Devin, but because of his child support issues, he was totally against it. He pestered her constantly about her birth control methods but refused to wear a condom when they had sex. Yadi finally just gave up on the idea of having any more children, which was probably a bad one from the beginning.

While Yadira and Jada were taking their bubble-bath, Devin suddenly appeared in the bathroom doorway. Devin was a Boris Kodjoe look-alike with his tall frame and bald head. Naturally, the love-addicted Yadi had fallen in love with him the first time she lay eyes on him.

They met at the Correction Academy during in-service training seven years ago. Devin thought that Yadi was gorgeous, as did most men. Devin thought that she would be another pretty face who was self-absorbed and conceited. However, after talking to her, he saw that she wasn't like most women. He trusted her so much that he shared some of the things that he went through with his other daughters' mothers. Devin thought that Yadi would be different.

They had a good run for a while and the sex was dynamite. Devin wanted to make her happy, and after awhile he found himself constantly doing everything to try to please Yadi. To his dismay, she whined and cried if she thought that he wasn't giving her enough attention. He thought it was cute at first but later realized that he couldn't get a moment to himself. If he tried to go out with his friends or even visit his mother, Yadi would go ballistic and accuse of him of cheating.

The accusations went hand in hand with the rants on his voice mail, and eventually, Yadi withheld sex from Devin as a form of punishment. She even began talking about him to anyone who would listen to her bullshit about how he mistreated her, which couldn't have been further from the truth. The end results were her parents not being able to stand him and Yadi was able to convince her friends and other family members that Devin was a piece of shit. Devin suffered in silence, because after all, he was a man. Nevertheless, behind closed doors, the bullshit Yadi put him through made him bitter.

When Devin finally realized that Yadira Cruz was not the woman he had grown to love, he made plans to leave, but it was too late; Yadi was pregnant and refused to get an abortion. Jada was born and Devin couldn't bear to leave Jada, afraid that he would never see her again if it was up to her mother. Not to mention Devin knew that the family court system would leave him with no paycheck. He was already getting thirty-five percent of his money taken out of his paycheck from his other two daughters' mothers.

At this point, Devin knew that if he left, Yadi would take him to court for child support. He had no other choice but to stay put.

Devin opened the bathroom door. The sight of Yadi's naked body didn't even turn him on anymore. He was emotionally and physically detached.

Devin frowned. "Um, you need to speed the bath up! I just came home from work and I wanna take a hot shower and go straight to bed!" he said to Yadi.

"Hi, Daddy!" Jada screamed out, oblivious to the harshness of her father's tone.

Devin smiled. His eyes lit up for his daughter. "Hi, princess," he replied, as he walked over to the bathtub and kissed her several times on her chubby cheeks.

"Hello to you, too, Devin," Yadira announced with an annoyed look on her face. She was tired of clamoring for his attention. Devin waved her off and walked out of the bathroom. He found it dreadful to be in the presence of the emotionally dependant Yadira.

Yadi and Jada finished their bath a few moments later and dried off. Yadi put on their bathrobes and cleaned out the tub so that "King" Devin could take a shower. Everything that Vanita said to her finally had an effect on her.

As she thought about it repeatedly, Yadi realized that maybe their lousy relationship was not worth saving. It was time to move on, but how could she? Yadi couldn't imagine being on her own. After all, she had never known what it felt like to be by herself.

Yadi stood up, tied her robe very tight, and walked out of the bathroom in a huff. She walked Jada into her bedroom and helped the little girl put on her pajamas. Being that it was only six o'clock in the evening, Yadi turned to the Disney channel for her daughter. After making sure Jada was comfortable, she walked out of the bedroom and closed the door. She knew that she and Devin were about to get into it.

When Yadi walked back into their bedroom, she brushed past Devin, almost knocking him into the wall. He was taken aback by her sudden abrasiveness. "What did you push past me for?" he asked with an angry look in his eyes. "Are you crazy?" Devin paused and smirked, while looking through some mail. "Oh yeah, I almost forgot. You are crazy!"

Devin threw the mail back on the nightstand and stood there, shirtless, preparing for his shower. He was a specimen of a man, standing at six feet three inches, with 200-pounds of muscle and a prominent six-pack. He towered over Yadi, with his pajama bottoms on, revealing that same six-pack that she used to love to run her tongue across.

"Go to hell, Devin, you bastard," Yadi said through clenched teeth, holding back tears. "I'm just so tired of livin' like this. You don't pay me any mind anymore. I know you got somebody else!"

"Oh, shut the fuck up, Yadira!" Devin replied. "You're always complainin' about somethin'. You wanted a baby, I gave you a baby. You wanted to live together, we moved in together. I gave you whatever you wanted and it was never good enough. You always wanted more."

"I'm just sick of you treatin' me like I'm a second-class citizen, after all the shit I do for you."

Devin laughed and pointed to himself. "Do for me? I put up with your lyin' ass all these years and you got the nerve to complain about what you do for me? I wanted to leave, remember? You threatened me with child support, knowing that my financial situation is fucked up! You told me that if I stayed you would hold me down and we was goin' to improve our relationship! You even tried to kill yourself! You used every manipulative gesture to get me to stay! Now I'm here, Yadira! I never once told you that I was happy with my decision to stay with your crazy ass! You're crazy and that's all you gonna ever be is a crazy bitch! I did you a favor by stayin' with you!"

Yadi was fuming as she walked up to Devin. She pointed her finger in his broad chest.

"Well, I'm gonna say this, motherfucker! If you hate me that much, pack your shit and leave! Go live with your other bitch or your mama, or whoever. Just get the fuck outta here!"

"I ain't goin' no damn where, Yadi! Why don't you fuckin' leave?" he retorted.

"Fine. Then I'm leavin'," she stated.

Devin thought about Jada for a moment. He knew that once Yadi left, she would try to keep him from seeing her.

"Well, you can do whatever you want, but my daughter stays with me!"

Yadi paused for a moment and looked for Jada, who was in her bedroom and unaware of their arguing. She didn't want to leave without her daughter but she had to go before it got out of control. She was tired of Devin. She figured nothing that she did at this point would ever save their dysfunctional relationship. Although she had never caught him cheating, she knew that he was probably feeling someone else. Her suspicions and jealousy were one of the reasons that she was so hostile to him.

"I'm takin' my daughter with me! She don't have no place here with you!" said Yadi.

Devin wanted to call her bluff. "Whatever, Yadira! You walk out of here with Jada, our relationship is definitely goin' to be over. Bet that!"

Yadi immediately went to her closet and pulled out an oversized Louis Vuitton bag. She hurriedly threw some of her and Jada's clothes in it, packing most of the items she needed for the week. She was hoping that Devin would at least stop her but he didn't try to. She got dressed, throwing on some form-fitting jeans and a shirt, along with a pair of UGG boots.

As Yadi grabbed her mink jacket from the closet and retrieved her pocketbook before heading toward the front door of their two-bedroom co-op apartment, Devin ran behind her and grabbed her arm. She gave him the look of death.

Devin began to worry about the impending child support case that would come behind the whole incident. "You're not goin' anywhere!" he yelled. "Where do you think you're goin'?"

"Gettin' the fuck away from you!" Yadi replied and snatched her arm from his grasp, a faint smirk on her face. His reaction to her leaving was the reaction she was hoping for. Now that she'd gotten the feedback she wanted, she felt powerful again. "Don't you ever put your hands on me again, Devin!"

Suddenly, Devin grabbed Yadi by her ponytail and dragged her 130-pound frame through their bedroom. He began slapping her but Yadi was not going to go down without a fight. She was worn out from him taking her for granted and she was going to show him how tired she was today.

Devin threw her against the wall and Yadi slid to the floor, feeling like her back was broken in several places. As he came toward her, she managed to get her leg up high enough to kick him in the nuts. As Devin fell to the floor, holding his testicles, she climbed on him and began clawing at his face. Yadi wanted to make sure she left her mark. Devin wrapped his large, calloused hands around Yadi's neck and began to choke her until she found the strength to punch him in the mouth. Devin instantly let go and his hand went to his bloody bottom lip.

"Oh, you wanna fight me like a man, huh?" Devin said, with fire in his eyes.

Yadi's chest heaved up and down. She was trying to drown out the cries of her daughter, who was banging on the other side of the bedroom door.

"C'mon, you bastard, I been wantin' to do this for a long time! And yeah, I wanna fight you like a man! I'm more man than your bitch ass could ever be!" she screamed, with her eyes bulging out of her head.

Devin looked at Yadi. *There goes dat crazy look again,* he thought. He had seen that wild-eyed look many times before. She crawled away from Devin, who was balled up on the floor, still holding his nuts with one hand and his mouth with the other.

Although she was exhausted and sore, Yadi managed to pick up the Bose CD clock radio and deliberately dropped it on Devin's head. His eyes rolled to the back of his head and for a moment Yadi thought she had killed him. After checking his pulse, Yadi breathed a sigh of relief. She bent down to put two fingers on his throbbing neck.

When Yadi finally opened the bedroom door, her crying daughter ran into her arms. Yadi held Jada close to her and ran into the living room. She didn't want Jada to see her father unconscious on the floor. She wrapped Jada, who was in her pajamas, in her fur jacket and she hightailed it for the door before Devin regained consciousness. She grabbed her duffel bag with her and Jada's things and ran out of the apartment. Yadi looked back at the building, half expecting Devin to be behind her.

When she finally pulled off in her Nissan Maxima, Yadi turned on some music in the car to soothe Jada, who was still crying hysterically. They were both shaken up from the ordeal but Yadi couldn't even find the energy to shed any tears. She was actually feeling liberated.

As Yadi turned onto Francis Lewis Boulevard, she figured that Devin was probably conscious by then, nursing his injuries and his ego. She was more upset at the fact that Jada was subjected to the chaos. Yadi realized that after that incident, she didn't want to expose her daughter to violence of any kind, if she had anything to do with it. Actually, Jada's presence in the household saved Devin's life. With Yadi's fragile mental condition, she would have definitely tried to kill Devin and that night was the opportunity to do it.

Not having anywhere to go, Yadi drove aimlessly through the streets of Queens for at least two hours. She finally ended up in front of Vanita's house, which was tucked away on a quiet block in Queens Village. Her home was very quaint and perfect for a single woman with no children. It looked dark inside and Yadi figured Vanita probably wasn't home, much to her dismay. She was hesitant to call Vanita, thinking that she may still be upset with her but she decided to take a chance anyway. She was desperate and Jada was cold and sleepy.

Yadi retrieved her cell phone from her bag. She noticed that Devin had called her three times since she'd left the house. The music in her car must have been so loud that Yadi hadn't noticed. She sucked her teeth when she saw his number but dialed Vanita's phone number instead.

"Please answer the phone, Nita!" Yadi said to herself. She turned around and smiled at Jada, who smiled back at her from the booster seat in the backseat of the car. Her daughter was a trooper.

"Hey, girl!" Vanita exclaimed happily. "What the business is?"

Yadi was surprised by Vanita's reaction to the phone call. She was even more relieved that Vanita had gotten over being angry with her.

"Nita, me and Devin had a fight tonight!" she said in a hushed tone.

Vanita brushed her off. "Y'all always fightin', Yadi—"

"No, Nita, we had a physical fight." There was complete silence on the phone.

"What?" Vanita yelled into the phone. "He hit you? Are you okay? Oh my God! What happened?"

Yadi's voice began to quiver. "We're fine, Nita. I'm just done. I know you heard it before but somethin' in me just snapped today. I'm tired of him callin' me out my name and just bein' so nasty to me. I mean, I know I have my issues but

I feel that I'm a good woman!" Yadi started to cry and Jada cried out from the back seat.

"Oh my goodness! Yadi, the baby is with you, too? That motherfucker!" she exclaimed. "You want my cousins, Day-Day and Jayquan and them from Marcy projects to pistol whip his ass? You know they will do anything for Yadi Cruz!"

Yadi burst out laughing and wiped her tears from her face. "Nita, I swear I love you! You are so crazy!"

"But where are you right now?" Vanita asked, sounding concerned.

"Um, in front of your house. The question is where are you?"

Vanita laughed. "Remember, I told you after Christmas that I was goin' away for the weekend in February with my new guy friend? That's why I wanted to go to the mall. I took off tomorrow and Sunday off from work and I won't be back until Monday evening."

Yadi slid down in her driver's seat. **Shit**, she thought. "I can't go to my parent's house. I don't want them in my business!" she said.

"Yadi, I'm comin' home right now, okay?"

"Hell no! You stay right where you are and have a good time. You're always bendin' over backward for me, girl. So just go ahead and have your fun. I'm gonna make some phone calls. I'll be all right."

Vanita wondered who Yadi was going to call. She didn't have many friends. "Make sure you call me and let me know where you're gonna be," Vanita said.

Yadi hung up the phone. She calmed herself down because her mind was all over the place. She couldn't think of a single soul to call because she didn't deal with too many people outside of work. Then she thought for a moment. Sean was doing overtime and she knew that he didn't get off of work until eleven-thirty that night. It was only nine-thirty but she was going to call him and leave him a message anyway. Hopefully, he would call her back as soon as he heard it. Otherwise, she didn't know what she was going to do.

Chapter 7

As he steered his Escalade over the Rikers Island Bridge, Sean rolled down the driver's side window. He needed the cold air to keep him awake for his drive home. He yawned loudly, exhausted from working overtime. The only thing he looked forward to was taking a soothing shower and climbing into his comfortable bed for some much needed shuteye. Sean let out a huge yawn and turned up the Joe song playing on the XM satellite radio station in his truck.

As Sean cruised on the Grand Central, he remembered that he hadn't listened to his messages. On one of his messages, which was marked urgent, he was shocked to hear Yadi's voice. He turned down his music and played the message over. She sounded like she was in desperate need of help. After hearing it a second time, Sean immediately called her back. Yadi answered the phone on the first ring.

"Hey, Sean!" Yadi said. "I am so glad you called me back! Everything just escalated and me and Devin got into a fist fight, and I have Jada with me. My daughter is in her pajamas and bathrobe and—"

Sean cut her off. "Whoa, girl! Spare me the details until later. What do you need?" he asked.

Yadi began to cry. "Can I please stay with you tonight, Sean?" she pleaded. "Me and Jada have nowhere to go and I just can't go to my family's house. Not like this. Vanita is outta town and I will be in jail tonight if I go back home."

"Yadi, you can come stay with me. I have an open-door policy."

"I'm so sorry to bother you, Sean, but—"

"You a'ight, baby girl. Meet me at my crib. 225 Hancock Street between Stuyvesant and Malcolm X Boulevard. I'll be home in like, twenty minutes."

"Thanks, Sean. You are a lifesaver!"

"Are y'all hungry?" Sean asked with genuine concern in voice. "Do you need anything?"

Yadi's heart fluttered at the kind gesture. "Oh, no, Sean we're fine, just tired. Jada is asleep in the back seat."

"Don't worry. I'm on my way home now." Sean sighed and stepped on the gas.

As he headed toward the BQE, Yadi's sexy-ass kept running through his mind. He felt bad about her ordeal but the little devil on his shoulder was telling him something different. First, his chance meeting with Brandi, and now Yadi was going to actually be staying in his house. What was a man supposed to do?

Twenty minutes later, Sean pulled his truck in behind Yadi's steel grey Maxima, which was parked in front of his house. He walked up to the car and Yadi jumped out of the driver's seat to hug him. She gathered her things and Sean unlocked his front door, carrying the sleeping Jada upstairs to his spare bedroom. Once Sean placed the little girl in the bed, Yadi entered the room and dumped her large bag on the floor. He looked at the bag and frowned.

Yadi saw Sean's facial expression and looked down at her bag. "Oh, yeah, I was only stayin' until tomorrow, Sean. Is that okay?" she asked.

"Nah, it ain't your bags. I was just buggin' out because I never thought you would be leavin' Devin."

Yadi sat on Sean's bed. "Yeah, I know, but it's over. Devin doesn't love me or respect me. And tonight he didn't have one problem with puttin' his hands on me." Yadi was distracted by her vibrating cell phone. It was Devin calling her again.

Sean stared at Yadi. He figured that it was Devin. He was happy that she didn't answer it because he didn't want to hear her argue with him all night. He just needed to get in his bed and get a few hours of restful sleep.

"I'm proud of you, Yadi. Once a nigga put his hands on you the first time, it only gets worse after that."

Yadi held her head down and pulled her long hair out of her face. "I know. I didn't think he would hit me after all these years but that goes to show how dumb I was."

Sean changed the subject. He didn't want her to be down in the dumps about her decision to leave.

"Get comfortable," he suggested. While pulling back the comforter on the bed, Yadi walked over and tenderly embraced Sean.

"Thanks, Sean. Thanks so much," she said. "You're a good friend."

She kissed Sean on the cheek and he kissed her back. Unexpectedly, they began to kiss each other passionately and after what seemed like an eternity, they stopped and looked at each other.

"Yadi, I can't do this," he said. "You know that I've liked you for a while now. But this is not the time to have sex with you. You just had a fight with your man and you're vulnerable right now.

I don't need to start messin' things up by bein' intimate with you."

Sean stepped back and took a good look at Yadi. Her face looked swollen and she had a black-and-blue bruise on her right cheek. Her hair was unkempt and one of her eyes was bloodshot red.

Yadi began to feel uncomfortable with her appearance. She attempted to push her thick mane into a ponytail .

Yadi blinked her bedroom eyes. "Sean, I know you like me and I like you too, but I need you right now. I've been waitin' for an opportunity to get with you."

Sean shook his head. "Yeah, but this is not the time. Get yourself together first, Yadi. You're in a relationship with Devin and this isn't gonna be the last of your problems with him. I'm goin' to keep it real, I don't wanna get caught up in your shit. You are my friend but no woman is worth me havin' to kill a nigga unless it's my mama. I don't wanna go through no bullshit with Devin, and you and him haven't really broken up with each other."

Yadi plopped down on Sean's bed. They looked at each other for a moment and paused until Sean finally broke the silence.

"I'm gonna go sleep now, Yadi. You can sleep in here with the baby. If you need anything, feel free to let me know." He paused for a moment and held out his hand for Yadi to shake. "Friends?"

She put on a fake smile and shook Sean's hand. "Yeah, friends."

Sean walked out of the bedroom and closed the door behind him. Yadi sat on the bed. She slid out of clothes and crawled under the goose down comforter. Yadi reached over and kissed Jada then turned off the lights.

She heard her cell phone vibrate in her bag again and sucked her teeth, while she fumbled around in the dark looking for it. When she retrieved her phone, she smiled when she saw Devin's cell phone number on her caller ID. *Maybe he really does love me* she thought. Not bothering listening to his messages, Yadi turned her phone off, slid in the bed, and fell into a deep slumber.

Meanwhile, it was past midnight as Brandi lay in her bed, alone and thinking about Sean. She was up late reading one of her Iyanla Vanzant books. Not accustomed to hanging out, Brandi did not mirror the woman she used to be. She was comfortable with just going to work and coming home every day rather than going out with every Tom, Dick, and Harry. She had to keep her mind positive because Lord knows, she didn't know if she could keep her sanity while Shamari was going through his drama on Rikers Island.

After pondering for a moment, something made Brandi get up and walk into her son's empty bedroom, which was looking exactly how he had left it before his arrest. The room was warm and she could almost smell the Allure cologne that Shamari wore as if he had just sprayed it yesterday.

She looked around the male-themed room and shook her head at the posters of Notorious B.I.G. and Jay-Z. Shamari owned almost every rap CD known to man and kept them stacked up neatly in CD racks that were nailed to the wall. She opened his closet and observed the abundance of sneakers and clothing that he had acquired over the years.

Brandi knew she was partly to blame for Shamari's sudden incarceration because not only did she lavish him with material things but she also spoiled him with love and nurturing. *What happened to him and where did things go wrong?*

Brandi walked out of the bedroom, feeling like there was a huge void in her life. Having done most of the things she wanted to accomplish, she couldn't help but wonder if she had selfishly put her needs before Shamari's. Needing some reassurance, she almost picked up her phone to call Sean, wanting to continue their conversation to take her mind off some of the turmoil in her life. Instead, Brandi climbed back into her bed and fell asleep.

Chapter 8

Shamari was awakened by what sounded like a search team of correction officers coming into his housing area. He glimpsed out of the cell window to see that the housing area was filled with COs, quickly hopping up to brush his teeth and wash his face. He wouldn't want the officers searching his cell to be subjected to his morning breath.

While Shamari looked in the mirror over his sink, he couldn't understand why people wanted to keep coming to jail over and over again. Just the regular routine shit had him about to lose his mind. Shamari had many regrets and ending up in there was one of them. His uncles had been through it and they had told him that it was somewhere he didn't need to be. Now that he was in the situation, Shamari finally understood everything they'd talked about. Unfortunately, he had no other choice but to man up and hold it down.

The search team came through Five North like a tornado. They tossed around the inmates' belongings and left without incident. Most of the inmates, including Shamari, were pissed about having to put their things back the way they had them arranged in the cell. After a while, everything returned to normal and Shamari decided to take a shower before he started his day.

As Shamari walked back to his cell from the shower, he hoped that Officer Daniels didn't work Five North again. He couldn't help but dislike the CO, although Sean had insisted on helping him with his transition. Shamari just hoped his mother didn't decide to fall for his bullshit. To step in his house after getting out of jail and seeing Sean's face would be a nightmare. He knew that Brandi had been alone and without a man for a while, immersing herself in school, work, and him. His mother did deserve to have a good man take care of her needs, although Shamari didn't want to even imagine his mother needing anything from a man. But why Daniels?

When he was a little boy, Brandi told him that some crooked cops in Virginia had killed his father. After that, Shamari secretly feared and hated any type of law enforcement officers because he felt they had the legal right to kill a nigga and get away with it. He knew how his father got the money he had, even though he ended up dying trying to keep it.

Shamari wanted to be smarter than his father and do it the right way, not knowing there was no such thing as a right way to make illegal money. Shamari was already disappointed in himself for not being everything his mother wanted him to be. He had hurt her dearly but he was always fascinated with making fast money. He was going to need some start-up dough, and ended up robbing trying to get it.

Shamari hooked up with Peeto, one of his father's old running buddies. On the strength of Shamari being Maleek's son, Shamari was going to pay for one half of a kilo in cash. Peeto was going to front the other half to the eager wanna-be hustler. Shamari succeeded in getting some of the money that was needed for the drugs he wanted to purchase, but couldn't come up with the rest of it.

He tried to get Peeto to give him the kilo on consignment and Peeto practically laughed in his face. Anyone who hustles knows that was a big no-no, if they were an amateur in the game. What Shamari didn't know was that if Brandi found out that he had a deal going with one of Maleek's boys, she would have tried to kill not only him, but Peeto too. Shamari was clueless about his mother's other side.

As Shamari exited his cell, he accidentally bumped into Born. Shamari made it his business to stay as far away from Born as he could, suspecting that the man, who was almost twenty years his senior, didn't like him that much. He knew that Born's reputation exceeded itself and although many in the jail feared him, he was loved just the same. Born stopped in front of the young Shamari and wouldn't let him by. Shamari's normally broad shoulders slumped.

"What's poppin', young one?" Born inquired. "Where do you think you goin'?"

Shamari swallowed and tried not to appear nervous. "Umm, I was goin' to check out my man, Ant."

Born smirked. "You ain't got no mans in here, little nigga. Remember that."

Shamari looked confused. "Huh?"

Born got in Shamari's face. "You heard me. You ain't got no mans in here. So don't you ever let me here you say that homo shit again, you hear me?"

Shamari stared at Born to see if he was serious. When he observed the veins protruding from the older man's bald head, he knew that it wasn't a joke.

"Yeah, man, I mean, a'ight, cool," Shamari stated. He didn't want to sound like he was being defiant.

"Good. And another thing, motherfucker, if I ever see you or hear about you violatin' my nigga, Daniels, I'll knock your fuckin' block off your shoulders, you hear me?"

Shamari felt his eyes water. *So that is what this is all about,* Shamari thought. He then nodded his head in agreement with the professional thug. Born looked at the teen and finally let him pass. Shamari looked back at Born, who was still staring at him from down the tier. Suddenly, he wasn't in the mood to check for Ant and decided to go back into his cell to sleep.

Later on that morning, Brandi sat on her king-sized bed, sipping coffee and reading the Saturday newspaper when the phone on the nightstand rang. She anxiously picked it up, knowing that it was Shamari. He would usually call her early in the morning on Saturdays, knowing that she would be awake. The operator on the phone announced, "Please hold," and when Shamari said something, the operator said, "Go ahead" Hearing her son's voice, Brandi smiled from ear to ear. She definitely missed her baby.

"Hi, sweetie!" she said loudly. "Are you okay? Do you need anything?" she asked, going into concerned mother mode.

"I'm straight, Ma. How are you?" Shamari asked. He didn't sound too happy and Brandi picked up on it.

"What's wrong, Shaki?" asked Brandi, referring to him by the shortened version of his middle name.

"I dunno, Ma, I just, I just regret even gettin' myself caught up the way I did. Word."

Brandi swung her legs on the side of the bed and sat upright. She didn't want her son to lose focus and do something stupid to get into more trouble.

"Listen, Shaki, hold your head up! I know it's hard, baby, but it's a lesson learned. I'm not trying to make you feel bad, but Shaki, you might have to do some time for what you did. I mean, I hired a great lawyer but you have to be strong, if you know what I mean."

Shamari was silent for a moment. His mother wasn't telling him what he wanted to hear. He wanted her to tell him that everything was going to be all right and that he would be home soon.

"Ma, I don't wanna hear nothin' about no lawyer right now. I just wanna get outta here 'cause I'm gonna end up hurtin' a motherfucker in here!"

Brandi moved the phone from her ear and cussed. She came back on the phone and tried to comfort her only child.

"Shamari Tashaki Wallace, you're a trooper so don't go out like a sucker! You're in there with murderers, rapists, child molestors, so do what you have to do to make sure you get back here in one piece. You must be strong, baby, because I can't be there to hold your hand on this one, I'm sorry. You're a man now and this is the path you chose to live so—"

Shamari cut her off. "So, what, Ma? What are you sayin'?" he screamed into the phone. "I ain't used to this shit! I came from somethin', I shouldn't have to live like this!"

Brandi smiled. "Exactly. You just said it yourself, but if you don't stop with this robbing, stealing, and hustling, your next stop is the graveyard!"

"Ma, some nigga in here is threatenin' me, talkin' about if I disrespect his peeps, Daniels, he gonna do me dirty! See what kinda niggas you tryin' to deal with? This dude got niggas in here threatenin' me!"

Brandi held the phone in complete shock. "What? Shaki, what in the hell are you talking about?"

"Me and CO Daniels had some words the other day and now some cat named Born wanna come up to me, talkin' about if I disrespect Daniels again, he's gonna fuck me up. This is the type of shit I gotta deal with, Ma. That's why I told you it was something about that dude that I didn't like from jump!"

Brandi felt herself get dizzy with anger. Sean reassured her that he was going to look out for her son, not get him killed. She thought back to the visit when Shamari was being disrespectful toward him. Was Sean trying to set Shamari up in retaliation for that day in visits?

Brandi looked at the time. It was nine a.m. "Shaki, calm down, okay? I'm gonna get to the bottom of this. Is this a visit day for you?" she asked.

"Yeah, Ma," Shamari replied. "It's A through Z visits today."

"Good! I'm on my way up there to see you!"

Brandi hung up the phone and prepared to go to Rikers Island. She wanted to find the underlying cause of this before she made any false accusations. In the meantime, Shamari hung up the telephone with a sinister smile on his face. He was going to have the last laugh after all.

Meanwhile, downstairs in visits, Sean walked the floor and chatted with random visitors and inmates. He was in a jovial mood and his joyful banter made the atmosphere in the area very positive. There were no arguments or fights that day and the children laughed happily. Even the COs fell back from harassing anyone.

Yadi was still at Sean's house, and apparently, was not in the mood to come to work that morning. She called off sick for the next two days, giving herself more than enough time to heal her emotional and physical wounds. Plus, her right eye had swollen up and her left was black and blue. She didn't need anyone at work seeing her in that condition.

Sean suggested she stay at his house until she got herself together and he quietly made a promise to himself to try not to touch her. He knew that it would only complicate everything and Yadi had too much emotional baggage to have casual sex with him or any man for that matter. Sean did have a lot of respect for Yadi, whom he thought was a very beautiful woman on the inside as well but Yadira's self-esteem and codependency were major issues for him. He was able to see the bullshit from a mile away.

Not wanting to deal with those problems, Sean made up his mind to concentrate on trying to get with Brandi. She seemed like a woman who had it all together. Sean just hoped that Shamari was no reflection of her parenting skills, or her as a woman in general.

Brandi arrived in the visit area and walked straight to the desk to get her registration card time stamped. She felt self-conscious as she noticed the dirty looks she got from the other inmates and their jealous girlfriends or wives. When Shamari called her, she had thrown on whatever, making her way up to the jail to get to the bottom of the alleged bullshit that was going on.

As soon as she sat in her assigned seat, she turned around and saw Sean, whose back was turned to her. She stared a hole in his back until he finally turned around and caught her eye. Sean was pleasantly surprised when he saw her sitting there with her arms folded. He didn't realize that she was angry until he walked over to her table.

"Hey, cutie. I didn't know that you were comin' up today," Sean said.

"Listen, Sean, I don't fucking appreciate motherfuckers walking up to my son and threatening him because of you! I can't see you getting somebody to try to cause bodily harm to my child while he's in here!" she whispered loudly.

Sean bent down to see if he had heard her right. "Whaaat in the hell are you talkin' about, miss? I wouldn't dare get anybody to threaten your son, let alone hurt him. What kind of man do you think I am?"

"Well, my son called me this morning and told me that some asshole named Born threatened him, talking about the next time that Shamari disrespects you, he's going to hurt him. Who the fuck is this Born character anyway?"

Sean gulped, just happening to observe Born sitting with his wife a few tables away from where Brandi was seated. He heard the metal doors opening and saw Shamari walking toward the table. *Shit,* thought Sean. He knew it was about to be on for real. He watched while Born talked to his wife and began kissing her. Shamari had made his way over to his mother with that infamous smug look of his on his face. Sean had an uncanny desire to wipe it off.

"Ma, are you still talkin' to this dude?" Shamari announced, talking about Sean like he wasn't standing there.

Sean's muscular chest began to heave because he was beginning to see right through Shamari's game. "Yo, Wallace, did you tell your mother that I had Born threatenin' you for me?" Sean asked.

Shamari rolled his eyes at Sean and pointed at him. "Ma, who is this dude talkin' to? I know he ain't talkin' to me!" Shamari stated.

Brandi was becoming annoyed with the both of them. "Where is Born, Shamari? Is he in this visiting room?"

Shamari looked around and made eye contact with Born who was staring in their direction.

Born gave Shamari the evil eye, as if he knew exactly what was being said about him. Shamari froze up and decided not to say anything to his mother.

"Nah, he's not in here. I'll be a'ight, but tell this dude to stay away from me and you, Ma!" Shamari replied, referring to Sean.

Brandi looked at Sean. He knew when he was being dismissed and walked away from the table. He was seething with anger and personally wanted to beat Shamari's ass for lying to his mother. He knew that Born called himself having good intentions but at what cost? Now, Sean's mood had changed instantly and he began walking around the visit area and making everyone with one minute over an hour get up immediately. His coworkers watched Sean with bewildered looks on their faces as if to say, "What happened?" He went from being pleasant to becoming a total jerk within a few minutes. Brandi tried not to make any more eye contact with Sean and felt bad about the accusations but she didn't know what was going on. Sean casually made his way over to Born's table. Born tried to give him a pound but Sean would have none of that. Sean greeted Born's wife instead.

"Yo, son, I gotta talk to you after your visit," Sean suggested.

Born knew what Sean wanted to talk about. "Yeah, a'ight."

An hour had passed and Shamari's visit was over. When Brandi walked out, Sean followed her through the metal doors. Not wanting everyone in their business, he grabbed her arm and pulled her to the side for a talk.

"Brandi, how could you accuse me of tryin' to get your son hurt in here? That's not anything I would do to anybody!"

"Sean, I don't know what's going on but if one hair on Shamari's head is touched, I'm personally holding you responsible. You said that you were going to look out for him, not get him killed in here!" Brandi replied, looking as if she was about to cry. She was seething with anger.

Sean sighed in frustration. "What? Brandi, don't believe Shamari! I wouldn't do that to him or anyone in here!"

"Don't you dare tell me not to believe my child! He wouldn't lie to me about no shit like this!"

Sean looked at Brandi and saw what the problem with Shamari was. His mother felt that he could do no wrong. It wasn't as if the young man was trustworthy. There was no honor among thieves and Shamari was locked up on a robbery charge. If he could steal, he could cheat, lie, and possibly kill. She was almost acting like she owed him something; like she was trying to make up for the loss of his father.

"You're right, Miss Wallace. You are so right. I'm gonna leave this alone and tell my man, Born, to fall back off your son. That's the least I can do since you don't believe me. I just hope you realize that Shamari is on his own now and I ain't gonna be his personal caretaker! And as for you, take care of yourself!"

Sean walked away and did not look back. As Brandi stood there waiting for the bus, she was beginning to think that she may have made a mistake.

Moments later, Sean decided to walk to the visit search area and approach Shamari. The COs who worked there saw the expression on Sean's face. The other COs noticed the peeved expression on his face. They knew what was about to happen. They conveniently walked out so that Sean could be alone with Shamari.

Shamari saw Sean and instantly began trash talking. "Yeah, motherfucker, you thought that you could get somebody to get at me, huh? Well, my moms done cut your bird-ass off so the joke's on you, you fuckin' lame-ass police!" Shamari announced.

Sean pushed the teen against the brick wall and Shamari winced with pain.

"Keep my damn name out your mouth, Shorty, 'cause I don't need none of these fuckin' crooks in here to do my dirty work, you hear me? If I wanted to whip ya ass, I'm a team by myself, nigga, and nobody is gonna stop me. You can call your mother, I.G., or God Himself and I will still lay your ass out. You ain't nothin' but a young fuckin' punk who can fool his mama but I don't care nothin' about you! Like you said, I ain't your fuckin' daddy, nigga!"

Shamari tried to bring some phlegm up and into his mouth, as if he wanted to spit in Sean's face.

Sean grabbed Shamari's face and held it very tight. "Oh, you wanna try spit on me? Huh? I'll bust your damn teeth out your mouth if you do!"

Shamari tried to squirm out of Sean's grasp but to no avail. Sean mushed his face and Shamari fell back onto the floor.

"I was gonna look out for you in here, and to tell you the truth, my man, Born was tryin' to show you some tough love. He wasn't gonna do shit but make you not wanna come back and forth to jail like he did when he was your age but since you don't appreciate shit, from now on, you little bastard, you on your own in here. Anything that goes down from now on is on you, big man!"

Shamari stayed on the floor and waited until Sean walked out of the visit area to get up. He brushed himself off and walked down the long corridor toward Five North. When he arrived back inside, an unidentified inmate who looked to be around Shamari's age punched him square in the face, knocking him on the floor. As Shamari lay out on the floor, temporarily unconscious, Born stepped over him and slashed him on the neck.

Chapter 9

When Brandi arrived home, she was still upset from Sean's comments. Was Shamari really playing her against the handsome correction officer? Maybe she was in denial and didn't want to believe that's what it was. Brandi knew that her son was a little selfish but she would be highly disappointed in him if she found out that he was wicked enough to accuse Sean of such an injustice. Brandi didn't want that false information to get back to the wrong person, especially if it would mean putting Sean in a bad position with his job.

Brandi thought back to when a person like Born would have been dead for fucking with her family. Her loyalty to her loved ones was never to be questioned and she would kill a nigga for violating anyone that was near and dear to her heart.

It was 1989. Brandi and Maleek were sitting in her Land Rover waiting for one of their connects, a guy named Justice. They were on the corner of Rockaway and Fulton Street. Brandi was uncomfortable with the surroundings. Even though she was from the hood herself, she felt uneasy as she watched the dope fiends and crackheads move around the poorly lit corner. Ironically, she couldn't help but wonder why everyone was looking like Night of the Living Dead with their zombie-like appearances. Maleek seemed extremely comfortable as he continued to rap along with Kool G. Rap on "Roads to The Riches." Brandi shook her head, removed her gun from her Gucci shopping bag, and lay it on her lap. Maleek gave her a strange look.

"What are you gonna do with that?" he asked.

Brandi looked over her shoulder and sucked her teeth. "What you think, nigga? I'm gonna put a cap in somebody's ass if I have to," she replied sarcastically. Maleek could be so naïve sometimes.

Maleek laughed sofly and kissed Brandi on the cheek. "My boo is so cute! She's gonna shoot somebody with her wittle gun?" he teased.

Brandi frowned. "No, see, Maleek! I'm dead-ass serious! You don't think somethin' is a little funny?"

Maleek looked around. "Man, fuck these motherfuckers! I don't see nothin' but crackheads and—"

Suddenly, one of the fiends put a gun to Maleek's head through the half-cracked window.

"Run yo' shit, nigga!" the fiend ordered. Brandi's eyes widened and her hand went for the .38 special sitting in her lap. The fiend never saw her make a move.

Maleek held his hands up and fear was written all over his handsome face. "Yo, son, look. Take the gun away from my head and I'll give you what you want!"

"I want your jewels and your bitch's jewels, too. And I know that you waitin' for that dude, Just, so I want Just's fuckin' money, too! Gimme your shit! Now!" The desperate criminal pushed the barrel of the gun deeper into Maleek's temple. Maleek grimaced in pain.

As Brandi reached for the small duffel bag filled with money, Maleek distracted the thief by taking off his jewelry. All of a sudden, Brandi reached across Maleek's face and pointed the gun in the perp's face. She pulled the trigger and hit the ornery rogue right through his eye. As the man fell backward into the street, his .45 caliber pistol went off in the air. He fell into the street, cracking his skull against the curb, with blood gushing from the gaping hole where his left eye used to be. Maleek stretched his head out of the window, and from the looks of it, the man was definitely a goner. The few people who were outside began scattering all over the place to escape the onslaught of gunfire.

Maleek started the truck and pulled off. "Oh, shit!" he yelled. "We gotta get the fuck outta here!"

He skidded off and headed down Rockaway toward Broadway. Maleek made a right turn onto Chauncey Street, not knowing where they were going to end up. After riding for fifteen minutes, they finally managed to pull over on Brandi's block on Quincy Street.

Maleek attempted to catch his breath. He looked over at Brandi in the passenger seat, who looked calm as hell.

"Yo! You killed that motherfucker you know that, right?"

Brandi shrugged her shoulders. "Yeah, I know. So?" Maleek shook his head in amazement. "That nigga tried to kill us!"

Maleek caught his breath and smiled. He knew right then that Brandi was his rider chick, his gangster bitch for life.

Brandi was about to get out of the truck so that she could go upstairs and tend to their sleeping baby. Maleek was going home.

"Where you goin', Brandi?"

"I'm goin' upstairs to my house to see about Shamari. Why?" she asked, getting her Gucci bag out of the car. She threw the murder weapon in the sewer. Brandi thought that Maleek was going to get into his Benz and go to his own apartment.

"We're gonna park your truck. Let's get in my car and go home," he replied.

"Home?"she repeated, with a confused look on her face.

"Yeah, home. Tomorrow, we could come back and get Shamari. Y'all movin' in with me."

Brandi climbed back in the truck and wrapped her arms around Maleek's neck. She'd finally proved her loyalty to Maleek that night and she got her man. But at what cost?

Brandi stared at the large clock on her living room wall and was tempted to call Sean to apologize. He was right when he said that he wasn't Shamari's babysitter and she felt that because of her snap judgment, Shamari could be in even more danger. Brandi had to remember that it was jail and at any given time, anything could happen to Shamari. It wasn't fair to put that type of responsibility on Sean. She took a deep breath and picked up her cell phone to call him.

"What do you want, Brandi?" Sean answered on the third ring.

"Sean, wait, I wanted to apologize about today. I do, um, can you forgive me?" she asked.

"Nah, I'm not fuckin' with you," Sean replied flatly.

Brandi was shocked. "Why?"

"Brandi, I take my job seriously and you and your demon seed is playin' a real serious game. Personally, I regret the day I lay eyes on you and your fuckin' son! So do me a favor and just leave me alone!"

Brandi began to plead with him. "Sean, listen to me, don't hang up. Can we still go out tonight? My treat."

Sean was silent. He knew he had opened an assortment of problems by dealing with this woman, but he couldn't deny his attraction to Brandi. Though the situation with her son was a big turn-off, he decided to give her the benefit of the doubt and take her up on her offer to hang out.

"Yeah, a'ight, a'ight. On one condition," Sean said.

"Sure."

"We forget about what happened today and just move on. From now on, your business with your son is your business, I'm stayin' out of it. And two, don't ever think I'm conspirin' with that nigga, Born, again, okay? What I'm tryin' to say is that I'm feelin' that you wanna protect Shamari but you can't protect him all the time and neither can I. Just because you think he's special and you love him, everyone don't have to feel the same way about him. He is in jail for a reason."

Brandi leaned back into her couch. She always devoted her time to raising her son and now it was time to get her life ready for some happiness.

"Sean, I apologize once again and I'll be ready to pick you up at nine o'clock. Is dat all right with you?"

Sean looked at Yadira and Jada, who were lay out on his couch watching television.

"How about I pick you up instead?" he replied.

At Sean's house, Yadi sang along with BET videos that were showing on the forty-two inch plasma television in Sean's living room, while she cleaned up. Jada was busy playing with some toys that Sean had stored away for his nieces and nephews. Yadi looked around at the spotless house and was more than happy that she could do something to repay her friend for his generosity.

She was pleased that he told her that she could stay there as long as it took her to get on her feet, which was going to be in no time. She just needed to stay away from Devin, whom she didn't seem to miss at all. She plopped on the couch, touching the knot on her head and hissed, as the pain from the knot sent a shock wave through her body. She was bruised up and limping but was happy that she was able to get away. Some women never made it out of domestic violence situations alive.

"Mommy, is this our new house?" Jada asked, while coloring in a Snow White coloring book.

"For a little while, baby. For a little while," Yadi replied, while playing with Jada's shoulder-length ponytails.

"Daddy can't come here, right?"

Yadi smiled. Her daughter was no one's dummy. "No, he sure can't."

Jada looked at her mother with her doe eyes and inch-long eyelashes. "That's right, 'cause Mr. Sean gonna beat him up if he do, right, Mommy?"

Yadi tried not to laugh. "Yeah, Jada, somethin' like that."

"Mommy?"

"Yes, baby?"

"I don't like Daddy no more."

Yadi reached for her daughter and sat her on her lap. "No, Jay-Jay, don't say that. You supposed to love your daddy. Me and him had a fight but that doesn't mean that he doesn't love you or you can't love him back."

"I don't like him 'cause he was mean to you. I want Mr. Sean to be my new daddy. He nice 'cause he let us have this new house."

Jada climbed off Yadi's lap and began coloring again. Yadi looked at her daughter and silently shed some tears. She would just have to work on getting Devin out of her life for good.

Yadi walked upstairs as Sean was getting dressed. She quickly put Jada to bed in the spare room, only to return to the doorway of Sean's bedroom, which smelled like the Hugo Boss he had just sprayed all over himself. She was secretly envious of the lucky woman who was going out with him tonight.

"So, who is this female you're hangin' out with tonight?" she asked, without cracking a smile.

"Oh, a friend of mine. You don't know her," Sean replied while putting on his Kenneth Cole shoes. Yadi felt a sexual urge creeping throughout her body, as Sean checked himself out in the mirror.

"How do I look, Yadi?" he asked.

"You look really good. You must really be tryin' to impress this woman," she added.

"It ain't that, ma, I just like to look good, whether I'm goin' out on a date or not."

Yadi inspected Sean from head to toe. "Well, I can see that you're gettin' your grown-man on."

Sean smiled at himself, while still standing in the mirror. He started to sing "How Does It Feel?" Everyone said he was a dead ringer for the singer D'Angelo, and he didn't believe that until that moment.

"I think I'm gonna cut my braids off. I am thirty years old now so it's about that time."

Yadi shook her head. Why was she feeling so jealous? Was it because she wanted Sean for herself or was it because she resented the freedom of the woman he was going out with? Yadi figured whoever she was, she probably had it all together. All she knew was that she was going to be in the house another night, alone. All the years she had spent with Devin were mainly spent in the house. They rarely went anywhere together.

"Well, you have a good time, Sean. You deserve it. You work hard as hell."

"Thanks, baby girl. I will have a good time and I do deserve it. Shit, you need to be havin' fun too."

"Umm, I dunno if I'm ready to."

Sean looked at Yadi and laughed. "Yo, I'm not tryin' to hear that. You can have men fallin' at your feet. You can have a NBA or NFL star, you name it!"

Yadi smiled. "Yeah, I guess. I mean, you right."
But I want you to fall at my feet, thought Yadi.

Sean looked at his watch and scurried down the
squeaky steps. He waved at Yadi, who was right
behind him, and instructed her to lock the door.
She continued to watch him get into his truck and
pull off. Yadi sighed and fell back onto the couch
in the living room. It seemed that she couldn't do
anything right. She kept asking herself why Sean
wasn't paying her any attention now that she was
staying at his house. Yadi didn't want to come out
and ask him, especially since he had already given
her a nice living arrangement. He was showing
his devotion by allowing her and Jada to stay in
his home/bachelor pad. Her cell phone vibrated
in her pocket, startling her. She saw that it was
Devin again. This time, she mustered up the
strength to answer it.

"What, Devin?" she yelled. "Why the fuck do
you keep callin' me?"

"Yadi, you need to come home! Where's my
daughter?" he yelled back.

"She's with her mother, that's where. You
need to leave me alone, Devin."

"And if I don't?"

"You will regret—see, this is what I'm talkin'
about. I'm leavin' you for good, Devin."

"You're not goin' anywhere, Yadi. You're too
weak to make it without a man."

Yadi laughed at him. "You don't own shit, you broke motherfucker! That's my co-op, you were drivin' my car, and I pay most of the bills around there! As a matter of fact, you need to be gettin' the hell up out of my apartment!"

"Give me back the money you took out of my account last year!"

"Fuck you, Devin! You're not gettin' shit back! You owed me that money. I done carried your ass for too long!"

For a fleeting moment, Yadi thought about calling Vanita's cousins, Day-Day and Jayquan from Marcy. She had two brothers herself but they both lived in Baltimore. If she told them about Devin putting his hands on her, they would be on 95 North in a hot second with heavy artillery in tow. They would definitely finalize the beef.

"And you're goin' to get out my house, Devin, one way or another!" she yelled.

"You're threatenin' me, Yadi?"

Yadi squinted. "You're not even worth a threat, Devin! I'm promisin' you."

Devin laughed. "Wow. You left here and lost your damn mind, for real! Anyway, I'm not goin' no motherfuckin' where. You done put me through a lot of bullshit all these years and now when the tables are turned, you can't take it. You left me here, remember? Now if you don't mind, I just wanna see my daughter!"

Yadi regretted answering the phone. "Yeah, all right, Devin. You wanna play? You wanna try to take over my apartment? No problem. Oh, and don't think about seein' Jada!" He hung the phone up in her ear.

Yadi wanted to scream, she was so angry. Devin couldn't careless about having his daughter living elsewhere. He just wanted to do her dirty. Yadi's name was on the lease so Devin had no other choice but to leave, either dead or alive. He would have to make that decision or else she was going to make it for him.

Chapter 10

Brandi strolled out of her building, with her four-inch heels clicking against the pavement. At five feet four inches, the Charles David thigh boots she wore gave her ass a nice lift. The waist-length leather jacket she had on made her feel and look extra sexy. Brandi checked Sean out as he opened the passenger door for her and held her hand while she climbed into the passenger seat of his truck. She thought that Sean looked delicious and smelled so good that she wanted to taste him. Sean climbed into the driver's seat and pulled off. They rode in silence for the first ten minutes, just listening to the R&B slow jam that was playing on the radio, which was getting both of them in the mood. When a commercial came on, Sean finally broke the silence.

"You look nice, Brandi. You would never think that you were thirty-five years old!" he complimented.

Brandi blushed. "Thank you, Sean. You don't look so bad yourself," she replied, giving him the thumbs-up.

He smiled. "You like, baby? Yeah, I'm just gettin' my grown-man on."

Brandi laughed because she thought about that herself. "Mmmm, you are a grown man, hopefully, in every since of the word."

Sean glanced at the sexy woman sitting in the passenger seat of his Escalade. She wore some tight-fitting skinny jeans with some stiletto thighboots. Her hair fell over her eyes, as she subconsciously swept her bangs back with her right hand, revealing her beautiful brown eyes.

"You know you're sexy as hell, right?" he said.

She smiled. "And so are you. Where are we goin' tonight?"

"I thought you were takin' *me* out!" They both laughed and began to relax a little more. "Nah, but for real, I'm gonna take you to this spot in Queens I wanted to check out after we eat dinner. It's called Startini's. Ever heard of it?"

Brandi frowned. She hadn't been on a date in a minute. She was just happy to be in the company of someone decent.

"Can't say that I have but it sounds like fun. As long as I'm with you, I don't care where we end up," she said as she licked her lips.

As Brandi rode in the passenger seat of Sean's truck, she felt a surge of power. She felt like a fifteen-year-old girl again; that same girl that caught Maleek's attention back in the day. Brandi hoped that Sean was a keeper because she promised herself that she would make him the happiest man ever. She didn't play when she was younger and now that she was grown, she definitely knew what to do when it came to keeping her man satisfied.

Sean looked at Brandi. Sean wanted to make sure that Brandi was just as comfortable with him as he was with her. He was definitely going to take what she said literally. She was irresistible, as her expensive Bulgari perfume permeated his truck, causing him to become dizzy with infatuation. It wasn't just her perfume that made him feel that way. Brandi was also very intoxicating. He wondered if he was going to have a hard time trying to get to know the "real" Brandi.

They had a nice dinner and afterward proceeded to go to the lounge bar to have drinks over some good conversation. As the night went on, Brandi became more and more open with Sean. He didn't want her to feel uptight and before it was all over, Sean was going to make sure she would never have to feel uncomfortable around him again.

"These apple martinis are popping!" she exclaimed. She laughed at herself. "Damn, I sound like one of the kids! What am I doing saying 'popping'?"

Sean laughed as well. "Yeah, you do sound like one of the kids. You don't even sound right talkin' like that. You seem to be real prim and proper," Sean stated while taking shots of Patron and chasing it with a Corona beer.

Brandi looked at Sean. "Shit, don't be fooled, Mr. Daniels. I wasn't always like this. This took some grooming, man, you just don't know."

Sean was curious. "What do you mean?"

Brandi caught herself because she didn't want to tell Sean too much yet. She had to remember that he was a correction officer and her past would probably be a little too much for him to deal with. Although she had moved on from the street life, she still lived by the codes.

"Just believe me when I tell you. It's nothing crazy, just regular stuff."

"Well, I'm lookin' forward to knowin' everything there is to know about Miss Brandi Wallace." Sean picked up Brandi's left hand and massaged her ring finger. "Were you married before?"

"No, I wasn't. Shamari's father and I were together for some years but we were never married. Were you?"

Sean sighed. "Nah. I want to get married one day, though. I wanna have children, too."

Brandi looked into her martini glass. She could do the marriage thing but she wasn't so keen on having any more children. "I'm not mad at you, Sean. You are a young man and I don't see why you can't have the marriage and some babies," she said as she sipped out of the martini glass.

"Yeah. You're right." They were silent for a moment. "As far as my job goes, you know that I'm not supposed to be talkin' to you, right?"

"Why not?" Brandi asked with a look of confusion on her face.

"It's against the rules. Fraternizin' with a visitor is just as bad as an officer fuckin' with an inmate."

"Are you serious? I mean, I'm a woman of good moral character and a law-abiding citizen. I have a master's degree, for Christ's sake!" Brandi announced, with a look of confusion on her face.

"I know, ma, but those are the rules. They're fucked up, I know, but that's just their way to keep us in line. If officers could mess around with visitors freely, can you imagine how many problems that could cause? It would be crazy!"

Brandi laughed. She was feeling a little buzz from her drink. "You're right, Sean. Even though you have your rules, I'm glad that you decided to break them for me. Fuck the rules!" She held up her glass for a toast and so did Sean. "Cheers!"

Sean looked at Brandi with a lustful look in his eyes. "Cheers!"

Four hours later, after their night was over, Sean pulled up to Brandi's building in Delmar Loop in Starrett City. It was quiet in the neighborhood with the exception of a few cars driving by on Pennsylvania Avenue. She sat in the truck for a few before getting out.

"Thanks for a good time, Sean," Brandi said. "I really had fun!"

Sean put his hands on her upper thigh. His touch sent tingles throughout her body. "You're welcome, sweetheart. I enjoyed you, too." He paused. "So when am I gonna see you again?"

She smiled seductively. "How do you want to see me?"

Sean licked his lips. "I wanna see you any way you want me to."

"Why don't you come upstairs with me, Sean?" Brandi said, grabbing Sean's hand.

He looked at his watch, knowing he had to get up to go to work in the morning, but damn, Brandi was irresistible. Sean smiled at her aggressiveness but he had to show her that the pussy wasn't the only thing he wanted from her. He reluctantly passed her up on her offer.

"You know, Brandi. I can't, ma. I have to go to work in the mornin' and if I go upstairs with you, I might fall asleep and not wake up in time. I don't even have my uniform with me."

Brandi looked disappointed. "Damn, Sean, I really want you bad. I know you want me, too."

She started to kiss him, flicking her eager tongue in and out of his mouth. They kissed and groped each other like dogs in heat. Sean finally managed to pull himself away.

"Nah, ma, I gotta chill," he insisted as he looked down at his swollen rod. A large print was showing through his Paper Denim jeans and Brandi, who couldn't take her eyes off it, began to lick her lips. She looked as if she wanted to devour him. Sean had to hurry up and get her out of his truck before they ended up in her bed. "So do you agree? We should chill, right?" he repeated. Brandi appeared to be sulking.

"Yeah, okay, Sean. You got away this time but next time, I'm going to eat you alive!" she laughed. "I'm going to let you go home now so you can get some rest for work."

Brandi slid out of the passenger seat and Sean got out of the truck to give her a good-bye hug.

Unable to resist each other, they began kissing again. Sean watched her walk into her building, waiting until she was inside safely before he climbed back into his truck and pulled off.

When Sean arrived home, he kicked his shoes off in the family room, too exhausted to climb the stairs to his bedroom. He pulled out a comforter from the closet and stripped down to his Calvin Klein boxer briefs. Sean grabbed the remote, turned on the television and got comfortable on his couch.

Suddenly, Yadi appeared in the doorway of the living room. She looked at the clock and saw that it was only twelve-thirty in the morning. She sat on the loveseat, while Sean got comfortable on the couch. He tried to keep from staring at Yadi's nipples, which were protruding through her nightshirt. He could see her naked silhouette in the dim light from the television. He felt himself rising to the occasion under the heavy comforter.

"What's up, Sean?" Yadi asked. "How was your date?"

Sean flipped through the channels on television, avoiding eye contact with the sexy Yadi. "It was cool. She's a cool lady."

Yadi nodded her head. "So if she's so cool, why are you home at twelve-thirty?"

Sean yawned. "I know but I had to get up in the mornin' to go to work. You know I can't work that visit floor and be sleepy. I would be sick to my stomach."

Yadi yawned also. "Well, it seems as if the yawnin' is contagious, so I'm gonna take my butt to bed. I just wanted to find out about your date." She walked over and gave Sean a hug. "Thanks again for lettin' me stay, Sean."

Sean returned the embrace and pulled Yadi close to him. He knew that he shouldn't have sex with her at that moment but he was still horny from the brief episode with Brandi. Not to mention, Yadi looked quite sexy in her nightshirt with her hair all over the place.

They kissed each other and Sean felt under her shirt, and to his surprise, she didn't have on any underwear. He massaged her plump derriere and she pulled the comforter back to reveal his iron hard penis. She smiled seductively as she removed his briefs, putting his erect dick into her moist mouth. Yadi shined it up with her saliva and slowly caressed the shaft of his dick with her long tongue.

As she ran her tongue across nerve-endings that Sean never knew he had, he began to moan. His body squirmed with pleasure as she tickled the head of his rod. She deep-throated Sean's cock, sending his body into convulsions and making his toes curl. He grabbed her hair while she worked the oral and made some slurping noises that made his eyes roll to the back of his head.

Sean pulled Yadi's face from his groin and put his arms around her waist. He sat upright and guided her on top of his bigness. Her pussy was so hot, it felt like an overheated oven and his dick was the main course. She grinded on his dick as if her life depended on it, making his dick hit every wall in her pussy.

Sean stuck his tongue in her mouth, as they fucked each other into pure oblivion. He felt as if he was having an out-of-body experience while he was sexing Yadira, who was not only a pleasure to look at and be around but to have as some live-in pussy, too. She was bouncing up and down on Sean's rod like a cowgirl at a rodeo and moaning softly, not wanting to have an orgasm so soon. Her dark hair covered their faces and Sean touched her mocha-colored titties, putting them in his mouth, one by one.

"Oh, Sean, baby, it's so good. I needed this," Yadi whispered softly, followed by a sexy moan.

"Take it, baby. Fuck Daddy's dick," Sean ordered. "Is it good? Is Daddy's dick good to you?"

"Oh, yesssss," she replied. "I need Daddy's dick, right there, baby, right there—"

They continued to sex each other for the next hour. Sean did everything he wanted to do to Yadi, and she didn't hold back either. He stuck his finger in her ass while he sexed her and she went crazy. Yadi gently tugged his testicles, while riding him and flexing her muscles. Sean sucked on her pussy and flicked his tongue in and out of her wet crotch like a cat lapping up milk from a bowl. They had orgasms repeatedly until Yadi went to her bedroom for some restful slumber. Meanwhile, Brandi was at home alone with her vibrator, wishing that Sean was inside her.

Chapter 11

The doctors in the clinic awakened Shamari. Some white shirts, Captain Hall, and Assistant Deputy Warden Miller wanted to interrogate him. They were the area supervisor and tour commander, respectively. He was in no mood to answer any questions and he wished they would leave him alone. He didn't want to create any more problems than he already had.

His life had become a downward spiral, and as he fell in and out of consciousness, he felt as if he was teetering on the edge of insanity. He tried to turn his head but the cut on his neck was hurting him, as he faintly heard the doctor tell the white shirts that he had received twenty-five stitches on his neck. Shamari was lucky it didn't hit a major artery because he would have been dead.

Of course, the proper procedure was followed and a search was conducted in Five North. Officers came up empty handed and no weapon was found. The officer on duty told Deputy Miller that she was on the top tier, doing her rounds at the time that Shamari had been cut. Upon her returning to the desk was when she saw Shamari on the floor, holding his neck. Several inmates surrounded him, attempting to hold towels to his neck to stop the bleeding. No one would cooperate and that was the end of it. A few inmates were transferred out of the building, but unfortunately, Born was still there.

Shamari trucked back to the housing area by himself and noticed that the officers had packed his things. He was going to be moved across the hall to Five West for security reasons.

As he settled into his new cell, his bandages covered only the wounds on the surface. His other wounds were unseen and tears began to flood his eyes. His thoughts went back to the day he got caught trying to rob the bodega on Stanley Avenue at three a.m. by himself. He had it all planned out after realizing that was the only store in the neighborhood that someone could physically walk into at that time of the morning. All the other bodegas in the hood had customers make their purchases at the plexiglass window on the outside of their stores.

Shamari took his .45-caliber pistol and walked inside the cluttered store toward the back, trying to see if there was anyone else in the store with the young Pakistani dude at the register. He grabbed a Pepsi from the freezer and walked toward the front again. Shamari's eyes scanned the area once again, making sure the coast was clear. Suddenly, he pulled out the gun, pointing it in the face of the frightened cashier. The man instantly began praying to Allah.

"C'mon, Habib, gimme the fuckin' money!" Shamari ordered in a stern voice. Beads of sweat broke out all over his forehead. He was nervous as hell. "I want it all out of the register and wherever else you got some cash."

The man gave Shamari the money in the register and just stood there. Shamari smacked the person at the register in head with the side of his gun. "What you waitin' for? Where's the rest of the money, motherfucker?" Shamari asked.

The man stumbled toward the back of the store, holding his bleeding head. He opened a small safe that was concealed in the wall of the store. He pulled out two stacks of big bills and handed them over to Shamari, whose eyes were bulging out of his head. He knew that this was going to be the money for his package that Peeto was going to hit him off with and he could fall back from the robbing spree.

Unfortunately, that thought couldn't be further from the truth. Police officers ran up in the store and caught Shamari red-handed with the bloody gun and the money. When Shamari walked into the store, he didn't realize that the owner was in a back room of the store. The owner was watching the cameras and called the cops. He emerged when the cops came in and handcuffed Shamari.

As Shamari lay on the bare mattress, he tried to make sense of everything that was happening to him. He wasn't ready to change yet. He had to regain his reputation while he was on the Island and let these dudes know that he wasn't nobody's sucker. *I'm out here robbing motherfuckers for self, so jail shouldn't be any different,* he thought. The cut on his neck was going to be a constant reminder that he was supposed to do the time, not let the time do him.

Later that day, Sean made his way up to Five North during his lunch to talk to Born. He entered Five North and greeted the male officer at the desk, who was engaged in a heavy conversation over the telephone. Sean walked to the back of the housing area, where Born was occupied with a game of spades with some other inmates. Everything appeared normal from what Sean could see. Born noticed Sean and instantly got up from table to greet the officer.

"What's up, Dee?" Born said, extending his fist to give Sean a pound.

"What's good, Born?" Sean replied, as he returned the pound. "Yo, what up with you threatenin' Wallace and mentionin' my name, all in the same sentence?"

Born laughed. "Oh, man, I was just tryin' to man that little nigga up! I see that he ran and told his mommy like a little bitch!"

"I know you tryin' to scare him, but Born, you gotta remember that nigga is only nineteen years old. He's not his father, Maleek. He's new to this jail shit!"

Born sucked his teeth. "Man, fuck that nigga! After yesterday, I really don't like his ass anyway! I was gonna give him a pass until he started cryin' about it. I never even put my hands on his young ass, neither! Shoulda slapped the shit outta him, now that I think about it!"

Sean shook his head. Born was already institutionalized, so he could not rationalize like a normal person. Not every person who came to jail was built for those walls and Shamari was one of them. Born had seen it all, in prison and out. He'd been through jail riots, gang fights, and shootouts, you name it. Born's mother forced him to start hustling at nine years old in order to help her at home. Being the eldest of ten children, he wasn't in the streets for recreation. Unlike Shamari, he had to do whatever he had to do for survival.

Sean looked around and noticed that Shamari's cell was empty. "Yo, where is he at, anyway?"

Born looked around. "Oh, that nigga got transferred outta here to Five West."

Sean blinked. "For what? What the fuck is he doin' in Five West?"

Born was visibly annoyed. "Nigga, I dunno! I ain't his damn keeper. Take your ass over there and find out." Born eyed Sean with a suspicious look on his face. "Why you takin' a sudden interest in this lame anyway, Dee?"

Sean smirked. "Go ahead with your twenty-one questions, Born!"

Born burst into laughter. "Oh, shit! I know why now! I saw his moms on the visit yesterday. Brandi, that's it. She's a sexy bitch, too! She had that sweatsuit on, fittin' that ass real good, and yes, that ass was fat as hell! Wifey was madder than a motherfucker 'cause she caught me starin' at her when she walked in!" Born slapped Sean on the back. "Damn, Dee! You that nigga, you sneaky bastard! Fuckin' with shorty moms on the low!"

Sean tried to lie but streetwise Born was having none of that. "Yo, Dee, you can't fool me. I'm thirty-eight years old and I been around the block and back. But remember what I told you about Brandi. She was a loose cannon. Hopefully, she ain't like that no more!" he said.

Sean gave Born a pound and walked out of Five North into Five West. He eyed all the inmates in the area, who looked at him strangely. He still didn't see Shamari anywhere. He asked the CO at the desk and she pointed to a cell located in the back.

The cell door was closed when Sean tiptoed over. He looked through the small window. He was able to see Shamari, who appeared to be sleeping. When he turned over, Sean noticed the bandages on his neck and the remnants of dried-up blood that had stained his bleached white pillowcase. He marched out of Five West into Five North again, this time requesting that Born step outside into the stairwell for five minutes.

"Nigga, what happened to Wallace's neck?" Sean asked.

Born pretended that he was clueless. "Dee, what the hell are you talkin' about now?"

Sean was getting annoyed with Born's facetious behavior. He knew that the hardened convict had something to do with Shamari being cut. They had known each other for too long, with Sean having full knowledge on Born's grimey ways. Born was a slimeball to the tenth power.

"What really happened, man? You gotta tell me somethin'!"

Born leaned on the wall and folded his arms. "Looka here, ain't this about a bitch! Sounds like you gettin' all protective over this guy. Is he your long-lost son or you tryin' to be his stepdaddy?" Sean was silent as Born continued. "I'm gonna tell you what. Why don't you just go ahead and fuck his mama and let this nigga hold his own up in here! He wanna be Billy Badass, that don't have nothin' to do with you or his mother. He's gonna have to go through it 'cause this is jail, this ain't Daddy Day Care!"

Sean shook his head in agreement with Born. The problem was he really liked Brandi and he felt partly responsible if anything happened to Shamari. His heart went out to her because she was a single mother who had genuine concern for her only child.

"So you're not gonna tell me who did it, huh, Born?" Sean prodded.

Born looked at Sean. He had a disgusted look on his face. "Nigga, you're the police! I ain't tellin' you shit!" Born rattled the steel door for the CO to let him out of the stairwell. He casually walked back into Five North, leaving Sean standing there by himself and wondering what he was going to tell Brandi.

Chapter 12

It was an early Sunday morning and Brandi was in her bed, looking through her planner. She saw that tomorrow was Shamari's court date. She took off her glasses and fell back against the fluffy pillows. She had spoken with the lawyer, and the judge was offering Shamari a plea agreement of one to three years. The robbery charge had been reduced to attempted robbery in the third degree. Since Shamari was a first-time offender, the judge was going to be lenient, his lawyer had explained to Brandi.

The lawyer, Mr. Ronald Samuels, who Brandi had paid a pretty penny to represent her son, had managed to get one of his friends as the judge presiding over Shamari's case. She knew that if Shamari took it to trial, he would probably be facing a lot of time and they couldn't risk that.

What Brandi was trying to understand was why her son would try to rob a store in the first place. She jumped up out of her bed and began ransacking his room for clues.

Since Shamari had been locked up for the last six months, Brandi felt there was something fishy going on with him. At first she was in denial. Brandi didn't want to believe that her son was guilty of anything. Now that the reality of Shamari's incarceration had finally hit her, Brandi decided that it was time to get some answers. It was obvious that Shamari wasn't going to tell her the truth.

Brandi went into Shamari's room and turned over his queen-sized mattress. When she did this, she was surprised at what she saw. She saw a .357 Magnum and what appeared to be thousands of dollars in $100 bills. Brandi sat on the floor and counted approximately $15,000. She was more amazed than upset, wondering what would drive him to have this amount of money in her house. Or period.

Brandi found Shamari's old cell phone and turned it on. She never had it turned off when he got locked up, half-expecting him to come home. Brandi began to scan through the list of phone numbers he had stored in the phone.

She saw mostly girls' names and numbers but when she arrived at one name, she froze because she had not heard that name in years. Peeto. He was one of Maleek's cronies from back in the day and was the only dude she knew who was still hustling, with nothing legitimate to show for his money but cars. He was always a certified clown and Brandi never could stand his ass. What in the hell was Peeto's number doing in Shamari's phone? Smelling a rat, she dialed the number instantly. Peeto answered the call on the first ring.

"Yo, Shaki," Peeto shouted into the phone, calling Shamari by his nickname. "You home, little nigga?"

Brandi was livid and went into street mode on Peeto. "Nigga, what the fuck is my son doin' with your number in his phone?"

Peeto was quiet. "Who is this?" he asked, pretending not to recognize the familiar voice on the phone.

"You know who the fuck it is, motherfucker! Why is your number in Shaki's phone?" she screamed. She resorted back to her ghetto ways for a moment.

"Brandi, calm down, let me explain—" he began.

"Peeto, I'm givin' your fat ass two minutes to tell the truth. I ain't how I used to be but you know I can always go there. So be a man about yours and fuckin' tell me what's goin' on!"

Peeto took a deep breath. It was fortunate he never had the opportunity to front Shamari the drugs because this was what he was afraid of and that was Brandi finding out.

"A'ight, Bee! Chill out. Shaki came to me for a package, a start-up package. I was gonna front him half and I wanted $20,000 for the other half. To be honest, I really didn't think he was goin' to come up with all that money but when he told me he had most of the money for me, I was like 'Wow'!"

Brandi wanted to throw the cell phone across the bedroom. "So how did he get the money, Peeto?"

"Well, I heard through the grapevine that he was out here robbin' niggas and whatever else to get the money. He probably was havin' a hard time gettin' the last of it 'cause that's when I found out he robbed the bodega on Stanley Avenue. He kept comin' to me, asking me if I could give him some work on consignment and I sent his ass walkin'! I really thought he was bullshittin', though!"

It was 1989 and Brandi pulled up in front of Peeto's building on Gates Avenue. Peeto was one of Maleek's cronies and Brandi's drug supplier. She knew that Peeto had a huge crush on her. Unbeknown to Maleek, she would use sexual favors to get him to come down on the prices of the drugs that she copped from him.

"Yo, Peeto!" Brandi screamed from downstairs. She was sitting in front of Peeto's Quincy Street building, waiting for him to bring the

package she wanted to cop from him. "Bring the shit down here, man! I been waitin' for the last twenty minutes, you fat motherfucker!"

Peeto stuck his head out of the second floor project window. "C'mon, Bee, you don't have to talk to a nigga like that!"

Brandi laughed and shuffled back into her Land Rover and waited for Peeto to bring her brick outside. Looking at her Fendi watch, she rolled her eyes up in the air. It was exactly three o'clock in the afternoon. She had to meet up with some Queens cats at Carmichael's on Guy Brewer at four o'clock and Peeto was bullshitting.

On the other hand, Brandi couldn't deny that Peeto probably cooked up some of the best work on that side of Brooklyn. This was one of the reasons why she always went to him. Peeto would cook up the cocaine and his product went far; it made Brandi and Maleek a lot of money. The only problem was that he was just slow as hell.

As Brandi sang "Let's Chill " by Guy, Peeto ran out the building and slid into the passenger seat. He was sweating bullets and his breathing was heavy from running. Peeto's eyes immediately became fixated with Brandi's perky titties and she laughed.

"Excuse me! My face is up here!" she said, pulling his face up to meet hers.

"I wasn't—" Peeto stammered.

Brandi waved him off. Her low-cut Yves Saint Laurent blouse worked. Now maybe Peeto would give her better prices. "Whatever. Just tell me the damage, Peeto."

He pulled the crack-cocaine out of the bag. It was half a kilo. "Um, how much you got?"

"Look, tell me the damn price so I can pay you and bounce! I gotta get on this Belt Parkway to meet these niggas by four o'clock!"

"You goin' by yourself?" Peeto asked, as his eyebrows shot up.

"Yeah. I do that sometimes. Why?" Brandi asked.

"Maleek ain't scared to have you meet up with these cats by yourself?"

"Maleek? Please! He got his own thing and I got mine. Now gimme the fuckin' numbers, Peeto!"

"Gimme 10 Gs."

Brandi smiled at the price and took ten piles of one hundred dollar bills from her oversized Coach bag. Peeto handed her the bag with the drugs in it and he got out of her truck.

"Wait, Peeto, before you go, lemme do something for you for givin' me such a reasonable price," she said with a mischievous smirk on her face.

Peeto got back into the passenger seat and Brandi went straight for his zipper. She pulled out his fat, stumpy penis and began jerking him off right there in her truck in broad daylight. Peeto leaned the seat back to enjoy being touched by Brandi. Her soft hand felt good rubbing against his hard dick. Brandi looked around and chuckled to herself while watching Peeto gyrate in her hand. He must have been very horny because it took no time for him to ejaculate all over her air-brushed fingernails. After that, Brandi opened the glove compartment, pulled out a pack of Shamari's baby wipes and wiped her hands clean. Peeto finally caught his breath and shoved his stump back into his pants.

"Thank you, Bee! I needed that," he whispered. "I just wish you could give me some of that pussy and you can get whatever I got for free."

Brandi sucked her teeth. "Nah, this pussy belongs to Maleek, boo. I wouldn't want to put your ass outta business!"

Brandi shuddered at that memory. She had long erased those sexual interludes with Peeto out of her mind. She was so different then.

"Well, he wasn't and now he's suffering the consequences. Just stay away from my son, Peeto. That's all I ask," she said.

Peeto sighed on the other end of the phone. He felt bad about Shamari's situation and partly responsible.

"Look, Bee, I—" Brandi hung up the phone in his ear.

Brandi calmed down when she realized that she couldn't get mad at Peeto. Shamari was completely and unequivocally responsible for himself and he knew better. She was tired of blaming everyone else for Shamari's stupidity and she refused to have him hurt her any longer. It was time for him to be a man and she was going to show him that starting today. After hanging up with Peeto she put the phone down on the cherry wood dresser in Shamari's room. Before she could walk out, the cell phone vibrated, startling Brandi. When she looked on the caller ID and noticed a girl named Amber's name on it, she decided to answer.

"Sweetheart, this is Shamari's mother. Shamari is away right now, so he won't—" Brandi started to explain.

The woman cut her off. "Just the person I wanted to speak to," said the adult-sounding female on the other end of Shamari's Sprint phone. "My daughter, Amber, is about to have a baby for your son. When she told him about the pregnancy, he never called back or tried to arrange anything, just nothin'. Shit, I just found out about him gettin' locked up a couple of weeks ago!"

"First of all, ma'am, who are you?" Brandi asked.

"Oh, I'm so sorry. I'm Amber's mother, Carol Johnson. Please excuse me. I'm just sorry it had to be under these circumstances," the woman replied.

"Well, I'm Brandi Wallace, Shamari's mother. I don't think I ever met Amber."

"You probably didn't. She said that she wasn't really a girlfriend of his, just a real close friend, if you know what I mean. I put Amber on birth control when she turned fifteen years old and this year she decided she wanted to stop taking them because they made her sick to her stomach. Can you imagine how I felt when I found out she was pregnant, two months ago?"

Brandi frowned. "Wait, Miss Johnson, Shamari has been locked up for six months. That would be impossible."

"Oh, Miss Wallace, Amber is eight-and-a-half months pregnant! I found out she was pregnant when she was six months!"

Brandi shook her head. What more could her son have done? "Miss Johnson, I would love to meet with you and Amber. Can I come see you, to talk in person?"

"Sure. My address is 3302 Bristol Street between Newport and Riverdale. It's a private house."

"Okay. I'm on my way over." Brandi threw on some clothes, grabbed her car keys, and ran out the door, perhaps to meet the mother of her grandchild.

Chapter 13

Upon arriving at the Johnson's home, Brandi looked around and remembered this same block was one of her old stomping grounds. She had done many transactions there and it was ironic that Shamari was actually seeing a girl that lived there. She secretly hoped that Amber's mother was no one she knew from the past.

Brandi stopped in front of the house, which appeared well kept from the outside. She opened the metal gate and walked up the four stairs that led to the porch and the front door. Brandi heard a dog barking in the distance, praying that there were no dogs in this woman's house. She couldn't stand cats or dogs and didn't want to leave there smelling like either of them.

Brandi rang the doorbell and a young girl of about sixteen appeared in the doorway. She opened the door to the house but stood there, pausing to open the storm door for Brandi to come in. The girl looked at Brandi from head to toe, as if she was inspecting her. Brandi introduced herself and the girl finally let her in. Once inside, the teenager looked at her up and down again.

"You're Shamari's mother, huh?" the girl finally said. Brandi hoped she wasn't Amber because she looked a hot mess with her hair sticking up every which way.

"Yes, um, are you Amber?" Brandi asked. The girl didn't look pregnant to her.

"Uh-uh. That's my sister, she's pregnant by your son," she replied.

Suddenly, a short, voluptuous woman finally appeared. "Hello, I'm Carol Johnson, Amber's mother."

"I'm Brandi Wallace, Shamari's mother," Brandi said. "I do have to apologize for my son's carelessness. I didn't know anything about Amber's pregnancy."

Miss Johnson took Brandi's hand and led her into the small living room. Everything looked neat and in place.

"I'm so sorry, Miss Wallace, about all of this." Miss Johnson glanced at the staring girl. "Ashlee, get outta her face and go sit your grown behind down somewhere. As a matter of fact, go finish combin' that peasy head of yours!"

The girl huffed and walked upstairs. Miss Johnson called for Amber, and a few seconds later she came wobbling down the carpeted staircase. Amber was a thick girl, who Brandi could tell had a killer body before she got pregnant. She was cute, too, with her heart-shaped face and pixie features. Her hair was done in box braid extensions that she had pulled up into a neat bun on the top of her head. Brandi liked her maternity outfit, as well. Amber was wearing a cute baby doll top that covered her protruding belly and some leggings. Shamari did have some great taste in girls. *Maybe too much,* Brandi thought, because Amber ended up pregnant.

"Hi, Miss Wallace. I'm Amber Johnson," the young lady said, smiling sweetly.

Brandi stood up to greet Amber and held her hand. "Hello, sweetie. I'm sorry we had to meet like this but I didn't know anything about Shamari getting someone pregnant. I just happened to turn on his phone a little while before your mother called."

Miss Johnson spoke up. "Well, like I was sayin', Miss Wallace, my daughter is eighteen years old. Fortunately, for her, she was able to graduate from high school and start community college. Now she's gonna have this baby and I ain't gonna lie, I need the help. I have three older children who don't live in the home anymore and this here is the last two, Amber and Ashlee. My husband, their father, died last year and I been strugglin' ever since tryin' to maintain two jobs and deal with these girls. Ashlee is fifteen years old and to be honest, she's next to be pregnant with her grown behind!" Carol sighed. "You know how hard it is raising these girls, I'm sure!"

Brandi smiled. "Yeah, I know because I was pregnant with Shamari at sixteen but believe me, Shamari isn't anything to write home to mama about, neither, as you can see, being locked up and getting some girl pregnant and not telling his mother."

Miss Johnson laughed. "I know what you mean, child."

Brandi's face turned serious. "I also hope you know that I have to insist on a blood test, Miss Johnson."

Miss Johnson seemed taken aback by the suggestion but she understood. "Trust me, I understand completely."

Amber looked disappointed. "Miss Wallace, no disrespect. I ain't no ho. Shamari was the only person I been with when I found out I was pregnant."

"I do not doubt that, baby; it's just something to have in writing that says my son is the father to your child. You guys are very young and you're not married." Brandi didn't want to hurt Amber's feelings but unfortunately, taking a blood test was being realistic. She didn't know Amber from a can of paint.

"Are you comin' to the baby shower?" Amber asked, changing the subject.

"Why, yes, Amber, I'd would like that, but let me speak to my son first. I need to get some clarification about this situation. You understand, don't you?"

"I understand, Miss Brandi. If you want to come, it's two weeks from now, on Saturday, the twenty-first," she replied.

Brandi sighed. She always wanted a baby shower when she had Shamari but her mother would have none of that. Her mother felt that a sixteen-year-old girl having a baby was nothing to celebrate.

Brandi sat there with the Johnson's for two hours. She honestly liked Amber and her mother, too, who was nice enough. She was relieved that Shamari at least had the common sense to deal with a civilized girl from a seemingly decent family. Amber gave the impression that she was a young lady with a good head on her shoulders. Brandi liked the fact that she said that she still wanted to continue her education, even after having the baby. At Amber's age, she didn't know what she wanted to do with her life and her mother stayed on her back because of this.

"You better do somethin' with yourself, Brandi!" her mother screamed at her. "You spent the last five years in the street, sellin' drugs and gettin' into all kinds of trouble with that piece of shit, Maleek! Now you wanna come back here to live in this house with the same crap that you was doin' before? Well, I ain't havin' it, Miss Brandi Lynn Wallace!"

Six-year-old Shamari was asleep in her old full-sized bed. His head popped up, startled from all the yelling her mother was doing.

Brandi winced at the sound of her mother calling out her name; she only did that when she was pissed. A full year had passed since Maleek's death and Brandi came back home to live with her mother for a while. The houses that were Maleek's were long gone but Brandi still had some money stashed. Maleek's mother sold the homes, which were in her name, and gave Brandi some money to put to the side for Shamari. This gesture made Brandi feel guilty as hell. If only his mother knew what really happened to her son . . . .

"Mommy, you act like I just be here sittin' on my ass all day—" Brandi began.

Her mother cut her off. "Brandi, you are twenty-two years old now. Shamari is six years old. You can't stay here if you don't get a job or do somethin' with yourself. I'm sorry. You are a grown-ass woman and it would kill me if you went back out in them streets and continued hustlin' again! Your brothers did it and they almost put me in an early grave, but I would die if somethin' happened to you. You're my only girl!"

Brandi looked at her mother and then Shamari, who lay his head in her lap. Her mother was right. She had been in the streets, living the fast life for as long as she could remember. After Maleek was gone she realized that everything that she had done wasn't for herself, it was for him. He had consumed her mind into thinking that his way was the right way and she ran with it. No more. She had devalued her morals to be with a man and that made her become a heartless person. Now, Maleek was never coming back and she was left to deal with the harsh realities of the world alone.

Brandi felt her life had no significance any-more. She thought about killing herself after it seemed as if she had no other options but hustling. She had grown accustomed to that life, to having whatever she wanted and being in *control. All the while she knew what the risks of being out there in the streets consisted of but she was going too fast to care. Did she want to end up dead or in jail, was the question she finally asked herself. It was her first time thinking about the consequences.*

Brandi looked at her mother standing in the doorway of her bedroom with her arms folded across her chest. Even though Brandi's mother had a hardened look on her face, Brandi could tell that she was hurting inside. The Wallace siblings were about to put their mother in an early grave. The thought of her and her brothers being responsible for their mother's death sent chills down Brandi's spine.

After Brandi managed to put Shamari back to sleep, she tiptoed toward her mother's bedroom. The television was the only thing on in the dark bedroom. As the TV light shined in her mother's face, Brandi realized for the first time that her mother had aged, although she was only in her late forties. Brandi walked in the room, lifted the heavy comforter and quietly slid into the bed beside her mother. The warmth coming from her mother's voluptuous body made Brandi drowsy. Miss Wallace held Brandi and kissed her, lovingly, as her daughter went to sleep in her arms. The next morning, Brandi went to sign up for the General Equivalency Diploma. It was time to get her life together. She got her GED and then went to college, never looking back.

When Brandi was ready to leave, Amber volunteered to walk her to her car. Amber spoke unreservedly about Shamari, apparently knowing more about him than his own mother did. Amber knew that she was having a boy and she wanted to name the baby Maleek, after Shamari's deceased father.

Brandi couldn't help but wonder if Shamari knew about Amber's pregnancy and if he did, why didn't he tell his mother about it?

"Well, Miss Brandi, me and Shamari was good friends, we went to school together and you know, one day we just started messin' around. He would tell me all about you and his father. I didn't tell my mother everything but Shamari knew that I was pregnant from day one. I was ashamed to tell anybody because he was actually robbin' and stealin' tryin' to get some money up for me to have this baby. I tried to tell him that he didn't have to do that but he just said that his father did it for you and that he was gonna sell drugs to provide for me and his unborn. I swear, Miss Brandi, I tried to tell Shamari to just get a job, I mean, we both graduated from high school.

He said he wasn't about to work in nobody's McDonald's. He just didn't want to listen to me."

"So why did you wait to tell your mother that you was pregnant?" Brandi asked.

"Well, I knew that she wouldn't approve of it. I was gonna get an abortion but I don't have no job or money. I was goin' to enroll in college but after Shamari was locked up, I just couldn't bring myself to go anymore. I was upset because we lost contact with each other and I'm sure he assumed that I got rid of it. I surely didn't want to tell my mother I got pregnant by a jailbird." She looked at Brandi and apologized for the comment. "I kept the baby because I thought that Shamari would have been home by now."

Brandi hugged Amber. "Don't worry, Amber, you're gonna be all right. I'm gonna speak to Shamari and make sure he calls you, okay?" Brandi handed her one of her business cards with all of her information. "Call me anytime, okay?" Amber shook her head in agreement. Brandi smiled at her before leaving the house. She then got into her car and pulled off.

Brandi didn't know whether to be happy or sad about being a grandmother at thirty-five years old, but she couldn't wait until that son of hers called. She was going to give him a serious tongue-lashing.

Chapter 14

The next morning, Shamari arose from a sound sleep, feeling groggy. The Tylenol with codeine the nurse had given him for the pain was kicking his ass. His neck began to throb and his head felt as if it weighed a ton. He dragged himself out of bed and washed his face, which was a task. Shamari walked out of the opened cell door and shuffled his way toward the phones. As Shamari walked by, he noticed several inmates staring and whispering to each other. They were pointing at the bandages on his neck but he didn't care. He was no longer worrying about what the bird-ass dudes in there thought about him. He was doing his bid alone.

Shamari dialed his mother's number and waited as the phone rang several times. Before the operator could complete the sentence, Brandi began yelling into the phone. Shamari held his head because her loud-ass voice was making it hurt even more.

"Shamari Tashaki Wallace! Why the hell you never told me that you got some female pregnant?" she screamed. "Does a girl named Amber ring a fucking bell?"

"Oh, shit!" Shamari exclaimed. "She kept it?"

Brandi shouted in disbelief. "Yeah, stupid ass, she kept it!" imitating Shamari's voice. "The girl is about to have the fucking baby, Shamari! She's eight-and-a-half months pregnant!"

"Ma, I'm gonna keep it real. I thought that after she found out I got locked up, she was gonna have an abortion!"

"Shaki, that child don't have no damn money to get an abortion! You didn't even tell me so that I could have at least tried to help her out. I'm all over there with the girl's mother and that woman is probably looking at me sideways because of your dumb ass! But it's too damn late now! The girl is about to have the baby!" There was a silent pause as Shamari tried to register everything. "Who was this Amber? Was she your girlfriend?"

Shamari couldn't deny Amber if he tried. He really did care about the girl even though he never bothered to call her back after he was arrested. But because of his avoidant behavior and immaturity, he really assumed that Amber had an abortion. At least, he hoped that she had an abortion after he was locked up.

"Yeah, somethin' like that, Ma," Shamari replied, shaking his head in disbelief.

"Well, she's about to be your baby mama, too. I mean, I don't understand you, Shaki. You and I used to be so close. You used to tell me everything. Then you have Peeto, his grimy fat ass, ready to sell you . . . Anyway, I'm not even going to address this shit over the phone." Brandi quickly changed the subject. She knew that Shamari's phone conversation was being recorded. "You know you go to court tomorrow, right?"

"Yeah, I know, Ma. I'm gonna take the plea agreement."

"I know the fuck you are!" Brandi said, with a harsh tone. "I'm not going to be there that day because I have an important meeting at work and I can't miss it. So be on your best behavior, Mr. Wallace. The lawyer is going to call me with the details and you call me tomorrow evening when you get back to your housing area. Are you okay in there?"

"Yeah, I'm straight," Shamari lied. He put his hands to his aching neck. "Yo', Ma, are you still dealin' with that CO cat, Daniels?"

Brandi paused for a moment. "Why?"

"I just asked. You probably wouldn't tell me anyway. I'll call you tomorrow for Amber's number."

Brandi shuffled around for Amber's info. It was time for Shamari to take responsibility for his actions.

"Oh, no, honey! You're going to call her right the fuck now! It's time for you to be a damn man and handle your business!" She gave Shamari Amber's phone number and hung up on him.

Brandi went into the living room of her apartment and poured her a glass of merlot from her bar. As she sipped her wine, she looked at the time. She wondered when Sean was getting off work. Brandi wanted to call him, maybe leave him a sexy voicemail but didn't want to seem like she was sweating his fine ass.

Brandi knew that she had the qualities to get any man she wanted. Ever since the Maleek days, she had become very cautious about the men she allowed in her circle. Long gone was her thirst for thugs, gangsters, and bad boys.

As for women, she never was real fond of their company, only had one real friend growing up and that was Sheba. Of course, she still rolled with Sheba, who was always a delight to be around. After all, they considered themselves sisters. Brandi laughed to herself and dialed her number.

"Heeelllo? Is this Brandi Lynn?" Sheba yelled into the phone. There was some loud music in the background.

"Hey, Sheba baby!" Brandi yelled.

"Will you turn that music down?" Sheba laughed and turned the music down. "What's up, girlfriend?"

"Girl, I'm fine. I just came up outta that subway system and I'm tryin' to unwind. I was workin' overtime all this week."

Sheba was a train conductor for the MTA for thirteen years. She inspired Brandi to put her past behind her and get on the right track. Like Brandi, Sheba was a teenage mother. She gave birth to her child, Chanel, when she was only seventeen. Not too long after that, Sheba made up her mind to get her act together for the sake of her daughter. She was also very instrumental in encouraging Brandi to go back to school to get her GED, just like she did.

Seventeen-year-old Sheba walked down Stuyvesant Avenue, heading toward the A train and pushing a Graco stroller. Her daughter, Chanel, was only a few months old at the time and Sheba was taking her to a doctor's appointment. It was a cold, blustery afternoon, and out of the blue, Brandi rolled up on Sheba, pushing a black 1988 190E Mercedes-Benz with the Hammer rims . Shamari, who was eighteen months, was asleep in his car seat in the back.

"Hey, Sheba, baby!" Brandi called out to her friend. Sheba looked at Brandi and frowned.

"Hey, Brandi Lynn!" Sheba yelled back. "Who ride is that? Maleek's?" she asked.

"Hop in and I'll tell you."

Sheba seemed hesitant to get in the car with Brandi. She loved her friend with all her heart but after Brandi started dealing with Maleek, Sheba saw that she was definitely heading down a path of destruction. Not wanting to be associated with Brandi's newfound profession, Sheba didn't have to wait for any mother of hers to tell her to stay away from Brandi. The boosting and petty crimes that they had committed in their youth were nothing compared to the drug game, which, unfortunately, Brandi had embraced as her new hustle. Sheba wanted no part of it. She looked at her adorable baby girl tucked comfortably in her stroller and decided that that was a good enough excuse to not get in Brandi's luxury whip.

Brandi looked at Sheba strangely. "What's the matter, Sheba? You're gonna get on the train?"

Sheba sighed. Brandi was breaking her heart. "Look, Brandi, I can't, I can't cosign this shit. I know that car ain't Maleek's, it's yours and I know what you been doin'. I can't cosign that shit, Brandi, I'm sorry."

Brandi mean-mugged her best friend. "What the hell are you talkin' about, Sheba? I'm chillin'! I'm only gettin' money with my baby daddy, and trust me, it's a whole lotta money out there to be made! We can get fresh as hell. I mean, my baby is even wearin' Gucci shit! Chanel will be fly . . . oh, and you can move out your mama's house—" Brandi said.

Sheba cut her off. "Look, Brandi, you my sister and everything but I ain't tryin' to be out in these streets like that. I got my daughter and you got a son. I'm about to go to school, get my fuckin' diploma, then take my black ass to work at a regular nine to five gig. We did our boostin' thing but it's over now. We're mothers. You wanna do that hustlin' shit, which is not cool, but that's you. I will still love you, but don't call me until you made a decision ta get your shit together. Plus, I'm never gettin' in that damn overpriced death trap—ever!" Sheba then walked away with her head held high.

Brandi was stunned and felt like a lost little girl. Now that she didn't have Sheba by her side, she felt fucked up. She looked at the plush leather in her car and then looked back at Shamari, who was laced with designer clothes from head to toe. Brandi looked in the rear view mirror at herself and shrugged her shoulders. As far as she *concerned, she did have her shit together. That's why she was driving a Benz and Sheba's high and mighty-ass was walking to the fucking train station in the cold. Brandi laughed and pulled off, beeping her horn at Sheba as she drove by.*

"What's goin' on with my baby? Is he all right in there?" Sheba asked, referring to her godson, Shamari.

"Girl, please! That boy is driving me up the wall! Sometimes, I think that I'm being punished for all me and Maleek's dirt because he is giving me straight hell! Everytime I look around, I'm finding out something new about him."

"You see, Brandi? I told your ass that you done spoiled his ass!" Brandi agreed. "What the hell he done did now? Don't he go to court tomorrow?"

"Yeah, he's going to court tomorrow. Anyway, girl, I found out that he was trying to buy a kilo from Peeto and he had to try to get the money up for it. That's why he was out there robbing people. But that's not it. He got some girl named Amber pregnant! She's eight and-a-half months, Sheba. I'm just so through with his ass!"

"What? Pregnant? Peeto? Lawd, that's the last man that Shaki needs to mess with! You know the rumor is he's the reason Maleek got killed."

Brandi was unusually quiet with that statement. She was actually the one that started that rumor back in the day. A wave of guilt swept through her body. She never even told her best friend about her part in Maleek's death.

"What the hell is goin' on with Shaki? He graduated from high school just to go and mess up his life like this? First, Peeto, jail, and now this girl is pregnant!" Sheba said.

"Yeah, I met her today. Her name is Amber and she is a very nice girl with a good family and a good head on her shoulders. Honestly, she doesn't need to be with no Shaki. She's lucky that I didn't know about this sooner because I would have taken her ass to have an abortion."

"Well, Brandi, we love Shaki to death but it is what it is. He has to take responsibility for his own actions." They both paused to take everything in. "So you got a grandchild on the way, huh? You old biddy! How do you feel?" Sheba started cracking up.

Brandi laughed too. "Fuck you, Sheba! I don't feel old and I damn sure ain't gonna let no grandbaby stop me from doing my thing!" She listened to Sheba take a drag from a cigarette. "Oh, yeah, by the way, I met this guy. A nice guy."

Sheba yelled into the phone. "Aw, shit! Not you, Brandi Lynn! It's about time! But wait, umm, does he have a friend?" Sheba asked.

Brandi said with a laugh. Sheba always made her feel better.

"I dunno, child, with your thirsty self! I didn't even get with him like that yet. In case you were wondering what he does for a living, he's a correction officer. I met him while I was visiting Shaki on Rikers. And he's fine as hell, girl! I noticed him as soon as I walked through the door but I knew that I wasn't there for my own personal pleasure. You know how bad I hate going to Rikers, so I wanted to get in and get out. He must have seen me, too, because he made his way over to our table to speak and you know that son of mine acted like a damn fool. Shaki embarrassed the hell out of me! Anyway, the guy is a young tender. He's only like thirty years old and, Sheba, he got it all together."

Sheba smiled from ear to ear. "Wow, sounds like he's a good catch. Does he have any children?" Sheba asked.

"No. He doesn't have any children," Brandi replied.

Sheba was quiet. "Now that could be a problem. He don't have any kids? What if y'all get with each other and he wants to have some kids by you?"

"I didn't think about that. I don't know, Sheba, I like this guy, but I gotta take it slow. I don't want to get all involved with this guy and get my feelings hurt. It's been a while since I been in a serious relationship with anyone and of course, Shaki don't like him."

Sheba sucked her teeth. For years, Brandi had made Shamari her life. She was tired of it.

"Brandi, for once stop worryin' about what Shaki thinks! You need to live your life 'cause your son is damn sure gonna live his. He's the one runnin' around here tryin' to sell drugs, robbin', and havin' babies! You wanna talk to the CO guy? You do just that and have fun. You have dedicated yourself to Shamari all his life, making sure that he was well taken care of. Now it's time for you to find some happiness of your own and if that means talkin' to this man, then do that." Brandi sighed. Sheba was always giving her some great advice.

After they hung up, she managed to do some things around the house to keep her mind off Shamari and Sean. Thinking about what Sheba said, Brandi felt more rejuvenated than she had felt in years. The only problem was that she was scared of falling in love. She was in love with Maleek and when he broke her heart, he ended up dead. If Sean was the man for her, Brandi hoped he wouldn't break her heart. She would hate for him to end up the same way Maleek did.

Chapter 15

It was Sunday evening and Vanita was back in town from her excursion. She was surprised to discover that Yadira was staying at Sean's house. Curious to find out how that happened, she conveniently invited herself over to Sean's place just to see what was going on. When she saw Yadi's bruised body, she got angry all over again.

"That mangy bastard!" she said about Devin. "I told you the the next thing that he was goin' to do was put his hands on you!"

Yadi shook her head in agreement. She would never tell Vanita that she was the one that started the fight.

"Yeah, Nita. You was right, as usual."

Vanita looked around Sean's digs. "Girl, this house is nice! Is this Sean's by himself?"

Yadi smiled. She wouldn't mind living in the beautiful brownstone with Sean. Of course, she was fantasizing about something that was never going to happen.

"He does have a tenant that lives on the top floor. His grandparents passed and they left it to him. It's been in his family for forty years and it was passed down to their youngest grandchild, which is Sean."

"Wow, that's what's up!" Vanita replied, as she looked around at the decorating. She loved how Sean played with the sienna and brown shades, giving the brownstone an earthy feel. She admired the runners on the hardwood floors and the family portraits that seemed to be all over the house. His taste in artwork was excellent and it consisted of mostly abstract paintings, which Vanita loved. She would have never guessed Sean had such flavor.

"Sean's home is lovely but I think that you and Jada need to come and stay with me while you get yourself together."

Yadi put a large coffee mug to her full lips. "Why?" she asked, shrugging her shoulders. "We're fine right here; Sean said that I could stay here as long as I want."

Vanita looked at Yadi, with her eyes half closed. "You fucked him, didn't you?"

Yadi put the cup down and walked to the refrigerator. "Nita, don't start with me!" she said.

Vanita shook her head. "Here you are tryin' to leave one relationship and here you go startin' another one! What's wrong with you?"

Yadi swung her head around. "I can handle myself, Vanita! Why are you actin' like I don't know what I'm doin'?

Vanita sighed. "Yadi, think about it. You're very weak right now. If you gave up the sex, you gonna end up fallin' for Sean. I mean, look at him. He's handsome, got a good career, and look at this damn house! He don't have no kids or baby mama drama, and he is a single man and obviously, a real man to take you and your daughter in. Somethin' you have never experienced with Devin. You gonna start feelin' a way when he's out with other women and he starts treatin' you like a roommate again. You're workin' on your emotions right now!"

Yadi looked at Vanita. "We always liked each other, Nita, and you know that. You told me to talk to him!"

"Yeah, I did but look at what's goin' on here. You and your baby father had a physical altercation, then you talkin' about to stayin' here for a while. That's baggage that I'm sure Sean don't want or need right now. Be fair to him and be fair to yourself. Get your shit together and if he hollers at you then it's all good. You have to close one chapter of your life before you can move on to the next."

Yadi looked at Vanita. Once again she had managed to drop some jewels on her. Thinking about what Vanita said, Yadi figured that she was going to do it the right way. She would tell Sean when he came home that she decided to stay with her friend. She didn't want to be a burden to him anymore.

Later that afternoon when Sean arrived home from work, it was unusually quiet and he wondered if Yadi was there. For the days that they stayed, he had grown accustomed to little Jada running to the door, yelling "Mr. Sean!" to the top of her lungs. He came home, sort of looking forward to sweeping Jada up in his arms, looking adorable with her long jet-black pigtails and dark eyelashes to match. He walked upstairs, called out Yadi's name and she answered immediately. Sean stepped into the guest bedroom and saw Yadi packing her things.

"Where are you goin'?" he asked. "Where's Jada?"

"Jada's at Vanita's house," Yadi answered, as she continued to do what she was doing. She didn't look at Sean when she replied.

"Vanita was here?" he asked.

Yadi looked up. "Yeah, she just got back in town and she came over here to check on me and Jada. That's when we both came to the conclusion that it would be a good idea for me to stay with her."

Sean seemed disappointed. "Yadi, I told you it was no problem for you and Jay-Jay to stay here with me. I got all this room that I don't need and, and it's not like we on top of each other!" They both paused, as they recalled the night they had sex. "Well, you know what I mean," he quickly added.

"I know what you mean, Sean, but I feel we made a big mistake by havin' sex with each other the other night. I don't want to get the wrong impression and I definitely wouldn't want to give the wrong one, neither. You are a great person and a sweetheart but . . . it's not you, it's me."

"Oh, boy, Yadira, you makin' this shit sound like we was in a relationship. You're my buddy. I got mad love for you . . . ."

"That's why I gotta leave this house, Sean. I think I'm fallin' in love with you."

When she went to walk away, Sean grabbed Yadi by her waist. He pulled her to him and slowly began kissing her. They made out in the hallway and eventually the make out session led to Sean entering Yadi's wet pussy doggie style and sexing her from the back.

As Yadi stood by the stairs with her hair hanging over the banister, she played with her clitoris while Sean stroked her G-spot from inside her moist vagina. Sean gently planted kisses on her spine and she moaned with delight as the tears fell from her eyes. Yadi didn't want to leave but she knew that with the sex being as good as it was and her feelings for him, it was a deadly combination.

Sean felt himself about to climax while watching her plump ass ripple, as he slowly pumped in and out of Yadi's wetness. Yadi turned around to face Sean and they kissed as he re-entered her from the front so that he could feel the friction of her clitoris brushing against his dick. As Yadi pulled Sean closer to her, he went deeper inside of her. Their bodies moved simultaneously and the smacking of her soaked pussy could be heard throughout the quiet house. The sounds of their moans bounced off the walls. They both had back-to-back orgasms and ended collapsing against the banister.

When they finished, Yadi disappeared into the bathroom to freshen up. When she returned, she looked at Sean without saying a word. Sean cared about Yadi and he didn't want to lead her on but what Sean didn't realize was that he was giving her false hope by having sex with her.

At that moment, Sean felt that they had both served their purpose and maybe it was best that she left before things got out of control. Yadi brushed by him with her bags, and walked downstairs and out of the front door. Sean stood in the spare bedroom, staring into space while he listened to her pull off. He wondered if he had made a mistake by allowing the vulnerable Yadi into his home. Only time would tell.

After Yadi was gone, Sean walked into his bedroom and slammed the door. Just two weeks before this, his life was perfect. He was just another single brother with a woman or two, with no commitments and no headaches. Now he had two beautiful women tugging him back and forth, emotionally and physically. He didn't know what to do. How did he let this happen?

Sean was definitely physically attracted to Yadi. However, after leaving the bedroom, what did she really have to offer him but good sex? He wanted a woman who was independent and strong-willed, not someone who was emotionally needy, like Yadira Cruz. He needed someone he could depend on, a woman who could hold him down if things got rough. Being beautiful on the outside just wasn't enough for Sean. On the other hand, Brandi Wallace was a good catch. The only problem with her was that her son was a pain in the ass. Sean didn't have any children but he would never expect a woman to choose him over her child. He just thought that Shamari was very disrespectful toward him, as a man. If he and Brandi decided to be in a serious relationship, how was he supposed to deal with Shamari and that attitude of his? He was a man before he was a correction officer so Sean certainly wasn't going to allow anyone, especially some young punk, to disrespect him in any manner.

He didn't understand what was wrong with the youth today. Sean was raised to respect his elders, and because of Shamari's behavior, he had no other choice but to question Brandi's parenting techniques. What if Sean wanted to have a child of his own? How would that fly with Shamari, who seemed selfish, thoughtless, and inconsiderate? That wasn't a good look.

Even though Yadi's confidence and self-esteem were shot, her parenting skills seemed exemplary. She seemed liked she took great care of Jada and Jada was a delightful child to be around. Although Jada was only four years old, he could only imagine what Shamari was like at her age. People probably hated to see his ass coming.

Sean's cell phone rang and he smiled as he looked at the caller ID.

"She's gonna live a long time," Sean said, when he answered the phone. "I was just thinkin' about you."

Brandi chuckled. "Oh, really? I've been thinking about you too. What are you doing?"

Sean stood up to slip out of the dark blue uniform. He stood in the middle of his bedroom with his underwear and wife beater on.

"Comin' out of this monkey suit. You sound like you're real relaxed," he said.

"Yeah, I am. I was sitting here sipping on some merlot and listening to my Jamie Foxx CD," Brandi replied.

Sean was turned on. "What do you have on?" he asked, while grabbing himself, still horny after having sex with Yadira.

"Umm, let's see. Nothing special. Just a pair of boy shorts and a tank top."

"Oooh, that's sounds good. Why don't you come over?"

Brandi was excited but played it off. "I don't know, Sean."

"Please. Come on over, baby. I wanna see you." Sean gave her the address.

"I'll be there in twenty minutes," Brandi said.

Sean gathered his stuff and ran into the shower to wash Yadi's scent off his body.

Chapter 16

Brandi pulled up in her Lexus and parked in front of Sean's house. She had on an ankle-length mink, with a fuzzy beret on her head to fight the winter cold. Her chocolate brown, thigh-length stiletto boots clicked on the sidewalk as she opened the metal gate and walked toward the stairs that led to Sean's front door. The double doors were made of oak and glass and she could look right into his foyer from outside. She leaned over the banister and tried to catch a glimpse inside his living room but heavy drapes covered the huge windows. She turned around and Sean was standing at the door, with a wife beater and sweats on.

"C'mon, girl!" he shouted, while waving her inside. "It's colder than a mug out here!" They both walked in and Sean guided her into the enormous living room.

"Your house is gorgeous, Sean! Did you decorate it yourself?" she asked.

"Some things I picked out but my mother and aunt helped me wit' da rest," he replied.

"Okay. So do your brother and sister live in Brooklyn?" she asked, while looking around Sean's living room.

"My sister, older sister, Mena, lives in West-chester with her husband and their two children. My brother, Twan, the police officer and he's divorced with three kids. He lives in Harlem."

Brandi nodded her head. "All right, Harlem world! So y'all pretty close, huh?"

"Yeah, we are. I have a big family. My mother has like five brothers and a sister. We're real tight. What about you?"

"Well, my mother and I talk from time to time. She didn't agree with a lot of things I chose to do when I was growing up and I think I hurt her a lot. She's just getting over them, actually. I have three brothers who, you know, are your typical street guys; getting locked up, hustling, kids everywhere, but other than that, we just kind of do our own thing. We get together for holidays and family events and stuff like that, though."

Sean shook his head. Now he saw where Shamari got his attitude from. Sean insisted Brandi take her coat off.

"Girl, are you nervous or somethin'?" he asked. "Take that hot-ass fur off!"

Brandi stood up and threw her coat on the couch. To his delight, she had on Frederick's of Hollywood cream-colored booty shorts and a frilly see-through baby doll shirt to match with thigh boots. Sean was stuck on stupid.

"Oh, shit!" he uttered, as Brandi walked toward him. She pulled down his sweats and squatted on the floor so that she could take his dick into her mouth. Sean's head fell back onto the couch, as he enjoyed the excellent head that Brandi was giving him. Sean watched the head of his dick disappear in her mouth and threw his head back, moaning with pleasure. Brandi's tongue swept across the shaft of his Johnson and she gave him a little tug of his testicles. The house was quiet so Sean was able to hear the slurping noises while she was giving him oral. Brandi shined Sean's dick up with thick saliva, becoming more and more excited by the minute, thinking of how much she wanted him to fuck her. Brandi sucked and slurped until he ejaculated into her pretty, glossed-up mouth and she swallowed every drop of his cum. She then licked his rod until it was bone dry. All Sean could do was just stare at her. He was not even bothered by the fact he had just had sex with Yadi an hour before the sexual encounter with Brandi.

"I . . . I don't even know what to say," he exclaimed. "That shit was good!"

Brandi then reached into her large Fendi Spy bag and pulled out a Magnum condom. She put it on Sean's erect penis with her mouth then he removed the lingerie, keeping the boots on. She climbed on top of Sean and slid his dick inside her. She was so wet from the anticipation of fucking Sean that she instantly began to have multiple orgasms after a few minutes of grinding on him. Sean looked like he was having an out-of-body experience and Brandi smiled because it was turning out exactly the way she wanted it to. She let him hit it doggie style and he lost his mind as he watched Brandi's juicy ass jiggle while he pounded her soaking wet pussy. He loved that. As they fucked all over the house all that could be heard was him smacking her ass.

Meanwhile, Yadira had double-backed and was in front of Sean's house. She had forgotten to return the key he had given her. Wanting to surprise him, she took it upon herself to put the key into the door and walk in. Before she could call out Sean's name, she heard Brandi's moans coming from upstairs. Embarassed and hurt, Yadi just shook her head and left the key on top of the oak banister in the foyer. She ran outside and back to her car with tears in her eyes.

***

Later on, after an evening of passionate love-making, Sean and Brandi made their way down-stairs. They were so turned on that they couldn't keep their hands off each other and stayed in bed for hours. Sean made Brandi something to eat, feeding her morsels from his plate while she did the same. Aside from the sex, Sean really dug Brandi. Brandi finally decided to open to Sean and talk to him about her past life.

"Sean, I have to confess, I was a wild chick back in the days," she said, out the blue, while they sat in the living room to drink some wine after their dinner. "I was a straight-up 'hood chick. I didn't drink or smoke but I used to sell my drugs, get my money, my cars, my jewels, my clothes; I was a mess! I had a Porsche, a Benz, a BMW, and a Land Rover. I didn't have them at the same time but I had them all."

"What about the feds? You never been locked up?" he asked.

Brandi sipped her wine from the champagne flute. "No, and this was because I always hid behind my brothers and Maleek. They never even suspected I was hustling because they just looked at me as some young chick that was living off her man's and her older brothers' hustling money. Plus, I was smarter than them. I had my clientele that I dealt with and I didn't put myself

out there with new people like that. That life is
no way to live because you can't trust anyone.
Who doesn't want to trust one single person in
their life? That's a very lonely life."

Sean agreed. "You're right, but what made you
go back to school?"

"When Maleek was killed, I had to go back and
live with my mother. She said to me, 'Brandi,
this little boy already lost his father, does he
deserve to lose his mother, too?' I thought about
what she said and she was right. My best friend,
Sheba, was also my biggest insipiration when it
came time for me to get myself together."

Brandi paused, remembering the tough time
she had adjusting to life after hustling. She
continued after a few moments of reflection.

"Sean, I was not the most religious person in
the world at the time, but I prayed. I prayed for
my son, and my mother because I had put her
through so much, and myself. I really, really hurt
my mother over the years and I could see how
it took a toll on her and our relationship. I even
prayed for Maleek's mother because she had
lost her son. For a while, it seemed like God had
given me a clean slate because I started doing the
right thing for once. That is, until Shamari began
to act like a fool. Just when I thought that the
Lord had forgiven me, here goes my son with his
mess. Now I know how my mother felt."

"Do you think Shamari is pickin' up where you left off?"

"Definitely. Fortunately, I have never been locked up. I was lucky enough to get away with my crimes and indiscretions back then. But I made my mother cry many a day because she expected so much more from her only girl. I was her last hope because my brothers was into their bullshit. Now that I'm in my mama's shoes and being that Shamari is my one and only child, he is last hope." Brandi shrugged her shoulders. "It's karma, I guess."

Sean sat back for a moment to analyze their conversation. The more she talked about her past, the more he felt that he could relate to her. There was more to Brandi than just beauty. It was the brains and street smarts that gave her brownie points. To hear it coming from her own mouth, Sean would have never believed that she was a former drug trafficker. Narrowly escaping death and incarceration, Brandi was the phenomenal woman.

What Sean didn't know was that Brandi, at one time, was just as crazy for love as Yadi. Love for her was confused with borderline obsession. The last man Brandi was madly in love with was Shamari's father and when he crossed her, she wished death on him. With the help of counseling,

Brandi was able to rid of herself of those demons and become a better mother, daughter, and lover. Unfortunately, she still had to go through life with the memory that she was a vocal instrument in Maleek's murder, although she didn't physically pull the trigger.

After some years of emotional, psychological, and emotional abuse from Maleek, Brandi became a glutton for punishment. Even though she fought him tooth and nail, she still catered to his every whim, silently yearning for his approval. Brandi thought back to a time when she found herself working hard to please the narcissistic Maleek. Everytime she obeyed him, it only added to his over-inflated ego.

"I hate you! You fuckin' lyin'-ass dog!" Brandi screamed at Maleek. "I thought that you wasn't goin' to the fuckin' party!"

Maleek put his hand up like he was going to slap Brandi and she flinched. They had had their share of physical altercations, too.

"Shut the fuck up before I slap the shit outta you!" he yelled. "That ass whippin' didn't teach you shit, huh? And I ain't gotta tell you shit! You're my girl, so why are you worried about what I'm doin' out there in the world when I live with you?"

"Fuck all that! I wanted to go to the party, too! What is this new shit you on, huh, Maleek? You don't wanna be seen with me? I can't go nowhere with you now?"

"Get that shit out your mind right now 'cause you ain't goin'! This shit is strictly for ballin'—"

Brandi was livid.

"Nigga, I make just as money as you out there in them streets. I probably can make more than you but I don't wanna put your black ass outta business!"

Suddenly, Maleek slapped the hell out of Brandi, knocking her into the glass sliding doors of their closet.

"You fuckin' dumb bitch! Who do you think you are, dissin' me like that, huh? I made your ass what you are today! I fucked that pussy and made it shape to this dick. I put you on to this money out here in the streets. I let you have my fuckin' seed, bitch! You supposed ta bow down to me. I'm the king of this fuckin' castle! You here to serve me so don't ever tell me that you would knock Maleek out the box! You was nothin' but a thievin' ass, boostin' bitch when I met you!"

As she sat on the floor, holding her stinging face, Maleek picked up his mink jacket off the bed. He looked at Brandi, who was crying and stunned. From the slap and the way he was

*talking to her, Brandi realized that she was
back to square one; trying to please a man who
would never be pleased.*

"You owe me a fuckin' apology," Maleek spat.

*Brandi looked up at him towering over her.
"I'm sorry, King."*

"Yeah, you are sorry. Bitch."

*Maleek slammed the door as he walked out
of the house. The noise startled Shamari and
Brandi screamed in frustration as the baby
began to cry at the top of his lungs.*

Sean closed the front door, after making sure
that Brandi had pulled off in her car. He turned
off the lights downstairs. He made his way upstairs to his bedroom when suddenly his hand hit
the key that was on top of the banister, knocking
it to the floor. He looked at the key and frowned,
knowing that he had never put it there. He realized that it was the spare key that he had given to
Yadi! Sean looked around his house, wondering
if she was still lingering around somewhere in his
house. He figured that she must have come back
to return it to him.

"Oh, shit!" Sean said to himself, stopping in
the middle of the stairwell. He wondered if she
overheard him and Brandi having sex. *Yeah, she
heard it,* he thought. Sean shook his head and
walked back up to his bedroom. He knew that
getting involved with Yadi was a mistake.

Chapter 17

After leaving Sean's house, Yadi found herself on the way back to Queens. Yadi had to keep convincing herself that Sean was a bachelor and he was entitled to have any woman he wanted. The only problem was that Yadi assumed that he wanted to be with her, especially after the way they had made love to each other.

When Yadi arrived at Vanita's house, she was totally flustered and feeling like a complete idiot. She made her way upstairs, where Vanita was in the bed with Jada, reading her a bedtime story. They looked so peaceful that Yadi felt guilty about even feeling down about Sean Daniels. She looked at her daughter and her best friend and concluded that the world did not revolve around having a man, although she couldn't say that she hadn't always made it her business to be without one. Vanita looked up and acknowledged her presence. She saw the expression on Yadi's face and asked Jada to go into the other bedroom to watch the Nickelodeon channel while she talked to her mommy. After Jada gave her mother a tight hug and walked in the other room, Yadi threw her coat she had on onto the floor. She then collapsed into Vanita's arms and began to sob. Vanita immediately comforted her.

"What happened, Yadi?" Vanita asked, with a look of concern on her face. She passed the sniffling Yadi some Kleenex tissues from the box on the nightstand next to her bed.

"Sean had some woman in his house when I went back to return the key. He didn't know I walked in, he didn't know I heard them!" she replied through sobs.

Vanita rolled her eyes. It seemed as if Yadi was always putting herself in a position to get hurt. She didn't want to blame her for her own actions but she always tried to keep it real with her friend and this situation was no different.

"Sweetie, I am really tryin' to ride with you throughout this whole ordeal. I can see why you are upset with Sean and probably yourself because I would be, too. But baby, I hate to get on you but you walked in that man's house without permission, and it didn't matter if you was returnin' the key or not. That was a no-no. Why didn't you ring the bell?"

Yadi shrugged her shoulders. She didn't want to tell Vanita that she had plans to seduce Sean one more time before she left his home for good.

Vanita cut her eyes at Yadi. "I know why. You probably was goin' over there to screw him again before you left for good, wasn't you?"

Yadi couldn't contain herself and burst into a hysterical laugh, while wiping tears from her cheeks. They both laughed with each other.

"You know, Vanita, I can't stand your ass. You know me like a damn book!" Yadi smiled, as she blew her nose.

Vanita shook her head. "Girl, you're talkin' to an old pro! I have been there and done that with these triflin' negroes. But I can't live without them, though. They don't do anything but try to treat us like hot garbage sometimes but this is why we gotta be smarter than them. You have to emotionally disconnect yourself and not have too many 'high' expectations when it comes to those nasty mofos. Trust me, my method works!"

"How was the trip with your guy friend?" Yadi asked, attempting to change the subject.

Vanita rolled her doe eyes. "Please, girl. It was nice. I spent his money, got a free trip and shopped 'til I dropped. In the midst of all that, his thing wouldn't even get up!"

They both rolled with laughter. Vanita continued. "Girl, I told him to lose my number until he
got him a prescription of Viagra. Had the nerve to
have a fuckin' attitude with me because his dick
was limp. Shouldn't I have had the attitude?"

Yadi continued to laugh. She still had Sean
on her mind, though, but she was going to have
to learn to keep her emotions in check like her
friend told her to. If they were meant to be, it
would be. Unfortunately, that would be easier
said than done.

Chapter 18

The rattling on the cell door awakened the drugged Shamari. It was the CO on the night shift trying to get him up so that he could prepare for court.

"Wallace, wake up, son. You got court, baby boy!" CO Washington called out. She was a plump, short woman who had been an officer for twenty-five years and who was like a mother or grandmother figure to most of the inmates in Five West.

"Okay, Miss Washington, I'm gettin' up! I was tore up from that Tylenol with codeine," Shamari responded.

The cell door opened. Miss Washington stood at the door with her hand on her hip. "C'mon, baby! Take your shower and stuff, get your court clothes on and Miss Washington will make sure you have a li'l somethin' to eat before you go to the receivin' room! You need somethin' in your belly when you're takin' medication!"

Shamari gathered his shower supplies and dragged himself into the shower. He lathered up, careful not to wet the bandages on his neck. After completing the shower, he dried himself off and put his underwear on. He removed some Bacitracin ointment from his pocket that he had received from the nurse to put on his wound and put a glob on his finger. Shamari put the ointment on his anus and removed the skinny razor that was wrapped in small shreds of a ripped sheet with a small string on the end, looking amazingly similar to a woman's tampon. He winced but managed to put the small homemade weapon in between his ass cheeks. He made sure that he was comfortable and that it was well hidden.

He walked back to his cell with his sweatpants and wife beater on. Back in his cell, Shamari did a double check of the weapon to make sure that it was strategically placed. He simulated squatting and was pleased when he couldn't see the string hanging from between his ass cheeks. Shamari was officially armed, jail style.

After putting on the clothes that he was wearing to court, which consisted of a button-down Polo shirt, Polo khakis to match, and Prada shoes on his feet, he walked toward the front desk. Miss Washington was waiting there with some bread and jelly and a small container of milk for Shamari to eat.

"This should hold you until you get to the receivin' room. And good luck in court today, baby," she said. Shamari thanked Miss Washington and walked out of Five West with the rest of the court inmates.

As he got closer and closer to the receiving area, Shamari was a nervous wreck. The receiving room was a large area with huge holding pens where inmates were admitted into and discharged from the jail. The receiving area or "intake" was busy around the clock with several correction officers running around to ensure that every inmate was in their rightful place.

Male officers took several inmates to the back of the receiving room to strip search them. The inmates would have to remove all articles of clothing and stand there buck-naked. Shamari was in line to be searched and he closed his eyes when the muscular CO told him to turn around and squat. Shamari did as he was told and the officer told him to get dressed. He paused for a moment, in shock that he didn't get caught with the weapon that was secreted between his ass cheeks. The CO looked at Shamari strangely.

"Mothafucka, get dressed! What the fuck are you just standin' there for?" the CO boomed. The officer turned to his coworker, who was just as muscular as he was. "Dumbass crook!" he stated, as his partner nodded his head in agreement.

Shamari walked off with a slight smirk on his face. "No, dumb-ass police!" Shamari whispered to himself, as he walked back to his holding pen.

As the bus rattled on the Brooklyn Queens Expressway, Shamari shifted around in the hard metal seat. The ride was miserable because some of the inmates were going to meet their fate in court that day. Many were career criminals with long rap sheets who were finally going to be served with a lot of time so it was not a time for shit talking and jiving. Shamari was on his way to accept the plea agreement so that he could move on and do his own time in state prison.

Upon arriving in court, Shamari waited for his name to be called. He sat in the court holding pen, careful not to make eye contact with any of the ignorant assholes who were probably looking for a fight. He needed to make this court appearance and he didn't have time to get into a verbal or physical spat with anybody. He had to keep in mind that he had a baby on the way so he was going to have to start doing whatever it took to make sure he was in one piece when he came home.

Shamari looked up and was surprised to see Born staring at him. Shamari frowned, wondering how long the seasoned crook had been there watching him. Born had a sneaky look on his face. Shamari turned his head when he saw the hardened criminal walking toward him.

"What up, youngblood?" Born asked. "You look like you're in another world."

Shamari sighed. He didn't trust Born and he didn't want to talk but responded anyway. "Ain't nothin', Born."

Born stared at Shamari. He knew that the younger man didn't have any idea that he was sitting next to the man who cut him on his neck. Born wasn't about to tell him, either.

"Yeah, I'm here for some bullshit jail case I caught a few months back." Born looked Shamari up and down. "So, I can see that you're lookin' like a million bucks, shorty, no homo. You're ready to meet your maker?" Born asked, referring to the judge.

Shamari continued to look the opposite way. He couldn't bear to look Born in his face, nor did he care about why he was in court. Shamari's only question was why was Born talking to him in the first place?

"Yeah, somethin' like that," Shamari answered in a curt tone.

Born nodded his head while he inspected Shamari from head to toe. He looked at the bandages on his neck and wanted to laugh. Shamari was lucky that Born didn't cut him across his handsome, boyish face.

"Well, little nigga, don't be having me mixed up or associated with your bullshit again, or else I'm gonna straight murk your ass, you hear me?" Shamari turned around to stare at Born. "I see you went back and told your mommy some shit about me threatenin' you. The big boys don't run their mouth up in here, nigga. Snitches get stitches." Born got up and walked back to the other side of the pen.

Shamari was frozen with fear and anger. *Born was probably the bastard that cut me,* he thought because Born was talking real reckless. He couldn't really remember the face because he was semi-conscious from the punch that was administered to his jaw. From all the careless talking Born was doing, it had to be him. He thought about his weapon and had a good mind to open up Born's face up with it. He decided against it, though, remembering that part of being a man to handle his important business first. He was going to definitely handle Born later on and when he least expected.

Shamari walked into the courtroom and instantly began consulting with his lawyer, Ronald Samuels. Samuels was a diminutive Jewish man, with a year-round tropical tan. He wore expensive Mont Blanc spectacles and a tailored-made three piece suit.

More importantly, Samuels was a reputable defense attorney, who was dedicated to helping young, misguided men like Shamari get their lives back on track. He didn't believe lengthy incarcerations helped rehabilitate people, it only made them worse. Samuels also made sure that they got the help that they needed, inside of the jail and out.

When Brandi came to him with Shamari's situation, she was open and forthright about her criminal past, as well as Shamari's father. His heart went out to the single mom who had the opportunity to get her life back on track, for the sake of her son. Shamari's case was small compared to the other cases he handled, so he decided to take the case without putting a huge dent in Brandi's pocket. Samuels and the prosecutor stepped up to the bench and conferred with the judge.

"Yes, Your Honor, Mr. Wallace has decided to accept the plea agreement. Please take into consideration that my client has never been arrested before. In addition, he apologizes for his actions and understands the consequences of his measures. He is extremely regretful and wishes to do his time and return to society as a law-abiding and a respectable citizen."

The D.A. had a stern look on his face. "Your Honor, I am satisfied that the offer was accepted by the defendant. To take this case to trial would have been a waste of time and injudicious. He is a young man that made a mistake and hopefully, he will serve his time sensibly and return to society with a very different outlook on life, with respect for the laws of this city, as well as the laws of the land. That's all I have to say."

The judge shook his head in agreement and both of the attorneys returned to their seats, where they remained standing. The judge looked at Shamari.

"Mr. Wallace, you stand before me, a young man having all the opportunity in the world to be the best that you can be. It agrees between this court and the District Attorney that you accept this plea agreement. It is unfortunate that you have to serve time for your first offense, although I don't believe that it is your first time breaking the law; just the first time you've been caught. If I see you in this courtroom for any other felony offense, you will do football numbers and I am not talking about the NFL. I am going to ask that the Department of Correction produce you in the next three weeks for sentencing. Is there anything that you would like to say?"

Shamari swallowed and made sure he chose his words carefully. "Umm, sir, I mean, Your Honor, I apologize for my actions that night and I am grateful that no one was hurt. I won't do it again and when I get home this time, I'm gonna be a better citizen and a role model for young men my age."

The judge seemed impressed with Shamari's comments. Court was dismissed and the judge went to his quarters. Shamari watched as the judge disappeared behind the oak door. Samuels looked at Shamari's neck. "Mr. Wallace, what happened to your neck?" he asked, while putting some paperwork into his leather briefcase.

Shamari put his hands to his neck, as if he had to remind himself that it was there. "Yeah, I got cut on my neck," he replied.

Samuels sighed. "What happened, Mr. Wallace?"

"Somebody sucker punched me when I walked into my housing area the other day and while I was out cold on the floor, somebody cut me. I don't know who did it."

Samuels looked at Shamari, with a look of fatherly concern. "Wallace, you have to learn survival techniques while you're doing your time. It is going against the grain if I actually told you what you should do but you have to protect yourself at all costs. First of all, refrain from talking about your case to anyone. They have informants all throughout the system waiting to jam you up.

Also, do not participate in idle gossip about other inmates, which the guys in there call 'dry-snitching.' And remember, you don't have any 'friends' in jail. Your friends are the law library, the visits, social services, and the clinic, things that are provided to help you throughout your incarceration. One more thing, call your mother and family as often as you can. Write letters, read books, exercise and rest. Rest your mind, Wallace. You're going to need to think about what your next move is going to be. You don't have time to be a fucking carving board for some sorry sap behind those walls."

Samuels held out his hand and Shamari shook it. "See you in three weeks for sentencing, son, and remember what I said. I have a son your age and I don't wanna see you messed up. Don't look at this as being the end. This is the beginning of a change. A good change."

Shamari held back his tears. No man had kept it real with him in a long time and he appreciated Samuels for giving him some good advice. But he still wanted to get revenge on Born.

Chapter 19

The next day, Sean walked across the visit floor, making sure everything was running smoothly. It was Wednesday and Thursdays evening visits, which were eight p.m. to nine p.m. These visits were always less crowded than on the weekends. He was happy about this because most of the riff-raff stayed home on Wednesdays and Thursdays. Sean was preoccupied and didn't see when Captain Monique Phillips walked toward him to make sure everything was good. He instantly embraced her.

"What's up, Cap? You lookin' good in your white shirt!" he complimented.

She blushed. "Thanks, Daniels. You lookin' good, too. How you feelin'?" she asked.

"I'm good. What brings you through here?" Sean asked.

Monique sighed. "Well, I just got transferred back over here and I think I'm gonna go for this steady in visits. I like workin' with the visit crew."

Sean smiled. "Come through. That's what's up! How is your daughter and your family?"

"Everyone is fine, thanks for askin'. When was the last time you spoke to Sierra?"

Sean sucked his teeth. "I spoke to her last week. You know, her man don't like me since I knocked his ass out that time. But we try to speak as much as we can. She should be comin' back to work soon. Messiah is gettin' big, I'm sure."

"Hell, yeah. He's adorable, too. Well, when I have somethin' at my house, I'ma invitin' you 'cause you're my peoples, forget about what Lamont thinks about you!" Monique teased.

"You do that, Cap. You better."

"Well, lemme go back to the front. Holla at me throughout the course of the day."

Sean watched as Monique walked through the sliding doors. She looked good since she lost a few pounds and from what he saw, her round ass hadn't budged. She was a very different person since being promoted to captain and he was happy for her. Sean looked at the control room and caught Yadi watching him. She was making him uncomfortable because she hadn't spoken to him since returning his key. He went inside the control room to retrieve some count slips. Vanita was on her meal break and Yadi was doing everything alone.

"Yadi," Sean said, breaking the uncomfortable silence. "What's up with you? Why aren't you talkin' to me?" Yadi ignored Sean. She continued to work. He stared at her. "Do you hear me talkin' to you?"

Yadi turned around and glared at Sean. "What do you want, Sean? May I help you?" she asked with an attitude.

Sean's shoulders slumped. "What is wrong with you? You're not talkin' to me and you givin' me the cold shoulder. What did I do to you?"

"Sean, you're gonna stand here and act like you don't know what you did? I came to return your key and you was screwin' some random bitch upstairs in your bedroom!"

Sean laughed at the uptight Yadi. "Okay, so what, I can't have sex with another woman in my own house now?"

Yadi wanted to smack the hell out of Sean. "You don't get it, do you? You had just fucked me right before that!"

"So, I'm your man, now? I don't have no girl, Yadi. You are my homegirl. That's it. What happened between us was special because I've always been attracted to you but you makin' this more than what it needs to be. What were you expectin' from me, a marriage proposal?"

Yadi crossed her arms in frustration. "I expected you to be a little more sensitive to my needs. Damn, at least let me move out of your house good before you start bringin' other women over there!"

Sean began to pace. "Listen to you! You sound crazy! You stayed with me for two fuckin' minutes and we had a session or two and now you sittin' up here tryin' to tell me not to have any female company in my house? You must have lost your mind!"

Yadi began to get loud. "You know what, Sean, go to hell! I don't need you to tell me how I'm supposed to act! You wanted to get with me for the longest and now when you did, this is how you act toward me?"

Sean walked toward the door and stopped. He turned around and looked at Yadi, who was visibly upset and about to work herself into a frenzy.

"Yo, I opened my door to you and Jada, made sure y'all was straight and this is the fuckin' thanks I get. You should have never walked in my house with that key and I think you know better. So be mad at yourself, not me. But it's all good, baby girl, 'cause I'm not dealin' with your crazy-ass no more!"

Sean swung the door to the control room open and looked at the visitors that were sitting the waiting area. From the expressions on their faces, they overheard the argument, including Brandi, who was staring at him with a pained expression on her face. No one sitting there could imagine how Brandi felt inside. She was embarrassed and humiliated, assuming that she was the "woman" Yadi and Sean were talking about. Sean stood there with a stunned look on his face, holding count slips in his right hand. Brandi just shook her head. That was the cue for Sean to walk away, which he did.

Brandi's chest began to tighten up from anxiety. She knew that there was no escape, because after all, she was on Rikers Island. She would have to suck it up and be strong for Shamari because the visit was for him, not for Sean. Brandi just kept staring at the door, hoping to catch a glimpse of the woman Sean was arguing with but she never appeared. What made it hurt even more, Sean had sex with the mystery woman right before she had come over that night. She could have kicked herself for having high expectations for Sean. It only made Brandi think of Maleek and one of the several occasions when he hurt her so bad.

"Maleek, how could you leave me and Shaki like this? I love you," a lovelorn Brandi exclaimed with tears in her eyes. She was a female gangster in the streets but with Maleek, she was as soft as butter.

Maleek turned his head, avoiding eye contact with her. "Brandi, I love you too but I'm in love with somebody else, too! Shit, I just can't explain it!" he replied. Maleek put his hands on his head, frustrated and confused. "I, I just can't be with you anymore! You're gettin' just as much money as me in these streets. I mean, look at you! You act like a fuckin' nigga! You shoot, you kill mothafuckas, you hustle! I need a woman that knows how to be a woman. A woman that knows her place!"

Brandi wiped the tears falling from her pretty eyes. "Maleek, I don't understand! I am a woman plus I'm the mother of your son!"

"I respect that but Brandi; we done did too much dirt together. When we're out in the public together, we're constantly lookin' over each other's shoulders because we both got beef in these streets. And the sad part is if somethin' happen to one of us, we wouldn't know if it's because of my beef or yours!"

Brandi plopped down on the red leather couch in the living room of the East New York home that they both shared. She put her face in her hands, as she thought about all the years she sacrificed to be with Maleek. Brandi molded herself into the woman she thought she was supposed to be for him. Now the truth was Maleek had used her up and gotten exactly what he could out of their relationship. So all of sudden he was telling her that he had enough of her, without even telling her that anything was wrong from the beginning. That wasn't a good enough excuse for Brandi but she knew that she would only be the champion in the end. She was going to make sure of that.

Brandi wiped her tears. "You know what, baby, you are right," Brandi said in a condescending tone. "I'm addicted ta the hustle and the flow. It's a dog-eat-dog world out here and yeah, I had to act like a nigga to survive in this game. But I lost myself and in the midst of all da bullshit, I lost you, too." She got up from the couch and walked toward the bedroom. "Do you need me to help you pack?"

Maleek looked at Brandi suspiciously. He had just seen the mother of his child standing in front of him, crying like a baby. Now she was switching it up on him. He was taken aback by her behavior and his street senses kicked in.

"Brandi, you a'ight? Why are you so calm all of a sudden?" he asked with a hint of fear in his voice. He knew that Brandi was liable to kill him. She killed a man in front of his face before with no remorse.

Brandi smiled. "Maleek, I'm fine. I just realized you were right. It's time for us to move on."

Maleek brushed past Brandi and as he packed up his things, he kept a close eye on her. Meanwhile, her heart ached as she watched the man she had meshed with over the years removing himself from their world together. They had a mini-empire they had built but fortunately, Brandi kept a stash of money to the side for emergency. She would have thought that she would lose him to death or incarceration but never to another woman.

After leaving Brandi, Maleek ended up moving to Virginia with a young woman who attended Norfolk State University, a business management major. Down there, he continued to hustle, laundering the illegal money through real estate property and other assets. This went on for a couple of months, with him not attempting to contact Brandi or his son. He let Brandi keep the house in East New York that they had lived in together, which his mother eventually sold. Brandi moved back in with her mother. Everyone tried to talk sense into Maleek about Brandi and his son, including his mother, who was fed up with his criminal exploits and heartlessness. Nevertheless, Maleek left Brandi devastated by his refusal to acknowledge her and Shamari anymore.

One day, she contacted an old connect of hers from Norfolk named Smokey. He was one of her best customers back then and he kept her hustle going by referring her to other customers in the Tidewater area. Smokey was partly responsible for Brandi claiming her stake in Virginia, and in return, she would set him up with the best prices for some of her product.

Smokey was a typical country boy but he was well traveled having been there and done that. His skin was the color of coal and he had the darkest eyes, with jet-black, silky hair. Even though Brandi and Smokey were always attracted to each other, they just chose to keep it on a friendly basis, not wanting to mix their business with pleasure. He eventually became her confidante and friend, always making sure that Brandi was good. He got nothing but respect from Brandi because of that.

"Smokey, listen, I need you to do somethin' for me," Brandi stated. "I came down here because I didn't want to discuss anything over the phone but I really, really need this favor."

Smokey stuffed some of his food in his mouth. They were sitting in a small diner in Virginia Beach, talking over some breakfast. Brandi had just flown in from New York and Smokey had met up with her at the hotel she was staying at.

"What up, Brandi?" he asked between bites of his waffle. "What do you need?"

"It's Maleek. He left me for some college chick, Smokey, and he won't take any of my phone calls or contact his son. He's bein' real fucked up to me and Shamari and I'm not gonna lie, my heart is broken."

Smokey stared at Brandi and her eyes began to well up with tears. She went over her thoughts a million times. She cried and fretted over it so many nights, asking God to remove the thoughts of murder from her head. Smokey touched her hand and he summoned the waitress, paid for the food, and got out of that diner. He knew what Brandi wanted; he read her mind.

While they sat in his Infiniti Q45, he let Brandi cry, while he waited for her to catch her breath.

"I need you to kill Maleek for me," Brandi announced.

Smokey chuckled. "Brandi, do you realize what you're askin' me to do?" he asked, with eyes filled with sorrow. He handed her some tissues from the glove compartment of his car and she blew her nose.

"I'm askin' you to do that for me or get some-one else to do it, as long as it gets done!"

Smokey looked out the window, staring into nothingness. He stared at Brandi with a concerned look on his face. "You know what you askin' me to do, right? You askin' me to, to . . ."

Brandi cut him off. "I know, Smoke, but you are the only person that I can trust with this. You'll make sure it's done, right?"

"Whoa, whoa," Smokey said, holding up his hands. "I ain't said I was gonna do shit, little mama, but why you wanna do this to old boy?"

"Maleek left me and now he won't take no calls from me or his son. If I call from an unknown number, he hears my voice and hangs up the damn phone on me! Now he changed his number! He told me before he left, I don't act like how a woman is supposed to act, I'm out here hustlin' like a nigga and that's not lady-like. But, Smokey, he's the one dat created this monster. He's the one that got me started with this hustlin' shit."

Smokey sighed. "Well, Brandi, that may be a sign for you to give this shit up, shawty. You got a son to look after and bein' that this dude ain't doin what he's supposed to, you gotta be there for your little boy."

Brandi held her head down and looked out the passenger side window. Smokey turned her face toward him.

"Smokey, I'm hurt, though! I been with this nigga since I was sixteen years ol'. My mother practically disowned me when I got pregnant by him. He turned me on to the hustle game and now that I look at it, he ain't never had to do nothin' for me or my son 'cause I always made sure we had. He did nothin' but pimped me. I allowed him to turn me into this gangsta bitch, now he claims he's not feelin' me anymore! He just up and left me for some prissy college chick, who he's probably treatin' like a fuckin' queen, payin' her tuition and shit. That's somethin' I shoulda done, gone to college and live a normal life instead of dedicatin' my entire existence to this fool. But dissin' me is one thing. Now he's hangin' up on my son and I don't like nobody fuckin' with my child!"

"Damn, girl. The baby? Don't disrespect the baby, man. He don't even try to see his son no more, huh?"

Brandi mouthed the word "no." "His family tried to talk some sense into this pussy-whipped nigga and he won't even listen ta them. I just don't know what else to do . . . ."

Smokey hugged Brandi, while she continued to sob, loudly. "I'm sorry, baby. I feel your pain, man." He let Brandi go and held her face, wiping her tears. "Look, I got you but here's the deal. Your man got some beef with these cats from Portsmouth. Seem like he beat them outta some money and work and they pissed off about it, man. Well, just so happen, they my peoples and they been askin' me about Maleek 'cause they know he be in No'folk. I always see him, you know, he might gimme a li'l head nod and we keep it movin'. The only reason Maleek life is bein' spared is on the strength of you, Brandi. I never cared for him 'cause I think he a fuck nigga but now that you tellin' me this shit here, I think I'm gonna go 'head and let them Portsmouth niggas know to ride in on that ass."

Brandi felt her chest tightened suddenly. She instantly regretted what she told Smokey but it was too late to take it back. She knew that if anything happened to Maleek, she was going to be the cosigner on his death certificate. However, even though she would have to live with the unanswered questions and guilt, she just couldn't live with knowing someone that she was in love with had moved on to someone else after all she had done to be with him.

"Wow, Smokey, I didn't know about the Portsmouth dudes but oh well, that's how the game goes," she announced, wiping her runny nose with her hand.

Smokey shrugged his shoulders. "I know you feelin' guilty but just think of this thang bein' like, karma. You treat somebody that love you fucked up, you get what's comin' to you, man!"

Suddenly, Smokey kissed Brandi on the mouth and she reciprocated. He tenderly massaged her breasts and she unbuttoned her blouse to reveal her black lace bra. It got so heated in his car that Smokey pulled off and they ended up in her hotel room, where he performed some of the best oral sex on her that she ever had. Smokey was a country boy and they never failed to deliver when it came to lovemaking.

Brandi took off his shirt and she was pleased as she ran her hands over his ripped body. Smokey's coal complexion had a beautiful contrast against her mocha-colored skin and the distinction of the skin tones turned her on even more. She licked on his rod as if it was a piece of thick, black licorice. His body tasted like dark chocolate and Brandi's sweet tooth led her to explore every nook and cranny of his ripped body with his tongue. The husky moans escaping from his succulent mouth made her ride his thick country-boy dick even harder.

"Damn, baby, I didn't know it was this good!" he yelled, as he grabbed her. His dick worked her insides and Brandi squealed with delight, temporarily forgetting all about Maleek and his escapades.

The next day, Maleek received information that Brandi was in town and he was looking to

*catch up with her. Immediately after Smokey
got wind of this, he put her on a plane back to
New York. There was no need for them to speak
to each other anymore, he thought.*

*When Brandi got back home, she picked up
the ringing house phone. It was Maleek on the
other end. A sinister smile appeared on her face.*

*"What the hell was you doin' down here, in
Virginia? Spyin' on me?" he screamed.*

*Brandi looked at the phone. "Spyin' on you?
Nigga, don't flatter yourself! I had some business to take care of. And why are you so concerned anyway? You don't give a fuck about me
or your son!" she yelled back.*

*"I don't wanna hear about you bein' in Virginia
again, Brandi! You had to know somebody was
gonna tell me that you was down here!"*

*"Maleek, I don't give a fuck about anyone
tellin' you a damn thing! Oh yeah, by the way, I
fucked Smokey and his dick was so much better
than yours ever was. I guess what they say
about them country boys is true!"*

*Maleek gulped. "You what? You did who?
Smokey?" Maleek paused. "Oh, you're gettin'
down like that now?"*

*"Yep. I sure am! So fuck you and I hope you
burn in hell!" Brandi hung up the phone before
Maleek could say anything else. He continued*

to call her phone and leave obscene messages, even threatening her life but Brandi refused to answer the phone. Brandi smiled as she thought about how much better her life would be without him in it.

Apparently, the Portsmouth dudes didn't have to catch up to the young hustler, after all. Smokey gunned down Maleek a few weeks after Brandi departed Virginia. Apparently, they had some major beef over Brandi and Maleek shot at Smokey, barely missing him. One day, Smokey made a phone call to Brandi, letting her know where Maleek's remains were. Smokey told her how everything went down, which had Brandi totally upset, to say the least. At the same time, he proclaimed his love for her and insisted that she move to Virginia to be with him. She was physically attracted to Smokey but she knew that he was only a pawn in her dirty game of chess. She changed her phone number shortly after.

Now she would have to live with knowing that she was instrumental in Maleek's death for the rest of her life, eventually shunning his family members as well because of the excessive guilt. Some months afterward, she heard that Smokey was killed by some of Maleek's people, in retaliation for his murder. Apparently, Maleek had put a contract on Smokey before he, himself, was executed. The pressure of being partly to blame for the deaths of two people she cared for finally took its toll on Brandi and she went into a deep depression, even contemplated killing herself.

Brandi's daydreams were interrupted when she heard her last name being called for the visit. A female officer exited the control room and figured that she was the one that Sean argued with. The officer was exceptionally pretty and Brandi could understand why most men would find her irresistible.

Brandi walked up to the officer and fought off the urge to snatch the registration card from the woman's hand. She took a glimpse of the nameplate on the breast of her uniform shirt and it read "Y. Cruz." Instead, Brandi gently removed the card from Cruz's grasp and smiled pleasantly, as she passed her stamped hand through a UV light before entering the visiting floor. Brandi then got her card stamped and was instructed by an officer to sit at table seven.

While she waited for Shamari to come out, she attempted to make eye contact with Sean. He did everything he could to not to look her way, stealing an occasional glance or two at Brandi's disgruntled face. Brandi knew that she wasn't his woman, but she was disappointed in him nonetheless.

Chapter 20

Shamari shuffled out to the table where they would be sitting and Brandi totally forgot about Sean. She was mortified when she saw the bandages on the neck of her only son.

"Oh my God, Shaki, what happened to you? Who did this to you? Why?" Brandi asked, with her arms spread out.

"Ma, Ma, c'mon, I'm a'ight!" he said, covering his neck. "I'm okay, it's just a small setback, that's all!" he said, hopefully dismissing any further questions. He was wrong.

"Shaki, you can't live like this! Walking around with cuts all over you! Why in the hell didn't Daniels tell me what happened?" Brandi exclaimed, even more pissed off with Sean.

Sean was visibly annoyed. "Ma, listen, that nigga is not my keeper! I'm a grown man. I got myself into this jail shit and I'm gonna do my time and come home! He ain't my babysitter so everything that happen in here, don't expect for him to tell! He's a man, Ma. Real men don't be runnin' their mouth!" Shamari explained. He knew that he had run his mouth and he had to learn his lesson the hard way. Now he knew better.

Brandi was frustrated. "I can't take you being in here. You're getting cut, fighting, it's just too much!"

Shamari took his mother's hands. "Ma, I understand that me bein' in here is tough for you. It's hard for me, too but I gotta do what I got to do. I was scared at first but I'll be fine, don't worry."

Brandi sighed. She was stressed out. "Shaki, I have to worry, you're locked up and you have a baby on the way. Now you're in this dump getting cut up, it's a lot for me to handle."

Shamari looked around and noticed Sean looking at his mother. "Ma, can I ask you somethin' and I want you to be honest with me."

Brandi blinked. She wondered if he had heard anything about her shady past. She worked hard to keep Shamari sheltered from any harmful information about her. "What is it, Shamari?"

"Are you involved with Daniels?" Brandi frowned. "Yeah, I wanna know if you're involved with Daniels."

"No, I'm not," Brandi stated, lying through her teeth. "Why are you asking me that?"

Shamari held his head down. "Please don't mess around with none of these CO cats, Ma. They try to screw any woman that walks through these doors and Daniels ain't no different. I just don't want my mother to be caught up in nothin' with these birds."

Brandi agreed. "I understand, Shaki, it is a conflict of interest."

Shamari paused. He didn't know what else to say to Brandi so they sat quietly for a moment. Brandi finally broke the silence by asking Shamari about his sentencing.

"I can't wait to go upstate, Ma. I just wanna get this over with," he said.

Brandi agreed. "That's true. At least, you know you'll be a step closer to freedom."

Sean walked over and spoke to Brandi, who was forced to speak back, not wanting to give Shamari any inkling that she was pissed with him.

"Hey, Miss Wallace. What's up, Mr. Wallace?" Sean greeted, giving Shamari a unenthusiastic head nod.

Brandi spoke to him in a curt tone. "Hello, Mr. Daniels." Shamari didn't say anything. Sean felt the tension and dismissed himself. Brandi's eyes followed him.

Shamari smirked. "I think you like that dude, Ma."

Brandi laughed. "Boy, please. I have too many things on my plate as it is and there's no room on it for Daniels."

"I hope not 'cause I overheard him arguin' with Miss Cruz in the control room. He's pluggin' her and you don't need to be a secondary side piece to nobody."

Brandi held her head down. She knew that Shamari was right but she had feelings for Sean, feelings that she hadn't felt in a long time for a man. She was tired of being in her bed alone and she was tired of being horny. Most men she met were threatened by her career and her independence. With Sean, he made her feel alive again, even though it has only been two weeks since they had actually known each other.

The rest of the visit with Shamari went well and Brandi returned to the registration area to remove items from her locker. Sean crept up behind her, startling her.

"Brandi, I apologize for what happened earlier. That wasn't meant for your ears," Sean explained.

Brandi huffed. "No, what you want to say is that, I wasn't supposed to be sitting in the visit area when you were arguing with this woman. I mean, what are the chances of that, right?" she replied.

Sean looked at the ground. "Let's talk. Tonight."

"Sean, I don't think that you're ready for a woman like me. You still looking to fuck different women and put some notches in your belt. I refuse to be some side action and I'm damn sure not trying to be your jump off."

Brandi looked outside and saw the bus. She began walking toward the door and Sean grabbed her arm. "I'm comin' over tonight, Brandi." She snatched her arm away from his grasp and walked away. Sean turned around and saw Yadi standing there, staring at him.

"So you fuckin' the visitors now, Sean?" she asked with her arms folded across her chest.

Sean looked at Yadi with a look of disgust on his face. "Why are you worryin' about me and what I'm doin'? And why the fuck are you stalkin' me? Damn!" Sean replied, attempting to brush past the love-struck Yadi. She grabbed his arm, and not wanting to make a scene, Sean stopped in his tracks.

"What do you want from me, Yadi?" he asked, with a serious look on his face.

"I want you, Sean, and you need me. I'm gonna do whatever it takes to prove that to you, do you understand me?" Yadi replied.

Sean snatched his arm away from Yadi's grasp and walked back toward his post. Yadi stood there with a smirk on her face. She was a woman who put a lot of effort into getting what she wanted. In this case, Sean was going to be the prize.

Chapter 21

Later on that evening, Yadi sat in her car parked in front of her co-op apartment that Devin still lived in. The evening was tranquil, except for an occasional wind that swept through. Yadi stayed put, patiently waiting for Devin to walk out of the building. She was curious to see what he was up to and had been watching him occasionally after she left her apartment.

During one of her "visits," she had considered doing major damage to his truck but decided against it. She just wanted to retrieve some more of her belongings from the house. First Yadi had to make sure that Devin was not at home at the time. That would perfect because Yadi wanted to clear everything out of the apartment and she didn't need to get into any more altercations with him. She also didn't want to give Devin the satisfaction of staying in her apartment and have access to the furniture she purchased.

Upon speaking with the cooperative board, they agreed to notify Devin and tell him that he would have to leave. Until then, Yadi was still financially responsible for the maintenance. The thought of him living rent-free in her place while she stayed elsewhere pissed her off. Nevertheless, she was going to do whatever she had to in order to remove Devin from her place and from her life, once and for all. She had to work on getting with Sean Daniels, the man that she was in love with.

Yadi sat upright in her Maxima when she noticed Devin walking out of the three-story building. She didn't know where he was going but she knew that she had to make it quick. She held her breath at the sight of him, almost forgetting how good he looked. Devin seemed as if he didn't have a care in the world, as he hopped into his Excursion and pulled off, totally oblivious to Yadi's watchful eye.

Knowing that she had no time to waste, Yadi jumped out of her car and gestured for the movers to follow her. It was 5:00 p.m., after hours for movers, but the people she hired for the job were more than happy to help Yadi (after being promised a nice piece of cash to do her the favor). They skillfully packed up her belongings and put the things into their truck. They removed her living room and bedroom furniture, dishes, linen, everything that Yadi told them to. Two hours later the job was done. Yadi stood in the middle of the empty apartment shaking her head.

Yadi purchased the co-op when she completed her probationary period with Department of Correction. For the first time in her life, Yadi was so proud of her accomplishments but only one thing was missing and that was a good man. Then she had met Devin and fallen in love, but now it seemed as if she was back to square one.

Yadi sighed thinking that she should have gotten the locks changed, but she wanted Devin to come home and feel her wrath. He would enter the empty apartment after a hard night's work, with no bed to sleep in, no couch to sit on. She laughed wishing that she could be a fly on the wall when he walked into total emptiness. Payback was a bitch.

After seeing that her things were properly placed inside the storage area she was renting, Yadi paid the movers generously for their work. She watched them drive off then she made her way back to Vanita's house in Queens. Yadi sighed thinking about Sean, wishing that she were on the way to his house instead of Vanita's. She needed his companionship but tried to wipe that thought out of her mind.

Yadi turned up the radio in her car and tried to hum along with the music. She finally called Sean's phone several times but he wouldn't answer. What really had her tripping was that she observed Sean talking to some female visitor, a visitor with whom he seemed extremely comfortable. She'd seen the woman visiting inmate Wallace on a regular basis.

Their familiarity with each other had Yadi extremely curious about the connection they had with each other. Yadi overheard Sean apologizing to the visitor about something. What reason did he have to apologize to her?

She would hate to have to put Sean on blast if he was involved with the woman. Would Sean be stupid enough to push her to the side for some bitch coming to visit her lowlife son in jail? Yadi felt that he knew better than that. He knew that having a personal relationship with an inmate's family member was against the rules.

When she walked into Vanita's house, Yadi was shocked to see Devin sitting in Vanita's living room, playing with Jada. Yadi looked out the window and cursed herself for not paying attention to his truck that was parked across the street from the house. She would have kept it moving. Yadi saw Vanita and made an angry gesture. Vanita had a confused look on her face and walked out of the room. Yadi followed her.

"What the fuck is he doin' here, Nita? I thought I told you that it was over between me and him!" Yadi whispered, peeking at Devin from the kitchen.

Vanita eyes darted all over her neat kitchen. She needed a shot glass for the Patron she was about to drink. "He came over to see his daughter, what was I supposed to do? Not let him in?" Vanita asked.

Yadi looked at Jada, who was more than happy to see her father. She began biting her nails. "How the hell this mothafucka even know where you live, anyway?"

Vanita shrugged her shoulders. "I dunno, Yadi! I was gonna ask you the same thing. I guess he must have followed you over here one day. But when he rang the doorbell, Jada was standin' there and I didn't want to make a scene in front of her. She was actually very happy to see him."

"Why didn't you call me and at least warn me, Nita?"

"'Cause you would have came in here, doin' the same shit you tryin' to do now, and that's flip out. Your daughter is happy to see her father so let's just leave it alone for now, okay?"

Yadi looked at Vanita and rolled her eyes. She walked into the living room and sat in a huge armchair. Devin looked up at Yadi, immediately wiping the smile from his handsome face.

"I'm playin' with Jada, alone, if you don't mind," he stated. "Can we be alone?"

"No, you can't. I'm not botherin' y'all. Go ahead and play with your daughter."

Devin glared at Yadi. He felt like smacking her ass all over Vanita's living room but refrained from doing it in front of Jada. She had been through enough already. Yadi sucked her teeth and when Devin stood up, so did she. He looked at Yadi then looked at Jada and smiled.

"Jada, Daddy has to leave now. I'm gonna see you later, okay?" Devin told his daughter.

Jada nodded her head and jumped up. Devin swept the little girl up into his arms and kissed her all over her chubby face. He then put Jada down and walked toward the front door. He turned around and faced Yadi.

"It ain't over yet, you little bitch," he whispered. The tone of his voice sent chills through her body.

"You threatenin' me?" she whispered back.

"No, I'm promisin' you," he replied, repeating exactly what she had told him a week ago. Devin walked out the front door and hopped in his truck. Yadi stood in the doorway with an evil expression on her face until he pulled off.

"You're lucky I don't kill your black ass," she said, under her breath.

Chapter 22

Later that night, Sean tossed and turned in his bed. He didn't know what to do or who to call. Yadi wouldn't go away and Brandi wasn't fucking with him at all. He wanted to see Brandi badly but he decided to sit it out for a few days, hoping she would at least calm down and call him. Suddenly, Sean hopped out of bed and got dressed. He decided to hit Brown Sugar for a couple of drinks to get his mind off Brandi Wallace and Yadira Cruz. Hopefully, he would run into one of his boys.

When Sean pulled up to the lounge bar, he was surprised at the amount of cars parked out front. It was a Wednesday night and a couple of cats were standing outside, smoking cigarettes and talking shit. Sean gave them all a pound and walked inside the bar where people were singing karaoke.

When he got inside, his boy, Unique, was playing pool and trash talking. Unique was a childhood friend of Sean's, who was also a successful accountant in Atlanta. They had been through hell and back with each other and Sean was happy to see him.

Unique got one of his balls in the hole. "Yeah!" he screamed at his opponent, lifting his hands in the air. "You about to pay up, my dude!" Unique shouted at the man, while continuing to play. He looked up to see Sean standing nearby and smiled. "Yo, Shiz, what up, homeboy?"

Sean walked over to the table and slapped the men five. They all hugged each other, too. "What up, Unique? When did you get back in town?" Sean asked. "Better yet, when was you gonna tell me that you was back in town, motherfucker?!"

Unique concentrated on his game while talking to Sean. "I came up this past Monday," he replied, with a smirk on his face. "I had a few meetings in Manhattan this week and you know how we do, homeboy! I had to get that monkey off my back and then I came here and got caught up with this pool game. Niggas act like they don't remember how Big U.E. gets down on some pool!"

Sean laughed. "You're a fool, kid! How's everybody doin'?" he asked

Unique smirked. "They're all good, man. Moms and Pops is movin' to Atlanta in a few months. They bought a house not too far from my condo. Oh, yeah, my brother just left outta here a minute ago."

Sean laughed aloud. "Oh, word? Damn, I ain't seen Wise in a minute."

Unique chuckled. "Yeah, well, Wise ain't seen himself in a minute. That dude is a dope fiend. He sniffin' that shit like crazy."

"Oh, word? Wise is on dope? Not fly-ass Wise!"

Unique continued to play his game. "Yeah, man. Found out a few months ago that he's been doin' that shit for a minute. Thought we had got through all that mess, the drugs . . ." Unique wandered off into deep thought for a brief second. "But, he gotta deal with that. I got my own problems, nah mean, Shiz?"

"Yeah, I know, U, I know. I got an asshole full myself."

Sean sat on the side and watched Unique's opponent finally lose the pool game. The man paid Unique his money, gave them a pound, and walked out the door. Unique sat next to Sean, counting money. "What's poppin', my dude? You look upset."

Sean folded his arms. "Yeah, man. My dick done got me into some trouble once again. I got these two chicks and I can't call either one of them to come over and take care of me, man."

"What happened, boy? Don't tell me that you lettin' some chicks stress you out, son. You must be gettin' old!"

"Nah, man. I got this one bad chick at work that I was cool with, right. She had some problems with her baby daddy so I let her and her daughter stay with me for a few days. We had sex with each other and now this heffer thinks that I'm her man!"

Unique took a swig of his Corona and shook his head. "You playin' that Captain Save a Ho shit again, Shiz?"

"Then I got this female I met while she was visitin' her son on Rikers."

Unique looked at Sean. "Damn, son, you messin' with old visit broads now? How old is she?"

Sean laughed. "Brandi is like thirty-five and her son is nineteen years old. He's a little bitch made dude, too. I wanted to fuck this dude up the other day because he was tryin' to play Billy badass in front of his boys. He's lucky I wanna holler at his moms or else I woulda lay his silly-ass out!"

"Yeah, man, he don't know that them things is registered weapons?" Unique said, pointing at Sean's scarred-up hands. "Don't kill the little young whippersnapper now! You tryin' to get in his mama's drawers!" They both laughed loudly.

Sean got back on the subject. "C'mon, nigga, I'm stressed over here! Both of these women are bad as hell. They ain't no regular chicks.

But chick from work is stressin' me. We got into this big argument at work the other day while my visit chick was sittin' right outside in the waitin' area. She was comin' to see her son. She overheard everything me and my coworker was arguin' about! Now she ain't really fuckin' wit' me!" Sean banged his fist on the bar. "Damn!"

Unique ran everything down in his head. "Yo, I can't believe you're messin' with a visitor broad! Can't you get into trouble for that shit?"

Sean shook his head. "Yeah, I can, man. Homegirl at work ran up on me while I was trying to talk to my visitor honey. I felt like a piece of shit, man."

Unique was getting impatient. "Yo, man, what are you gonna do, then? You can't be sittin' around feelin' sorry for yourself! You don't have no girl or no kids. You a free agent to do what you wanna do. Actually, why don't y'all all have fun in the sack? Have a threesome!"

Unique's suggestion sounded like a good idea but Sean wouldn't disrespect the two women like that.

"Nah, man, I wouldn't do that. They're both cool but they are two very different women. My coworker, Yadira, is a sexy half black, half Latina, who, I'm not gonna lie, everytime I see her, she makes my nature rise. She was straight, at least I thought she was, until we started havin' sex with each other. Brandi, on the other hand, is very attractive, mature, and she's got it goin' on, too! She has a master's degree, and she's a good woman. She got street smarts, too. She may have a son whose locked up in jail but she dealin' with it. I guess what I'm tryin' to say is that I like Brandi. Yadira is turnin' into a crazy bitch, man."

Unique looked at his friend and ordered some more Coronas for the both of them. Unique was no stranger when it came to drama; he already had his share of it.

"Damn, Shiz, I dunno, man. If you really like Brandi, what's stoppin' you from fuckin' with her? I know you're not going let her son stop you from messin' with his moms."

Sean looked around. "Hell no! It ain't the son that's the problem. It's Yadi, man. This broad has been givin' me grief at the job and I don't know what's gonna happen next. I don't trust that bitch."

Unique laughed. He could see the fear in Sean's eyes. "What? You scared of a chick, Shiz? I never thought that I would see the day that my man got fear in his heart over some broad!"

"Yo, U, man, you don't understand. It's somethin' about Yadi that makes me real uneasy. She used to always complain about her baby father and shit but now that I dealt with her myself, I don't think it was the baby father that was the problem. It's her ass that's crazy!"

Unique took a swig of his beer. "I don't know what to tell you, Shiz. I ain't never had that problem with none of my women."

Sean laughed. "I know you ain't had that problem 'cause you ain't no fly-ass dude like me, nigga, that's why."

They both laughed but Sean was still uneasy. There was something unsettling about Yadi and he knew that he would have to be careful with her.

At work the next day, Yadira watched Sean's every move. Sean made it his business to ignore Yadi and talk to everyone except her. At one point, Yadi was so desperate for his attention; she stomped out of the control room and walked out onto the visit floor. She didn't know what else to do and everyone was starting to notice her fixation with Sean Daniels.

The gossip mill began and tongues were wagging all through the jail. Some male officers in the male locker room even prodded Sean for information about Yadi's sexual prowess, by asking questions, like "How was the pussy?" or "Does she give good head?" Sean was annoyed with all the queries from his male coworkers but he managed to keep his temper in check. Yadi was only making it worse with her erratic behavior. Secretly, Sean still had an insatiable urge to sex Yadira again, but at what cost?

Sean walked into the officer's lounge area and sat at a table with a few female coworkers he talked to from time to time. While they were sitting there having a good laugh, taking a break from the stress of their daily routine, Yadi walked in. She walked over to the table and stood there, staring at Sean.

"What are you doin'?" Yadi asked, pointing her finger at the two female officers, like they weren't supposed to be around there.

Sean looked at the women and they looked just as bewildered as he did. "What are you talkin' about?" Sean asked.

"I'm talkin' about you sittin' here, talkin' to these bitches!" she exclaimed, loudly.

The women looked at each other but only one stood up. "Wait a fuckin' minute, bitch, I will—" one of the female COs yelled and attempted to come at Yadi.

Sean stood between the Yadi and the woman. Inmates stopped serving the food and the kitchen staff rushed to the front to observe the ruckus.

"Yo, Cruz, step outside. We don't need nobody in the business!" Sean said.

"In the business? You don't want them in the business?" she yelled. "Should I tell them about us, Sean? Should I?"

Sean began to get angry. Yadi was making their encounter into a relationship that never was. "What the fuck are you talkin' about, man? Why are you actin' like this?"

The crowd grew. Everyone was anticipating a big finale and wanted to be around to watch. Yadi pointed her finger in Sean's face. "How you gonna fuck me and you're fuckin' with a visi—"

Sean grabbed Yadi's face and pushed her out of the lounge area and into the corridor. Some officers followed them to watch and some intervened. They managed to separate Sean and Yadi before any supervisors walked up on them. Sean struggled to get away from his coworkers' vice grip and some females pulled Yadi away. They continued to yell down the corridor but were long gone before one lone captain stepped into the hallway to see what the commotion was about.

After the altercation with Sean, Yadi walked to the female locker room with two of her fellow coworkers. They were tenured officers and had seen many fights and arguments over the course of their lengthy careers between officers who decided to hook up with each other.

"Cruz, you need to get yourself together, baby!" stated a female officer named Cook. "You done lost your rabbit-ass mind approachin' that man like that! What is wrong with you, girl?"

Yadi was pacing back and forth. She felt like she was losing her rabbit-ass mind. "I dunno, Miss Cook, I just want to get outta here right now!" she replied.

The other woman spoke. "Do you need some kinda help, because you can't be comin' to work with this kind of drama, sweetheart. Trust me, we all have been there before. You gotta have some self-respect!" she said.

"You ain't lyin', Mayes!" Cook replied. "Shiiit, I done had me a few men back in the day. We came from a time where mothafuckas would come to your post and whip your ass over these sorry people up in here, man or woman. But you are a beautiful young lady; you can't let no man take you outta your character. It ain't worth all that, ma."

"I know but I really am in love with Daniels. He just isn't payin' me no attention right now and I feel like a fuckin' fool," Yadi said.

Cook looked at Yadi, with a frown on her smooth, brown face. "Why? I mean, have you looked at yourself lately? You can have any man you want, in this jail, on Riker's Island, and out in New York. Why are you limitin' yourself to Sean Daniels? A man that you claim isn't givin' you the time of day?" Cook paused. "Girl, please, if I had your looks, mothafuckas would be payin' me just to sniff it, let alone fuck it. You got some serious shit to think about, sis!"

Mayes shook her head in agreement. "Don't play yourself, Cruz! You know these women are already hatin' on you and the men are hatin' that they're not with you. You can't get mad at Daniels 'cause you gave it up to him. Y'all were friends and you know you messed up when you lay up with him and caught feelings!"

Yadi sat on the wooden bench. "You ladies are right. It's like I can't control myself. Me and my man broke up and it's like, I'm scared to be by myself. I ain't never had to be by myself."

Yadi began to cry and the women comforted her. They both had been where she was and it took maturity and experience to get to where they were now.

Shortly after, the women left and Yadi stayed in the locker room by herself. She went into the bathroom to look at her face in the mirror, which was beginning to swell up from rubbing her tears away.

An hour later, Yadi managed to walk through the corridors of the jail without any incident, knowing that people were probably talking about her and calling her crazy. Yadi didn't feel that she was crazy. She was just in love with a man named Sean Daniels and no one could tell her that she was wrong for that. When she finally made it back to her post, Vanita looked at her sideways and shook her head. There was an uncomfortable silence between the two friends, as they continued to work side by side.

Chapter 23

In midtown Manhattan, Brandi arrived at work, emotionally drained from thinking about her personal problems. She spoke to her coworkers and casually strolled into her office and shut the door. When Brandi closed her door, it was the message to her staff that she was in no mood to be bothered. She looked out the window, staring at the weathered buildings that faced her office. The people below were scurrying around on the streets like roaches, but for some reason she would have rather been down there with them than in her office. She swiveled her chair around toward her desk and sighed as she stared at the mountains of paperwork she had to look over. She had to make sure that the clients of Administration for Children Services were given the services that they needed. As she put on her Prada spectacles and began to do her work, she heard a knock on the door. It was Mrs. Pritchard, the septuagenarian, who worked at the front desk. She was holding a giant bouquet of colorful roses in a glass vase.

"Wow, Miss Thang," Mrs. Pritchard began, looking over her rimless glasses. "You must got somebody whipped!"

Brandi smiled. Mrs. Pritchard made her day with that comment. "These are for me, huh?" Brandi asked as she took the bouquet out of the older woman's shaky hands. "They are gorgeous!"

Mrs. Pritchard continued to stand in the small office, waiting for Brandi to open the enclosed envelope. "Hurry up, child! I'm waitin' for you to open the letter!" Brandi chuckled and hurriedly opened the small envelope.

"A woman like you deserves something that's just as beautiful as you are, Kisses, Sean," Brandi read.

Mrs. Pritchard clapped while looking over her eyeglasses. "Brandi, who is this sendin' you the beautiful arrangement? It looks like it cost them some money!"

Brandi smiled and held the note. "Someone very special to me, Mrs. Pritchard."

"Hmm, that's obvious. He sounds like he's worth keepin'. Maybe he could help take your mind off Shamari." Mrs. Pritchard walked toward the door and turned around. "Um, helllooo! I don't see you makin' that 'thank you' phone call!"

Mrs. Pritchard walked out of office and closed the door. Brandi giggled, while she hurriedly picked up the phone to call Sean. She couldn't even stay angry with Sean for long. She looked at the clock and realized he was still at work so she just left a seductive voicemail instead.

"Hey, Sean," Brandi began. "I received your flower arrangement and I would love to thank you in person, you know, to show you some real appreciation," she said, in a seductive whisper. "Call me back, baby."

Later on that afternoon, Sean listened to his voicemails and instantly got a hard-on after hearing Brandi's voice. He knew that she would love the bouquet of roses that he had delivered to her job. What he really wanted to do was go straight to her house and work that pussy over real good, but he couldn't do that yet, he didn't want to seem too eager to have sex with her. He was leaving it up to her to suggest that. He picked up the phone to call Brandi.

"Hello?" she answered on the first ring.

"Hey, cutie, wassup?" Sean asked. "Oh, yeah, I got your message."

"I hope you did," Brandi said. Sean got the joke and laughed.

"I know that I've been apologizin' a lot and I wanted to make it up to you. I need to talk to you in person about what's goin' on so, if you wasn't busy, you wanna come out tonight?"

"Out where? To your house?"

"Nah, girl! Slow down! I'm goin' to meet my man, Unique, at Brown Sugar's tonight, you know, kick it and have a couple of drinks and what not. You wanna meet me over there?"

"Sure. Can I bring my friend, Sheba?"

"No doubt. As long as I don't have to do the matchmakin' thing, especially since I'm tryin' to get with your sexy ass. Ain't nobody fuckin' up my chances with you!"

"Sweetie, nobody is gonna mess up your chances of getting with me!"

"Hmmph. I hope you mean that, ma. I hope you really mean that," Sean replied, thinking about his situation with Yadi. He wanted to meet with Brandi to tell her about Yadi before things got serious. Sean didn't want anything or anyone to come between him and Brandi, especially some love-struck drama queen like Cruz.

He realized that he was already taking a chance on being involved with Brandi because Shamari was locked up in the jail and he was a correction officer. The wrong person, which was Yadi, had gotten wind of Brandi, and his career could be on the line.

"So Brown Sugar is on Marcus Garvey, right off of Fulton Street, right?"

"Yeah. I'll be there at nine-thirty. See you then."

Brandi hung up with Sean and called Sheba. "What's up, girl? Get dressed, we're going out for a little while." Brandi moved the phone away from her ear, as Sheba yelled into her ear about why she didn't call her earlier and how she would have gotten her hair done and so on. Brandi had forgotten how vain her friend was.

"Sheba, just get dressed! Damn, it's only a freaking lounge bar! You're fly, girl! Get creative and I'll be over to pick you up in an hour!"

Brandi laughed and hung up the phone. *Same old Sheba,* she thought while shaking her head.

Sean and Unique sat at the bar in the Brown Sugar lounge, nursing some Hennesy and Coke. When Sean turned around, Brandi was standing behind him, along with her friend, Sheba. Sheba was an inch taller than Brandi, with long hair and just as fine as Brandi. Sheba looked so much like Brandi, they could pass for sisters. Happy that they were there and looking good, Sean immediately introduced the duo to Unique. They stood up and offered the women the bar stools that they were sitting on.

Brandi was impressed by the gesture. "Thank you! You guys are such gentlemen," she said.

Sensing that Sean wanted to be alone with Brandi, Unique excused himself and walked toward the pool tables and beckoned Sheba to follow him. Sean and Brandi stayed put for a much-needed talk at the bar.

"You look good, as usual," Sean complimented, admiring Brandi's tight-fitting Liberation jeans that hugged every curve of her body, and her low-cut blouse. "I'm real glad you came out tonight."

Brandi blushed. "Yeah, me too, Sean. I really wanted to see you, especially after you sent that bouquet to the office. That was really sweet of you."

"Thank you, sweetheart. That's only the beginning." Sean paused and sipped on his drink. "Brandi, look, I needed to talk to you. I need to be up front about me and my coworker, Yadi Cruz."

She was silent. "Could you order me a drink first?"

Sean ordered Brandi a cosmopolitan. Brandi was curious to hear his side of the story even though she felt that it probably was only the half truth.

"Okay, where do I start?" Sean said, with a sigh. "Okay. Yadira Cruz was a friend, a coworker, and a woman that I found very attractive. She had a fight with her daughter's father the week before last and she asked me if she could stay with me for a while, so I agreed to help a friend. I told her that she could stay for as long as she liked because I have that big house to myself and she needed a place to stay. The night that we hung out, I came home horny and she just happened to be waitin' up for me. One thing led to another and we had sex."

"But that was no reason to have that kind of an argument. Why was she arguing with you?" Brandi asked, sweeping hair out of her eyes.

"She was upset because when she came back to my crib to drop off my house key, she let herself in and overheard us havin' sex with each other upstairs."

Brandi put her hand over her mouth. "Oh, shit! I would have felt like an idiot, too, but you know what it is? She got caught up in her feelings, Sean. You can't get mad at that woman for that and why would she let herself in your house anyway?"

"I asked her the same thing. But, damn, I never said I was gonna be with her and I never said that I'm her man. She just threw it at me," Sean said.

"And you caught it, didn't you?" Brandi asked.

Sean laughed. "Yeah, I ain't gonna lie, I did," he replied.

"Mmmhmm, I thought you did. So now she's acting all crazy, huh?"

Sean sighed and sipped his Hennesy. "Yeah, she is. She's just flipped on me for some reason." Sean paused. "She even threw you in my face!"

"Look, you knocked her boots because you wanted to and the opportunity was there. You know how you men are; guys are opportunists." Brandi shrugged her shoulders and slurped on her cosmo. "Well, what can you do? It was the wrong place, wrong time with the wrong person."

They continued their conversation, switching it from subject to subject. Sean enjoyed talking to Brandi, who seemed mature and confident. Not accustomed to having a meaningful conversation with women, Brandi was like a breath of fresh air for him but how long would that last with Yadi in the picture?

Chapter 24

"Daddy, where we goin'?" Jada asked. She was strapped to her booster seat in the back of her father's SUV.

"We goin' to Granny's house," he said, while driving down Hempstead Turnpike toward his mother's house. "Don't you wanna see Granny?"

"Yay! We goin' to Granny's house!" Jada paused. "Why Mommy can't come?"

Devin rolled his eyes. "'Cause Mommy gotta work, baby girl. She gonna let you stay with Granny for a little while, okay?"

Jada clapped. "Okay, Daddy. I like to stay at Granny's house, anyway. She make me cookies!"

"I know, baby. Granny got you a lot of cookies," he replied, with a smirk on his face.

Devin had taken it upon himself to pick his daughter up early from her day care. He was surprised when they allowed him to leave the facility with his daughter in tow. Taking his name off the authorized list was obviously one of the things Yadi had forgotten to do. Even better, Jada was more than happy to leave with him, allowing him to go ahead with his plans of trying to keep her away from her psychotic mother. Yadi had been calling him with death threats. It was because of Jada he didn't have her ass arrested for aggravated harassment.

Devin was on the phone with his mother. He'd called her to let her know they were on their way to her house. The phone beeped and he rolled his eyes, seeing that it was Yadira's cell phone number.

"Listen, Ma, lemme call you back. Here she is now." Devin clicked over. "Yeah, I got Jada. She's goin' to my mother's house."

Yadi screamed into the phone. "Motherfucker, bring my daughter to me, right now! You took her outta school without my fuckin' permission! I will kill your ass if you hurt her!"

Devin looked at his phone. "Hurt her? Oh, Yadi, please. She's mine, too! Ever since you left, you haven't tried to let me see my daughter! So if you wanna see her, then come to my mother's house to see her!"

"That's my mommy?" Jada yelled from the back seat. "I wanna speak to Mommy!"

Devin looked in the rear view mirror at his daughter. "Mommy will talk to you later, Jay-

Jay. She's gotta go now." Devin turned up the music in the rear of the truck. As Jada sang along with Ne-Yo, Devin spoke to Yadi.

"You know you been pushin' my buttons for a minute with all of your lies, Yadi. You got everybody thinkin' you're some goody-two-shoes and I'm just a piece of shit! Well, I'm not playin' with you anymore! You wanna see your daughter, take me to fuckin' court, I dare you! I will pull out those psychiatric papers quicker than you could spell your name! Does the judge need to know you tried to kill yourself?"

"Yeah, but I tried to kill myself over you, you bastard! Now I'm tryin' to figure out why! But I know one thing, I will kill you if you take my daughter from me! I will hunt you down and gut you like a fish, I swear. I want my daughter!"

"Whatever, Yadi! You tried that killin' yourself bullshit with every dude you was in love with and that was basically any that you dealt with. You know I know! Like I said, if you wanna see her, she'll be at my mother's house." Devin hung up the phone and turned it off.

When Yadira crawled into the bed, the tears started flowing. She felt as if she didn't have any control over her anger anymore. Devin had taken Jada away from her and she was beginning to believe he had every right to. Sean was backing away from her and she couldn't say that she blamed him, either. Yadira refused to call her family because they would only make her come home with them.

Later that night, she finally managed to get out of the bed and look at the time. It was eleven p.m. She peeped out the window and saw Vanita's car parked in the driveway. Yadi shrugged her shoulders and threw on a long down coat and some boots. She crept down the stairs and got into her car. She wanted to take a drive to clear her head.

As Yadi traveled on the Conduit, she knew that she was heading to Sean's house. She wanted to apologize for the way that she'd been acting toward him. Sean was a good catch, like Vanita told her, and it would be a shame if she allowed some other woman to get with him.

When Yadi pulled up on Sean's quiet block, she smiled when she saw his truck parked in front of his house. The house looked dark inside but Yadi was unfazed as she rang the bell. Little did he know, she made a spare key to his house, never knowing when it would come in handy. But she wasn't going to use it this time. She rang the bell like a maniac and Sean came to the door, rubbing the sleep out of his eyes, with a robe on. He swung the door open when he saw Yadira standing on the stoop.

"You comin' over here unannounced now?" Sean shouted. He stood there holding the door but didn't bother to invite her in.

"Sean, I ain't come here to cause no problems. I just wanna talk to you for a moment," Yadi said. "Can I come in?" she pleaded.

Sean leaned against the door and sucked his teeth. If he let Yadi in, he knew that he was going to end up having sex with her. He couldn't allow himself to think with his little head anymore. He had to get Yadi out of his area, for the last time.

Sean reluctantly let her inside, and as she was about to walk upstairs toward his bedroom, he stopped Yadi dead in her tracks.

"Yo! Where the fuck do you think you're goin'?" he asked. "You have anything to say, you can say it right here at the bottom of these steps."

Yadira leaned against the banister of the staircase. "Sean," she began, "I don't wanna be your enemy. I want us to call a truce. I know that it's been a rough two weeks and I understand that maybe I got a little outta control with everything but . . ."

Sean rubbed his unkempt head. "But what? You want us to be friends again? How the fuck can I trust you, Yadira? I open the door for you and Jada and in return, you caused all this friction in my life? Not to mention, you're harassin' my friends and shit?"

Yadi licked her lips. "I'm not causin' nothin' in your life, Sean and I damn sure ain't harassin' none of your friends. You're the one that insist on playin' games with me."

Sean hit the wall in frustration. "Playin' games with you? I was never your man, though. We shacked up for a few days and you're tellin' me that I'm your man? How does that shit sound to you?"

"Okay, but you can't deny that you were feelin' me at one point, right? You wanted to holler at me, didn't you? And you had to be feelin' me some kind of way if you're gonna let me and my daughter stay in your house, right?"

"Listen, you were a coworker and a friend, a friend that was in need. That's it. Yeah, I wanted to holler at you at one time but you told me out of your own mouth that you was with Devin and you don't creep on him. I respected that. Now when you stayed here, I'm not gonna lie, the physical attraction and the lust got to me and we had sex. That's it. It was just sex!"

"What is it, Sean? Is it that bitch, Brandi? This Brandi broad got you open, huh?"

"Brandi? Why is Brandi even a part of this conversation? This is between me and you. She don't know you, she's not thinkin' about you so why don't you leave her name out of your mouth?"

Yadira crossed her arms and stared at Sean with an earnest look on her face. She felt lost now that their friendship was officially over and she could not bear to see herself without him. Yadi walked up to Sean and hugged him. She could feel his body stiffen. There was no mistaking the erection under his robe, though. She smiled and loosened the embrace.

"Hmmph. I see that I didn't lose my touch, huh?" she proclaimed, while looking down at Sean's stiffness.

Sean looked down, too, without cracking a smile. "Yeah, but you know what? That down there has a mind of its own. This fuckin' head on my shoulders says that I wouldn't touch your crazy ass with a ten foot pole, in this case, my ten foot pole."

Yadi looked at Sean sideways and dropped to her knees. She attempted to pull his hard rod out of his boxers and he pushed her away from him. She fell on her back, with a stunned look on her face.

"Do me a favor, Yadi, get your ass up off my fuckin' floor and outta my crib! That shit ain't workin' on me no more. Five minutes of pleasure ain't worth a lifetime of aggravation!"

Humiliated, Yadi got up and brushed herself off. She stood there for a few seconds and looked at Sean, who calmly guided her toward the front entranceway. Yadi felt the butterflies floating in her stomach as she opened the door to leave.

"Sean, you gonna regret the fuckin' day you ever lay eyes on me!" she exclaimed, with tears falling from her eyes.

"Too late, bitch, I already regret it!" he replied, escorting her out the door. By the time Yadi turned around to say something else, his door was locked.

Chapter 25

Shamari walked out of the cell into the housing area. He rubbed his eyes and looked around for someone to play a game of cards with him but everyone was still asleep. The CO on post was chatting on the telephone and not paying him any attention. He stood up on a chair and turned on the television. It was Saturday morning and cartoons were in full effect. Shamari sat back and watched them, thinking back to his childhood and missing his father.

Maleek lifted the four-year-old Shamari in the air, as the child laughed with delight. They were in Disney World and Shamari was happy because his father said he could have whatever he wanted while they were there.

"Go ahead, Shaki," Maleek said, as he nudged his son while standing in one of the many novelty shops. "What you want, li'l man?" Shamari's young eyes widened as he watched his father pull out a knot of money.

Brandi frowned. "Maleek, don't tell that boy that! You know he is gonna go ape shit up in this store. Look at all this stuff!" She looked around at the Mickey Mouse paraphanalia and sighed. "How the hell are we gonna get all this shit on the plane?"

Maleek waved Brandi off. "Brandi, let the boy have what he wants! Shit, it ain't every day a nigga get a chance ta be with his boy in Disney. I don't hustle for nothin'!"

Shamari happily grabbed up whatever he wanted and his father purchased it all. Shamari gave his father a big hug and a kiss.

"Thanks, Daddy! I love you!" Shamari said as he hugged Maleek.

Maleek picked him up and gave him another kiss on the cheek. "I love you, too, Shaki, and no matter what happens to me, I don't want you to ever forget me, okay?"

Shamari shook his head. He was only four years old at the time but he would remember those words for the rest of his life. Even though his father died when he was very young, he was never the same. Shamari loved his mother, and as he matured, he started feeling different things, things that he knew he couldn't share with Brandi. Only a man.

Right now, Shamari felt like he had no one to go to, refusing to let his guard down, especially while he was on lockdown. Any sign of sensitivity was a no-no when a nigga was incarcerated. It would be perceived as a sign of weakness. Darkness became a prisoner's enemy because this was the time that they were the loneliest. It was when they had time to think and all those demons resurface. The morning time seemed as if it was a step closer to freedom.

Shamari got up and walked toward his cell, but not before he heard his name called.

"Wallace, you have a visit, son!" an escort officer shouted. Shamari ran in his cell, grabbed his slippers, and walked out the door.

When he arrived downstairs, he was surprised to see a very pregnant Amber waiting for him. Since meeting his mother, Shamari and Amber had been speaking to each other every day. A smile appeared on his face, as he briskly walked over and hugged her tightly. Her stomach was huge and her once slim face had filled out from the pregnancy. Her attire and her neatly done hairdo were very becoming and Shamari was immediately turned on by her appearance.

"Hey, Amber! Man, I didn't expect to see you up here this soon," Shamari exclaimed, kissing her on the lips. "I'm happy that you're here, though!"

Amber smiled, displaying a beautiful set of white teeth. "Yes, Shamari, I know you didn't. I'm about to burst!"

Shamari rubbed her stomach in amazement. "Look at this. This is us, huh?"

Amber put her hand on her protruding stomach as well. "It sure is. I know when your mother told you that I was havin' the baby, you probably was talkin' shit."

Shamari waved the thought off. "Nah, Amber, you know you was my girl. I mean, I did my thing with other people but I always loved you. I still do."

"Mmhmm. You better, Mr. Shamari Wallace, 'cause I love you too. That was the problem. I loved you too much. Now look, we got this baby on the way."

Shamari held his head down. The tears began to flow freely. The stress of being locked up was starting to get to him. Shamari had too much going on to be behind those walls. He had his mother, Amber and now a baby on the way.

Amber made him look at her. "What's the matter?"

Shamari looked around to see if anyone was watching. "Amber, I'm sorry for puttin' you through this. I was runnin' around actin' a fool when I shoulda been on my A game and takin' care of my responsibilities. I love you, Amber, and I promise I'm gonna be there for our son. When I come home, I'm gonna do what it takes to be a good father!"

"Okay, Shamari, I know you are but why are you cryin'? I believe you, I always believed in you."

Shamari wiped his tears. "I know, shorty. I been thinkin' about how much I need my pops in my life."

Amber rubbed Shamari's arm. "I know but you're gonna be there for yours. I see that. Just gotta get outta here."

Amber looked on Shamari's neck and saw the healing cut. "Oh, shit, Shamari, who cut you?"

"Long story. We'll talk about that later. Isn't your baby shower tomorrow?"

Amber smiled. "Yeah. I just had to come see you before it got too crazy. I might be havin' this baby any day now." Amber paused. "I love you, Shamari. Don't leave me again, okay?"

Shamari hugged Amber and whispered in her ear. "Nah, ma. I promise this is the last time. I'll ever leave you or my son." Shamari sat back in his seat and took Amber's hand. "By the way, Amber, do you wanna get married?"

Chapter 26

Two weeks later, Devin parked his truck in front of Jada's school. He looked around to see if Yadi was anywhere in the vicinity. She'd been leaving threatening voice mails on his phone all night and finally, he decided to go to a precinct that morning to make a complaint report for aggravated harassment. The next step was an order of protection so that he could build a case against Yadi for custody of Jada. He wanted to get her before she got him.

When Devin walked into the school, he ducked and dodged children, who were running around him trying to get to their parents. He approached Jada's classroom and her teacher had a surprised look on her face.

"Oh, Mr. Marshall," she exclaimed. "I didn't know that you were going to pick up Jada today!"

Devin looked around. He didn't see Jada anywhere in the classroom. His heart dropped.

"Yeah, I've been pickin' her up every day for the last two weeks. Where is she?"

The teacher swallowed. She sensed that there was a custodial problem between Jada's parents and didn't want to be involved. "Umm, her mother picked her up a half hour ago. Didn't she tell you?"

Devin rubbed his bald head. "Damn!" he said under his breath. "Hell no, she didn't tell me." Devin looked at the shocked teacher. "I apologize, Miss Tina, it's not your fault. Thank you anyway." Devin hurriedly walked away and ran back to his truck. He couldn't get his cell phone out fast enough.

"Where the fuck is my daughter?" he screamed into the phone.

Yadi laughed hysterically. "With her mother, like she should be! You didn't have no right comin' in her school to take her away in the first place. Now you know how the hell it feels to have her taken away from you right under your nose. So take me to court, stupid, so that I can take your ass for child support and take the rest of your sorry-ass paycheck that you bring home every two weeks!"

Devin banged his hand on the dashboard. "You know what? I'm comin' to Vanita's house." Devin disconnected the phone call and stepped on the gas.

Meanwhile, Yadi rushed out of Vanita's house with Jada in tow. She wanted to leave before Devin came over. It would take him all of five minutes to get there so she had to be quick about it.

"Mommy!" Jada sulked, while holding her crotch area. "I gotta pee!"

Yadi was desperate. "Jay-Jay, you can't hold it until we stop at a McDonald's or something? Don't you want Mickey Dee's?"

Jada shook her head. "Mommy, I can't! I gotta make number two!"

Yadi's nose began to flare as she took Jada to the bathroom. She ran back to look out the window and saw Devin's truck pull up in front. She would have to leave out the back door but she cursed as she thought about the gate and the neighbor's pit bull on the other side of the fence.

"Shit!" Yadi said aloud.

"Oooh, Mommy, you said a bad word!" Jada shouted from the bathroom.

"I'm sorry, baby. Don't you repeat it, okay?" Yadi replied. Jada continued to talk but Yadi was too aggravated to listen as she watched Devin come to the door. She heard the bell ring and sucked her teeth.

"Mommy! The doorbell!" Jada shouted again.

"I know, Jada, just use the toilet, okay?" Yadi retorted. She ran downstairs and watched Devin from the window. He looked angry. Yadi was unsure if she should call the cops on his ass or not.

"I know you're in there, Yadira!" he shouted. "Gimme my daughter!"

This dirty motherfucker! Yadi thought. He was out there screaming for the whole neighborhood to hear.

"I want my daughter!" he yelled again. All of a sudden, five minutes later, she heard keys and voices downstairs. *Damn,* she thought. She had forgotten to warn Vanita about Devin before she came home.

Yadi ran to the bathroom and told Jada to be quiet. She lied and said that they were playing hide and seek and that Aunt Nita was it. Yadi helped Jada off the toilet and they hid in the shower.

"Yadiiii!" Vanita yelled. "Damn, she must have left with somebody. Her car is outside."

Yadi cringed when she heard Devin's booming voice. "I know the bitch is in here. Why you let her stay with you anyway?" Devin asked Vanita.

"'Cause she's my friend, that's why. I know you feel otherwise but I really care about Yadi."

Devin laughed. Yadi stepped out of the tub so that she could stand up and put her ear to the door. She hushed Jada, who was clueless and enjoying the hide and seek moment.

"Nita, stop frontin', girl. You let her move in here 'cause you probably felt guilty about me really tryin' to get with you! Now you done went and moved her crazy-ass in your house!"

Vanita chuckled. "Negro, please. I never was tryin' to get involved with the likes of you! You aren't anybody I would want!"

"You know I always wanted to get with you, Vanita. Why you never let me holler at you the right way?"

"Devin, Yadi is my friend and I am not goin' to violate her or myself like that. I didn't tell her about all the passes you made at me 'cause I didn't want to break her heart!"

Yadi slid to the floor in complete shock. She was not surprised that Devin was trying to make a pass at Vanita. She was angrier at the fact that Vanita never told her. How could Vanita be trusted now? Jada tapped Yadi on the shoulder from behind the shower curtain.

"Mommy," she whispered. "Can we come out and surprise Auntie Nita now?"

Yadi shook her head, holding back tears. Jada had seen her cry enough but this time she was going to be strong.

Yadi told Jada to be quiet, picking her up in her arms. She cracked open the bathroom door and looked outside in the empty hallway. She heard Devin and Vanita's voices in the kitchen, as she crept down the stairs, with her daughter in tow. She couldn't concern herself with them right now; she had to think about her and Jada. Yadi quietly walked out the front door of Vanita's house and pulled off in her car.

Chapter 27

A few weeks after Shamari asked to marry her, Amber was wheeled into the maternity ward of Kings County Hospital with her contractions coming every five minutes. She had never felt a pain like that in her life and she knew from that moment, she didn't want to feel it again. It was midnight and her mother was by her side, coaxing her every step of the way.

Once Amber was in the triage, her doctor, Dr. Samaj, checked her cervix to see if she was dilated. She was eight centimeters after having been in labor for a few hours. Amber screamed to the top of her lungs as Dr. Samaj immersed his gloved hand into her vagina. She grabbed her mother's hand tightly. Suddenly, Dr. Samaj looked at the fetal monitor that the triage nurse had managed to hook her up to.

"Nurse, get her prepared! This patient is showing signs of fetal distress!" Dr.Samaj announced.

Amber was immediately prepared to go into the delivery room. She was placed on a gurney and was wheeled out of the triage and whisked down the hall. Dr. Samaj was going to do an emergency cesarean because the baby was losing oxygen. Amber cried out for her mother, who was not allowed to come into the delivery room with her. She was given anesthesia, and seconds after she was unconscious, they began the C-section. As Dr. Samaj carried out the grueling procedure, one of his assistants notified him that Amber was losing oxygen, as well. They had to be quick because now they had two lives to save.

Dr. Samaj was able to pull the baby boy out of Amber's womb just in time. The baby's face was completely blue from the umbilical cord being wrapped around his neck. The newborn was resuscitated and began to cry.

The nurse looked at the flat line on the monitor. "Doctor! Doctor! Oh my God, we're losing his mother!"

The crew worked quickly and began massaging her heart. A nurse then bought over the defibrillators, giving her electric shocks to the chest. Amber's body jumped but her heart did not start back up. After several attempts to bring the young girl back to life to no avail, the crew gave up. They had exhausted everything and their eyes suddenly went to the crying baby who was already cleaned and swaddled in a baby blanket. A nurse ran out the delivery room in tears. Dr. Samaj threw his gloves across the room and went to the sink to scrub his hands. Unfortunately, he had to tell Amber's mother the good and bad news.

Dr. Samaj dragged himself down the long hospital corridor. He entered the waiting room and attempted to smile a little. Ms. Johnson stood up with a smile on her face. Brandi and Amber's little sister, Ashlee, accompanied her. They all were excited.

"Hey, Dr. Samaj, are my babies all right?" Ms. Johnson asked. Dr. Samaj gently held her hands.

"Ms. Johnson, you are the grandmother of a healthy baby boy! He was seven pound, nine ounces," Dr. Samaj replied.

They all rejoiced. "Wow, that's big! Shamari is gonna be so happy!" Brandi said. "How's Amber doing?"

Dr. Samaj held his head down. "I am so sorry but Amber didn't make it. We did everything that we could but Amber passed—" Dr. Semaj said. The wails from Miss Johnson didn't allow him to finish.

Amber's mother fell to her knees. "Noooo! Not my baby! Not my chillld!"

Dr. Samaj comforted her. "I am so sorry, Ms. Johnson!" He looked around at the crying women and wanted to escape. Brandi suddenly took over and asked Dr. Samaj what happened.

"Well, Amber experienced what we call septic shock. There wasn't enough blood flow and her organs shut down. Her baby's umbilical cord was wrapped around the neck and we had to do an emergency C-section. Fortunately, we were able to save the baby but Amber, well, Amber was in distress as well and we were unable to revive her."

Brandi looked back at the crying mother and her chest tightened up. She couldn't help but feel guilty because if it weren't for Shamari getting her pregnant, they probably would have still had Amber. She summoned Dr. Samaj to leave and she walked over to comfort the distraught Johnson women. She shook her head as she thought about how Shamari was going to react.

On her way home, Brandi couldn't stop crying. She displayed every emotion that was humanly possible the moment she walked into her empty apartment. Once again, she was left to live with some agonizing guilt. There was no way she would be able to face the Johnson's after the horrible catastrophe but after having a few drinks, she realized that she was going to have to grow up and face the music. She would have to be strong for

Shamari, who was going to be torn apart from the mind-blowing news that she would have to deliver.

Back at the jail, Shamari thought about how he missed his family; he missed his bed and home-cooked meals. He missed hanging out with his boys, going to parties and talking to girls on his cell phone. All the things that he had taken for granted were no longer accessible to him. Now that he was having a son of his own, he was going to have to devote his young life to his son, making sure that he was a positive role model for him.

Returning from the barbershop, Shamari exited the staircase. There, he ran into Born, who was entering the staircase at the same time. Born pushed Shamari back into the stairwell, while the COs in the control room weren't looking. Shamari's back hit the wall.

"Yo, if you feelin' a way about me, you talk to me!" Born stated, through clenched teeth. "I'm tired of you puttin' my name in your mouth, nigga !"

Suddenly, Shamari charged the man into a metal banister. Born cringed then punched Shamari in the face. Shamari, who was much younger and quicker than Born, immediately sprung into action after the punch. He might have been scared as hell but that didn't stop him from protecting himself. Shamari's adrenaline was flowing, as he and Born went for each other like savage beasts. All that Shamari could think of was that any minute Born would start cutting. Shamari kicked Born dead in his nuts, causing the hardened criminal to wince in pain.

As Born fell to his knees, Shamari kicked him in the chin. Born's head flew back and Shamari stood over the seriously injured man. He removed a homemade weapon made of sharpened metal from his pocket and cut Born across his face, from his ear to his chin. Born was in excruciating pain, as he flopped all over the hard, cement floor like a fish out of water. Shamari knew that if he bolted now Born wasn't going to tell anyone what he had done to him, for fear of being labeled as a snitch. Born was a proud man and it would scar his reputation if he told that Shamari, an amateur jailbird, cut his ass. All of the years of Born's criminal career, no man was able to get close enough to administer a slash to any of his body parts.

Shamari hid the razor in a large crack in the wall and casually ran back down the stairs to the first floor. The officers opened the door and let him out, not knowing that there was a man on the fifth floor, bleeding profusely from a cut that

Shamari had just given him. When the probe team responded, inmates, including Shamari, had to face the wall. Shamari complied with the orders and faced the discolored wall with a smirk on his face.

Shamari was taken along with other inmates to the receiving room and stripped searched. The officers on duty told their area supervisor that Born left the housing area unscathed and he apparently received his injury while he was outside in the hallway somewhere. The other inmates were clueless and Shamari was in question. Upon being stripped searched for evidence and none was found, Shamari was allowed to go back to Five West after a few hours. As he was being escorted down the long corridor by a captain, he felt good now that he had gotten his revenge. He didn't need anyone to hold him down; he was officially his own man now.

Chapter 28

Brandi made the trip to Rikers the next morning, which was miserable. All the things that she never paid any attention to were so annoyingly distracting that she almost lost her mind on the visit bus to Shamari's facility. There were women with uncontrollably crying babies and attention-seeking, wanna-be gangster boos who made most visitors coming to see their loved ones in Rikers look bad with their loud, shit-talking asses. Brandi rolled her eyes in her head and prayed that her old self wouldn't rear its ugly head. It wouldn't have been a pretty sight and her freedom would be compromised if it did.

When she walked on the visit floor, Sean had a smile on his face but Brandi could not muster up the strength to return the smile. She walked past him and plopped in the seat that she was assigned to, watching Sean make his way toward her with a look of concern.

Suddenly, Brandi saw the gates opening. She watched Officer Cruz walking over to Sean. She whispered something in his ear that stopped him in his tracks. Brandi watched the woman walk back out of the gate and back onto her post inside of the control room. Sean never managed to get over to Brandi after that. She silently wondered what that was all about.

Shamari marched toward his mother, not noticing the look on her face until he was seated. Brandi held her head up, with Shamari seeing that her eyes were red and puffy. He wanted immediate answers, answers that Brandi couldn't give at that moment.

"Ma, what's goin' on? Why are you lookin' like that?" he asked, rubbing her arm.

Brandi sighed. "Shaki, your baby was born last night. A boy, seven pounds and nine ounces," she replied.

Shamari clapped his hands. He turned to another inmate and told him the good news. The inmate congratulated him.

"Oh, yeah, I got my baby boy! I gotta get outta here, Ma, I got my son in New York!" Brandi shook her head and Shamari looked confused. "Ma, what's goin' on? Why you . . . How's Amber?"

All of a sudden, Brandi just broke down in tears. "Shaki. Shaki, she didn't make it. They couldn't save her but—"

Shamari pushed back his seat. "Wait, Ma, what the hell are you sayin'? You're sayin' my girl is dead? Tell me, Ma, are you sayin' that Amber is dead?" Brandi nodded her head. "Noooooo, Ma. She can't be dead . . . she just came to see me. She was my girl . . . my son's mother . . . I was gonna marry her . . . I was, noooo!"

Suddenly, Shamari stood up. He picked up the seat he was sitting in and threw it. The chair didn't go far and barely missed hitting the officers sitting at the desk. Sean ran over to where they were and immediately began to try to calm Shamari down. Shamari punched Sean in the face, barely missing his nose.

Brandi began screaming, as she watched an impending melee unfolding before her eyes. She ran to grab her son but some female officers grabbed her to try to calm her down as Sean and several other officers restrained her son. Yadi pressed the alarm and one minute later the response team entered the visit area with vests and batons. Other inmates joined the fracas and officers had to prevent visitors from getting hurt.

Shamari and the other detainees were led out of the visit area after five minutes and two waves of officers had to respond there. The inmates were immediately taken to the intake area and thrown into holding pens. They were to be held there until further notice, as per the warden.

Brandi was removed from the visit floor to the waiting area, when all of sudden, Yadi came out of the control room. Brandi thought she was imagining things when she saw Yadi watching the whole scene go down with a smirk plastered on her face. Unfortunately, she wasn't imagining.

Watching Brandi get removed from the area gave Yadi a feeling of self-satisfaction. She shrugged her shoulders and went back on her post, delighted that Brandi was not going to be allowed back on Rikers Island for a while. Maybe then Yadi could work on having Sean to herself.

Yadi walked back into the control room with her head held high. Vanita was worried about her friend. The day Devin came over, she was sure that she spotted Yadi's Maxima parked on the block, which was the reason she had let Devin in the house in the first place. Upon discovering that Yadi wasn't home, Vanita couldn't get rid of him fast enough.

"Wow! Did you see all that? I wondered what made Wallace wild out! His mother was about to lose her—" Yadi cut Vanita off. She could care less about Brandi and her loser son.

"Vanita, could you pass me some count slips?" Yadi asked. Vanita handed her the slips.

"Yadi, are you all right?" Vanita asked. Yadi looked at her and laughed.

"Why, of course, Nita, why do you ask?" she replied.

Vanita flopped in a large armchair. "I dunno. Why didn't you stay at my house the other night? Where did you go?"

Yadi turned around with her back facing Vanita. She didn't want her to see her expression. She put the total number of inmates in the visit area on the count slip.

"I went to a friend's house." Yadi smirked, knowing that Vanita would be curious about her "friend." Truth was, Yadi finally broke down and went to her parents' house on Staten Island.

Vanita frowned. "What friend? Sean?" Yadi swung around but managed to control her temper.

"A friend, Vanita. A friend, okay?" Vanita left the topic alone.

"Oh, okay. Umm, are you comin' to my house tonight?" Vanita asked. Yadi ignored her and Vanita went back to working.

Yadi's insecurities and paranoia were beginning to take control of her already unstable mind. Yadi suspected that Vanita always thought that she was better than her and was secretly envious of her relationship with Devin. She was imagining Vanita wanting Devin for herself, which was the reason she never told Yadi about the passes he made at her. Yadi laughed to herself as she thought about how an attractive, single woman like Vanita could be envious of her life. What Yadi didn't realize is that she was only imagining Vanita wanted Devin.

Vanita couldn't take it anymore. "Yadi, what's goin' on between us? You're not talkin' to me? Did I do somethin' to you?" Vanita asked, with a confused look on her face.

Yadi put her hand up and Vanita stopped mid-sentence. "If you want Devin, you can have him. And I should have seen it comin'. You always been a secretive bitch, Vanita, so this shit ain't much of a stretch for an undercover ho like yourself, now is it?"

Vanita cleared her throat. "Now, listen, Yadira, there is no need to call me out my name, all right! I don't know what the hell you're talkin' about!"

"Okay, he's a piece of shit, haven't you been listenin' to me? Haven't you heard me all these years? He knows, he knows that you are my only close friend! He's tryin' to use you against me. Plus, you never told me how he comes onto you! I dunno what to say about you, Nita. I always thought that you were a controllin' bitch, but man, I wouldn't have ever believed that you would keep this shit from me!"

Vanita frowned. "Yadi, what are you talkin' about? What did Devin tell you?"

Yadi laughed. "He didn't tell me nuthin'! Neither did you. You couldn't tell me that he tried to make a pass at you? What, you was savin' him for a rainy day?"

Vanita stood up. "I dunno what you talkin' about, Yadi, because I would never do anything to hurt you. Devin is no one that I would even consider havin' in my area, your man or not. If he made a pass at me, don't you think I could shut him down without havin' to drag you into it?"

Yadi laughed again. "I dunno, Vanita. I can't say who I can trust these days. Everybody is screwin' everybody. You could have been fuckin' Devin all along without me knowin' a damn thing."

"Now, wait a minute! What kind of lowdown, cheap hussy you're talkin' about 'cause you're not talkin' about me! I been there for you through thick and thin and you have the nerve to jump in my face about Devin? I could never stoop so low and sleep with my friend's man behind her back, knowin' how you feel about him and that you tried to kill your . . ." Vanita stopped.

Yadi's bottom lip began to tremble and Vanita got up and walked off the post. Vanita had reminded her of how fragile she was but the thought went right over Yadi's head. After shedding a few tears and feeling sorry for herself for a brief moment, Yadi regained her momentum, realizing that Vanita had left her in the control room to fend for herself.

Later on that night, the loud ringing of her house phone awakened Brandi. She came home and drugged herself, falling into a stupor after taking a few sleeping pills she had in her medicine cabinet. Without bothering to look at the caller ID, Brandi answered the phone.

"What? What is it?" Brandi managed to yell into the phone.

"It's me, Brandi. It's Sean."

Brandi paused. "What the fuck do you want, Sean? Why are you calling me?" she cried out.

"Look, before you curse me out, I was just callin' to give my condolences. I heard that your grandson's mother died. I, I just wanted to say that I'm sorry."

"You are sorry, Sean. My grandbaby's mother is fine in heaven. She was an angel. You, on the other hand, are full of shit. And tell your girlfriend, Miss Fucking Cruz, that I will bust her ass all up and through Rikers or wherever if I see her ass again!"

Sean sighed. "Brandi, she ain't my girl. She's a coworker, a friend."

"A friend? A friend? She isn't your friend, Sean! Don't you see what she's doing? She wants us to have conflict, Sean. She is a manipulative, possessive maniac and yet you keep having sex with her! What is wrong with you men?"

"Brandi, I'm not fuckin' Yadi."

"Stop with the bullshit, Sean. You're still fucking her. I know. She stopped you from coming to my table yesterday. I know she did. And guess what? You didn't come! I was going through it at that moment and I needed you. You didn't even come over to speak to me."

Sean was speechless. That day, Yadi waltzed her way over to him and told him that if he as so much talked to Brandi on that visit floor, she was going to go straight to the warden's office and tell him that he fraternizes with visitors. Now Yadi was holding his secret over his head and he was stuck in a difficult situation.

"Brandi, I'm sorry but Yadi threatened to tell the warden about our relationship with each other. That was the reason I didn't come over and speak to you. If you don't want me to call you, I won't. I just wanna let you know that I'm not gonna press charges against Shamari for hittin' me. Anyway, take care and my deepest sympathy for your loss."

Brandi hung up the phone. She cried herself back to sleep, thinking about Shamari and her motherless grandson.

Chapter 29

A few hours after the chaos in visits, Shamari was waiting in the intake area of the jail. His back was killing him from sleeping on the hard bench in the holding cell, which was located in the intake area. He looked around at the other inmates and they didn't budge, as he was being escorted out of the holding pen by the officer. When Shamari stepped out the cell, a CO with plainclothes on put cuffs on him and led him into the counsel visit area, located in the back of intake. Once inside, one cuff was removed and one hand was cuffed to an iron cuff bar that was on the brick wall. The CO sat in a seat across from him.

"Mr. Wallace," the CO began, "I see that you are a busy man."

Shamari looked at the balding Puerto Rican man as if he had two heads. "What? Man, I ain't got time for this shit!" Shamari replied, with an attitude.

"Well, Mr. Wallace you don't have any other choice. You are being re-arrested for assaulting an officer."

Shamari sucked his teeth. "Fuck is you talkin' about, man? Them fuckin' police fucked me up! You see my swollen face, man? I'm suin' y'all ass up in here!"

"I'm CO Rivera. G. Rivera. Your ass is in some hot water. You think that's all you are in here for, *puta*?"

"Who are you callin' a puta, nigga? I'll spit in your fuckin' face!" CO Rivera jumped up and held Shamari's face very tight. He loved assholes like Shamari; he would fuck them up all the time and get away with doing it. After all, there were no witnesses.

"You fuckin' *maricon*! I will rip your fucking lips off your face and feed those shits to my pit bull for dinner, *pendeja*!"

Shamari couldn't move and was struggling to get loose from the strong grasp of the muscular CO. He finally got himself under control and Rivera let his face go. He mushed Shamari back in his seat. Shamari saw that he was serious.

Rivera straightened himself out and looked at Shamari. "You like to put your hands on officers, I see. Also, I'm hearing through the grapevine you're into cuttin' mothafuckers, too."

Shamari held his head down. "I don't know what you're talkin' about, CO."

Rivera chuckled. "Born from Five North got a nasty little scratch on his face. Heard it was from you. Little get back from the cut he gave you on your neck." Rivera pulled back the collar to the jumper that Shamari wore. "Hmmm, you wanna tell me about that?"

Shamari sucked his teeth. "I ain't tellin'you shit." Rivera shook his head. He leaned back in the seat and took a good look at Shamari. Shamari was scared to death. Rivera had been doing this for almost twenty years and he knew when an inmate was nothing but a scared punk. Shamari fit that description to a tee.

"Well, Mr. Wallace. You're being moved to the Bing. When you go to your hearing, they can tell you exactly how many days you're gonna get."

"Y'all can't take me to the Bing now! That shit just happened a couple of hours ago!"

"Well, the god damn chief says that we can, motherfucker, and we are! You are a threat to this facility and as much as I don't want to believe that shit, it is what the fuck it is! Your ass is going to the Bing and all your shit is there in a nice cell waiting for you! So have a great vacation! Oh yeah, see you in court!"

Rivera got up and walked out of the area, leaving Shamari cuffed to the cuff bar. A few seconds later, two Bing escort officers came to re-cuff Shamari and escort him to the Bing. He was put into solitary confinement without further incident. Shamari looked at the four walls in his cell. He thought about Amber and screamed to the top of his lungs.

On Rikers Island, solitary confinement, better known as "the Bing," was like a jail within the jail. Inmates were locked in their cells for twenty-three hours a day and were mandated by the state of New York to be allowed out of their cells for one hour of recreation. Bing inmates had to be escorted in handcuffs everywhere they went, whether it was to visits or the law library or even to the shower. They were labeled as threats to their facility, locked down for various infractions, such as assault on staff members, slashings, and sexual offenses. There was no TV, no commissary snacks for the inmates, and they were allowed showers only three times a week.

Phone calls were another story. They were authorized to only make one personal and one legal phone call a week, which caused many inmates to complain. The officers who worked there were stressed out, overworked, and under-appreciated, having to endure constant verbal and physical abuse from the inmates who were plum crazy from looking at the four walls of their cells for months at a time. Female staff were subjected to offensive sexual gestures and comments from undersexed convicts who had no respect for themselves or for women in general. It was a world of its own and the Bing inmates' shouts of madness could be heard throughout the Island.

Shamari sat in his cell and listened to the banging and the yelling from the other inmates in the Bing housing area. He walked to his cell window and noticed they were doing the p.m. feeding, which was good because he was starving. There were two tiers and there were two COs doing the feeding with pantry workers in tow to assist. They pushed the food wagon around from cell to cell, which had warm food trays stored inside of it. On top of the tray, there was a large juice container. It contained the "murderous" fruit juice that inmates hated to love. It was never proven, but Rikers inmates claimed that drinking the fruit juice made them sterile.

Shamari's cell was located on the top tier and he watched the female officer doing the feeding. She would open cell slots, as the pantry worker put additional items on the already prepared trays. She filled up cups with the forbidden juice as well, closing the slots once the process was completed. Occasionally, an inmate would try to hold her up by asking stupid questions, purposely prolonging the feeding for the inmates on Shamari's side of the tier.

"Yo, son, get off her fuckin' bra strap so that she can feed us, mothafucker!" shouted the guy in the cell next to Shamari's. "Damn, we hungry over here, too, nigga!"

"Shut the fuck up, faggot!" shouted an inmate from across the tier. "You gonna eat, muhfucka! Feenin', starvin'-ass nigga!"

"You damn right!" the nextdoor neighbor retorted. "Your ass wanna sap rap and shit, do that shit some other time, nigga! Food gonna get cold!"

"As long as I got my warm food, nigga, I don't give a fuck about nobody else's food gettin' cold! Y'all niggas ain't shit to me!"

Shamari shook his head, embarrassed at the spectacle the inmates were making of themselves in front of the female officer, who seemed oblivious to the verbal jabs between the inmates. All of a sudden, Shamari's nextdoor neighbor started banging on the metal door.

"Yo, Miss Jones, you bitch, what the fuck is you doin'? You can't do the fuckin' feedin' for runnin' your mouth!" he shouted.

Shamari pressed his face against the cell window as CO Jones's scent seeped into the crack of his cell door. She was at the cell next door with the food wagon.

"First of all, Tucker, I ain't gonna be too many of your bitches, you hear me?" she exclaimed. "I'm the one doin' this up in here so you need to calm your bitch-ass down if you wanna get fed!"

Shamari smiled as he listened to her tell his neighbor off with no thought to it. He couldn't wait until she got to his cell so that he could get a good look at her. She sounded like she wasn't too much older than him.

Shamari heard the Folger keys unlocking the slot to his cell. He looked up and was mesmerized by the pretty CO standing in front of his cell. He was so stuck that he forgot to hand her the green plastic mug in his hand.

"Hello. If you want juice, you gonna have to give me your cup," she said.

Shamari finally snapped out his daydream and handed her the cup. When she took it from his grasp, her gloved hand touched his and he felt his body shudder.

"So, you're Shamari Wallace. The guy from visits, huh?" she asked. Shamari shook his head. "I'm sorry to hear about your baby mama. I could understand why you spazzed out like that."

Shamari smiled. "Word?" he asked. He was glad somebody understood how he was feeling. He had been crying ever since he found out.

"Yeah, word. Well, I don't know if you know it or not but the Warden has you on suicide watch. Not that you gonna do any harm to yourself, it's just procedure 'cause of your situation and all." She looked around his cell and shook her head. "Okay, your cell is in order, that's how it's supposed to be. Anyway, go ahead and eat and I'll be back to talk to you later, okay?"

Shamari watched as Jones walked away, with her ponytail swaying from side to side. Even for the environment she worked in, Jones seemed to hold it together amidst the yelling and screaming. After eating his dinner, Shamari managed to lie down on the thin mattress and continue to grieve the mother of his son.

Chapter 30

The following week, Brandi entered the Woodward Funeral Home on Troy Avenue. There was a big turnout for Amber's wake and Brandi felt out of place walking inside alone. She was saddened that Shamari couldn't be there. She stood in the middle of the funeral home looking for a familiar face but didn't see one. She finally mustered up the strength to walk in and view the body.

When Brandi finally walked up to the front, she greeted Amber's mother. Amber's sister, Ashlee, and her other siblings, were crying silently. She walked over and hugged Mrs. Johnson. They stayed in that position for a minute, as the siblings looked on. Brandi greeted everyone with a hug, and after viewing Amber's body, her mother invited Brandi to come sit next to her. It was a sad occasion watching young teenage girls, apparently friends of the deceased, run out of the room after seeing Amber in the cream-colored casket. Brandi felt a lump in her throat but managed to sit through the service, composed and serene.

After the service was over, Brandi spoke with the family. She had assisted the Johnsons with the cost of Amber's funeral and they were more than grateful.

"Miss Carol, if you need anything, you call me. I'll be by to pick up the baby this weekend," Brandi said.

"Brandi, we are fine! You have been more than good to us ever since the day we met, child. You're like family. In fact, you are family. We are the grandmothers of a little baby boy that needs us."

Brandi smiled. "You're right, Carol, you're right. I'm gonna come and get the baby . . . wait I was so busy running around; I never even thought to ask my grandchild's name. What did you all name him?"

Miss Johnson chuckled. "Now, child, you know better than to even ask me that question. His name is Shamari Maleek Johnson, but we call him Shamari, of course."

Tears came to Brandi's eyes and she hugged Mrs. Johnson tightly. "Oh, thank you, Carol! My son is going to be so happy!"

"Well, you just tell Shamari Sr. to make sure he gets home in one piece. He and his son need each other."

Brandi said her good-byes and walked toward the exit of the funeral home. Standing there, to her surprise, was Sean Daniels, with flowers and a card in his hands.

"I wanted to pay my respects too," he stated. Sean handed her the flowers. "I hope you don't mind."

Brandi took the items from his grasp. "No, Sean. I don't mind. After all, it is a wake."

Sean held his head down. "May I walk you to your car?" She agreed. They walked to Brandi's Lexus and Sean slid into the passenger seat.

"I miss you, Brandi and I want to apologize for lettin' this woman manipulate me. I don't wanna lose you as a friend."

Brandi looked straight ahead. "Well, Sean, that's up to you. I mean, it's pretty hard to get rid of someone that you're physically involved with. That woman, Cruz, is going to be a pain until she gets what she wants and what she wants is you."

Sean leaned his head back on the leather headrest. "Brandi, I can't shake this chick! She's at work with me all day and then she pops up at my house sometimes and sits outside. I should kick my own ass for fuckin' with her!"

Brandi shook her head. "The sad part is a lot of you men seem to like mentally unstable women. You like the drama, the excitement. See, a woman like me is too predictable, but don't get me wrong, I've been there. I was a drama queen for your ass! That's how I know about women like Cruz. She's a jealous, conniving sister whose out for your blood and any woman she feels that you're interested in. I know I'm definitely on top of her list."

"Nah, she's not gonna—"

Brandi cut him off. "Sean, I want you to knock it off! You see, right there is what I'm talking about. You're underestimating this woman. Women have all kinds of tricks up our sleeve, and you need to remember that we work on emotions. We will sit there and stir up a concoction on how we could get a motherfucker back, you know, a bitches' brew! We are always cooking up some scheme. Don't sleep!"

"Brandi, I really like you and I can't stop thinkin' about you. Look at all the shit I've been through. I even got assaulted by your son, and I still wanna be with you!"

"Well, Sean, if you wanna be with me, take care of your business. I have no room for any of that bullshit in my life. I'm a thirty-five-year-old single parent of an incarcerated male, who is the teenage father of my motherless grandchild. So what room do I have in my life for mess? None. So if you got some, don't bring it this way."

Sean looked at Brandi, taking his finger to sweep the hair out of her eyes. "I'm gonna clean all of this up, and after that, I'm comin' for you. I don't care who you're with!"

Sean kissed Brandi on the forehead and got out of her car. He watched her pull out of the parking lot and fly down the street. He looked at the time, climbed into his truck, and headed home.

The next morning, Brandi walked toward her car, which was parked in the garage directly across the street from her building. She had her Coach briefcase in one hand and a Starbucks coffee mug in the other. She was pressed for time but was unable to walk quickly in her three-inch pumps. As Brandi approached her vehicle, she was surprised to see Yadi standing near the driver's side. Startled, Brandi dropped her metal coffee mug and watched as it rolled down the sloped driveway in the garage.

"Well, well, well! If it isn't Miss Brandi Wallace. So, you're off to work this mornin', huh?" she said.

Brandi was furious. She didn't know whether to kick Yadi's ass or be afraid. "Why are you standing by my car? Why are you even fucking here?" she yelled.

"I'm here to reclaim my spot!" Yadi explained, leaning on the hood of Brandi's Lexus. "I'm here to tell you to stay away from my man!"

"Girl, please! Who is your man? Because if you're talking about Sean Daniels, I have absolutely no interest in him being with me! So I don't know what you're talkin' about!" Brandi replied, hoping she could get through to Yadi. "So if you here for him, you can leave. He's not here!"

"Yeah, that's what I wanna hear. Stay the fuck away from him. I fuck with him now and it's final. Don't need common street trash like yourself to interfere with our relationship. You wouldn't want to put his job on the line by continuin' to deal with him, now would you?"

Brandi brushed off the verbal jab from Yadi and smiled. She walked up to Yadi, resisting the urge to punch her dead in the mouth, until she remembered that Yadi was a correction officer. She didn't want to be arrested.

"Trash? If I'm not mistaken, you're the bitch that's standing in front of my car at six-thirty in the morning talking about some man that doesn't belong to you. Now which one of us is a trashy bitch?"

"Mmm," Yadi began, looking at Brandi from head to toe, in her business suit. "So proper, such a fuckin' lady! You know what? I see why

Sean would like you, but unfortunately for you, he loves me and you're a distraction, so leave us alone!"

"Oh, leave you two alone? First of all, I don't bother him. He loves when I call, and as for you, you're the furthest thing from my mind. So if Sean is your man, like you think he is, tell him to stop calling me and see if he listens to you! Now excuse yourself so I can go to work!"

Yadi slowly moved away from Brandi's car, slightly brushing by the woman. Yadi didn't know much about Brandi, because if she did, provoking a fight with her would have been the last thing she would have wanted to do. The old Brandi would have emerged and scraped Yadi's face against the concrete.

Yadi stood nearby as Brandi opened her car door, determined to get the last word. She knew that Brandi really liked Sean and she wanted to make sure that she was done with the handsome officer finally.

"Well, I'm pregnant with Sean's baby!" Yadi lied. "So you can do what you wanna do. This is Sean's first child, so you know I'm gettin' the queen treatment from him!"

Brandi laughed loudly. "Damn, you are the most pathetic bitch I have ever encountered! You just won't stop at nothing, will you? My son is almost twenty years old and look at me, do I need to have another baby? I have too much going on to be tied down with a crying-ass baby bouncing on these hips! So, go right ahead, if you want to. You'll be sitting at home with your titty in your baby's mouth every night while me and your baby daddy'll be traveling the world together!"

Yadi pushed her hair out of her face. "You sorry bitch!" Yadi yelled. "I will whip your ass!"

Brandi posted up and stared Yadi down. Brandi was so close to her that she could feel Yadi's breath on her face.

"Bitch, do you know who you're fuckin' with?" Brandi asked, pointing her finger in Yadi's face. Yadi didn't know that there was another side to Brandi's professionalism.

"I had heat for hoes like you back in the days! You better do your fuckin' homework and ask about me. I'm pretty sure some of them fuckin' crooks right in the jail you work in know how I used to get down back in the day! So if you gonna come at me, you better come at me the right way, you scandalous bitch, or else I will split your fuckin' wig! Now get the fuck outta my way and don't ever let me see your ass around here no more!" Brandi put on her Chanel shades, got into her car and pulled off, leaving Yadi standing there to sulk alone.

Yadi stomped her feet and marched down the steps in the garage. She just had to get Brandi back; she had to win. As Yadi started her car up, she suddenly had an idea. She remembered that Brandi's son, Shamari, was in the jail and smiled as she came up with a plan to make Shamari pay for the comments his mother had just made.

Chapter 31

Later on that evening, Brandi came home from work an emotional wreck. Her day went well although the run-in with Yadi still had her shaken up. She didn't understand what was going on and why was she at the center of the controversy between Sean and Yadi. Sean wasn't even her man, although she wouldn't have minded them working on something.

The situation with Yadi was starting to turn Brandi off every time she thought about it. It was like Yadi was trying to awaken the dead, with the dead being the old Brandi. The old Brandi would have demolished Yadi and her pretty face without a thought. It was disheartening to Brandi to work so hard at being the person she was today only to be sucked back into past behavior by some possessive lunatic of a woman named Yadira Cruz.

It was 1990 and Brandi was on Pennsylvania Avenue in East New York, checking on a few of her workers. It was a cold, winter night and

Brandi wrapped her mink jacket around her body, practically running to her red BMW so that she could blast her heat. Suddenly, Nikki stepped out of a building in front of her.

"You need ta step off, Brandi!" the woman shouted. "My name is Nikki and Maleek is my man and I'm tired of you gettin' in our way!"

Brandi was confused because she had never seen or heard of a Nikki until that moment. She was taken by surprise when the woman approached her.

"Excuse me?" Brandi exclaimed. "Who the fuck are you?"

"I'm Nikki! I know you know me! I know all about you and your son, Shamari. I been in your house and everything with your red leather sofa and your king-sized bed! Yeah, I know you real good!"

Brandi remained composed. Maleek was definitely a womanizer but women in their home was too much to bear. She was pissed but she wasn't going to give Nikki the satisfaction of knowing how much.

"Okay and . . . What do you want me to do?"

"I want you to disappear, go away, go find another man 'cause Maleek is mine. Remember all the nights he told you he was with his nig-gas? Well, he was with me!"

Brandi laughed. "Well, if you are so important ta him, why do he have to lie to me? Are you
sure that you're his girl or is it his turn?"

"What are you sayin, bitch? You sayin' that
I'm his ho? No, baby, you're his ho with that
monkey-lookin' baby of yours!"

Brandi stopped. She was going to let the bitch
off until she disrespected her son. Shamari was
an innocent toddler who had nothing to do with
his father's escapades.

"What the fuck did you just say?" Brandi
asked, with her hands in the pocket of her mink
jacket.

Nikki put her hands on her hips. "I said,
you're his ho with that monkey-lookin'baby! I
didn't stutter!"

Before she knew it, Brandi pulled out her
chrome .22 pistol and shot Nikki in the thigh.
The young woman fell to the sidewalk, screaming in pain. Brandi's workers ran around the
corner to see what had happened. They put
their hands over their mouths when they saw
Brandi standing over Nikki. Maleek's jump-off
was lying on the ground with blood oozing from
a gunshot wound. One of the workers ran over
to Brandi and snatched the gun out of her hand.
The others hustled Brandi to her Benz as quickly
as they could, but not before Brandi kicked the
wounded Nikki in the face.

"Go tell that, bitch, and I'm gonna come back and kill you! Talkin' about my baby! You must be out your mind!" Brandi shouted.

After that incident, Brandi never saw Nikki again. She was rumored to have moved out of the neighborhood and down to Georgia, never showing her face in East New York. Maleek never said anything about it and neither did Brandi. She made her point when she plugged that bitch, Nikki, in the thigh. She was lucky that Brandi didn't kill her ass.

Careful not to disclose her past to anyone, Brandi never really got close with too many men anyway. After Maleek's death, she chose to dedicate all of her time and energy to making a productive living situation for her and her only child. Now that she was much older and wiser, Brandi felt that she was being tested. Could she suppress her inner gangstress and let the confrontation with Yadi slide? That was yet to be confirmed.

She knew that Sean was a good catch and she needed someone she could enjoy being with without all the drama. Sean was young, had a good career, and he seemed extremely comfortable with her. He was the antidote that she needed. She normally threatened most men and Brandi couldn't understand why. The phone interrupted her thoughts and Sean's deep voice came through the phone after she answered it.

"Hello, miss. How are you?" he greeted her warmly.

"Hello, Mr. Daniels," Brandi responded in a curt tone.

"Whoa, you sound a little short. What's the matter now?"

"I got an early morning visit from your friend."

"What friend?" Sean asked cluelessly.

"Sean, don't play with me!" she replied. "Yadira Cruz, that's who!"

Sean sighed and wiped his face. "Where did you see her?"

"Standing near my car in my garage parking space! What is wrong with her?"

"Do you wanna make a complaint, Brandi? You can, you know!"

"I know but I don't want to drag you into this!"

"Brandi, don't worry about me. I'm a big boy. I can handle what comes my way."

Brandi hesitated. She didn't want to tell Sean that she still lived by the code of the streets. She didn't want to involve the police; she would rather handle it herself before she got the cops involved.

"No, no. I'm just gonna watch my back. I don't want that woman to do anything stupid. I would hate to have to whip her ass!"

Sean suppressed his laughter, as he thought back to what Born told him about Brandi. He was hoping that Brandi would save him the trouble and release her street side on Yadi. She deserved every bit of the ass whipping that Brandi would give her. He didn't tell Brandi that Yadi popped up at his house that morning as well. It would only complicate matters.

"Look, Sean, could I call you back? I just walked in the house from work and I wanted to get settled."

"Are you really gonna call me back, Brandi?" he pleaded.

"Of course, Sean, I'm gonna call you back," Brandi replied, then ended the call.

Brandi sat on the bed for a few more moments. The whole situation was starting to wear on her and she didn't like it one bit. It was like history repeating itself all over again only this time it wasn't about no man. It was about maintaining her dignity and she was about to pass that test with flying colors.

The day after the brief encounter with Brandi, Yadi was able to return to her co-op apartment. She successfully had Devin moved out, with the assistance of the co-op board. Yadi was equally relieved when she discovered that Devin had to move back in with his mother. It served him right for trying to screw her over. She watched as the moving men put all of her furniture and the rest of her household items back in their rightful places.

Now that her relationship with Devin was officially over, she could work on her and Sean. She felt that they could finally be with each other now that she had removed the number one problem from her life and that was Devin. Brandi should have caught the hint when Yadi ran up on her in the garage that morning. The next time Yadi wasn't going to be so nice. Sean was hers and hers only and she was determined on letting bitches know it, especially Brandi.

Her phone rang and she looked on the caller ID at the familiar number. It was her parents' house. Yadi sighed loudly and answered the phone.

"Hi, Mommy," said the small voice on the other end. "When are you comin' to get me?"

"Hi, angel!" Yadi beamed. She knew that the love from her only child was unconditional and she relished that. "Mommy will be there soon. Where's your granny?" Yadi asked.

Yadi's mother came on the phone. "Yadira? Are you okay?" she asked.

"Yes, Mommy, I'm fine. How are you and how's Papi?"

"We are okay. Devin was here earlier, visitin' Jada. I didn't let him take her anywhere, just like you told me to."

"Oh, really? What did he have to say?" Yadi asked.

Mrs. Cruz sucked her teeth. "Now you know he didn't say anything to me, child. I just don't wanna be involved with this mess. Seems like you two are always goin' through some craziness with Jada bein' in the middle!"

Yadi rolled her eyes in her head. She couldn't have a five minute conversation without her mother putting her two cents in her affairs.

"Mommy, could you please? I'm gonna get Jada soon and you won't have to be in the middle of our craziness!"

"Well, that's what I wanted to talk to you about. Why not let Jada stay with us for a little while? Let us help you, Yadi."

"Help me with what? Jada and me are goin' to be fine—."

Mrs. Cruz cut her daughter off. "Now, Yadira, you and I know why me and Papi need to have Jada stay with us. You've been down this road with almost every man you've dealt with. Now that you have a daughter, it's a whole different ball game! It's only a matter of time before you meet your next victim!"

"Victim?" Yadi balked. "Victim? What about what they do to me, Mommy? What about them?"

"Well, Yadira, if these men treat you so bad, why do you always have a new one? Why do you go through these different relationships one right after the other? Give yourself some time to re-group before you get involved with anyone else but, but if I know you like I do, I know that as we speak, you are gettin' all wrapped up in somebody else! That's why Jada is stayin' here with us! Do I need to take you to court and get grandparents' rights?" her mother threatened.

Yadi began to cry. "Yadira, I'm not tryin' to hurt you, I'm tryin' to help you. I love you and I love Jada very much but you need help. Who knows you better than me?"

"Mommy, I have to go. I can't discuss this right now!" Yadi hung up her cell phone. One of the moving men came over with the receipt and he stopped when he saw her crying.

"Miss Cruz, are you okay?" he asked. "Do you need a moment to yourself?"

Yadi shook her head and signed the receipt. She gave the man a money order and they left immediately after. Yadi put fresh sheets on her bed and lay down. She stared at the ceiling for a moment, trying to fight her demons.

Years ago, Yadi had been diagnosed with bipolar disorder and dependant personality syndrome. She had taken medication for a while, which she had grown weary of, and in one of her manic episodes, she decided that she was well. Unbeknownst to her, she wasn't well and she was only getting worse. She felt the blood boiling in her veins as her mind obsessed over Sean and Brandi, as well as Devin and Vanita.

From Yadi's standpoint, she didn't know anything about being alone and equated that with being lonely. She knew that men clamored for her attention because of her unique looks and with her visions of grandeur, she just couldn't understand it when someone she wanted didn't want to be with her. In her mind, a man should have felt honored to be with her and that no other woman could compare. Unfortunately, Yadi's mental condition was going to be her downfall. It was only a matter of time.

Chapter 32

The visit area wasn't too busy that Wednesday afternoon. A few inmates were seated with their visitors and the correction officers were free to relax, as opposed to the weekend, when the visit area was crowded. Afternoon visits were a hassle, due to the rush hour and excessive traffic on the Grand Central Parkway at that time of the day.

Yadi remained calm throughout the day, going on as though nothing had ever happened on her days off. Sean watched her closely, preparing himself for the storm. They had maintained their professionalism toward each other while they were at work, because, after all, enough people were in their business as it was.

The male officers who were once attracted to Yadi were beginning to shun her. After hearing about Sean's situation, they were happy that they were not the object of Yadi's affection. They empathized with Sean and kept their distance from Yadi.

Yadi didn't care about the male officers not giving her the attention that they used to. Her eyes were on Sean and no one else. She was going to get him, no matter what it took, even if she had to put her self-respect on the line to do it.

Vanita tip-toed around Yadi, even though Yadi still attempted to converse with her while on post. Vanita had not forgiven Yadi for accusing her of trying to maintain a secret rendezvous with Devin behind her back. The assassination of her character had affected their friendship, with Vanita being unable to erase their prior conversation from her mind.

Unknowingly, Devin had finally managed to break the bond between the two friends and Vanita was saddened by it. No more would she be the social worker to the stubborn Yadi, who had apparently digressed and was in a losing battle to win Sean Daniel's heart.

Yadi waited until Vanita left the post to make a phone call. She had hatched a plan to get back at Brandi for trying to get smart the day that she approached her in the garage. Now the plan was to get to Brandi through her jailbird son. She looked on the roster and saw that Shamari Wallace was being housed in the Four South housing area, which was the Bing. Yadi called up Four South and used her fingers to press her nostrils together, disguising her voice.

"Four South. CO Taylor," the officer who picked up the phone announced.

"Hello, Officer Taylor?" Yadi said, in a nasally tone. "This is Captain White. I'm gonna need you to get an escort to bring Inmate Shamari Wallace to the visit area."

A rookie officer and eager to please a supervisor, Taylor jumped at the opportunity. "Oh, um, yes, ma'am, that's fine. Um, when should I bring him?"

"How long have you been on the job, Mr. Taylor?" Yadi asked, trying to keep from laughing. She couldn't stand "New Jacks," a nickname that tenured officers used for rookie officers.

"I, I been on the job, for, let's see, five months. I just came out the Academy two months ago!" he said proudly.

Yadi smiled. This was going to be easier than she thought. "And your partner? How long has he been on the job?"

"Oh, he came out with me. So we're both kinda new!"

"Okay, that's fine. Here's what I need you to do, Officer Taylor; I need you to bring Mr. Wallace to the general population visit area."

"But, wait, with all due respect, ma'am, isn't he supposed to go to the Bing visits? He's a Bing inmate."

Yadi sighed. *Dumb-ass rookie! Swear they know the job* she thought. "Look, Officer, this is a direct order! Cuff Wallace and bring his ass down to the visit area on the general population side. Upon your arrival, you uncuff his ass and put him in the visit pen with the rest of the fuckin'crooks, is that understood?"

Taylor hesitated. "Yes, ma'am. I mean, Captain White."

Yadi hung up the phone and put her feet up on the desk. She chuckled as she thought about how much trouble Taylor was going to be in and how Brandi's precious little angel was going to be in some hot water, as well. After doing some research, Yadi had gotten wind of the little tiff Shamari had with some G.P. inmates and she hoped they would be around to pound his ass out real good.

Some minutes passed and Yadi watched as CO Taylor came down with Shamari. Taylor uncuffed Wallace, who looked as if he didn't know what was going on, and Yadi opened the gate to the pen. She pretended as if she didn't see Shamari getting uncuffed, just in case anyone would ask her. Shamari walked in the visit pen looking around at the other inmates. They looked familiar to him, not realizing two inmates from Five North were waiting for a visit. Unfortunately, for Shamari, they were Born's cronies.

"Yo, ain't you that nigga, Shamari?" the taller one asked. "You used to be in Five North and Five West, right?"

Shamari posted up. "Who wants to know?" he asked.

The smaller one stepped in. "Nigga, we wants to know! You the lame-ass nigga we knocked out in Five North, that's why! Punk motherfucker!"

Suddenly, the taller guy punched Shamari in the face and he fell back against the metal gate. The smaller inmate kicked Shamari in the stomach and Shamari caught him with a left hand, causing the inmate to fall the other way. Another inmate got involved and pushed Shamari, who lost his footing and fell to the floor of the pen.

While on the floor, Shamari covered his face with his arms, not wanting to experience too much damage to his face. Luckily, all the inmates wore plastic slippers to visits so he wasn't hurt, but his pride was as they beat him mercilessly. As they were stomping Shamari out, a smirk came across Yadi's face. She even waited a few seconds before she pressed the personal body alarm and alerted the response team.

The response team came suited up with vests and batons and requested the gate to be opened, rushing into the visit pen to gather up the fighting prisoners. The three inmates, including

Shamari, were led out of the visit area with plastic flex cuffs pulled tightly around their wrists.

The visit supervisor, Captain Phillips, responded to the area and threw a fit after she found out Shamari Wallace was a Bing inmate.

"Who in God's name bought this inmate into my area?" she shouted, as she gathered up her staff in the visit control room. "Wallace is a bing inmate! Why the hell was he in general population visits?"

Everyone looked at each other. They were clueless. Captain Phillips called up to Four South.

"Who bought this inmate down here?" she asked the unknown person on the other end of the phone. "Who? CO Taylor? Who the fuck is Taylor? He's a what? Why did he leave . . .? Forget it! I don't even wanna kn . . . Who the fuck is Captain White? We don't have no captain named White in this jail! Stupid . . . Yeah, okay. Thanks. Bye." Captain Phillips hung up the phone with a disgusted look on her face.

"I hope that none of y'all is responsible for this shit! I hope nobody ain't play no trick on this rookie because he is in a lot of trouble!" she exclaimed.

The visit staff shook their heads, knowing that it was very dangerous to do what Taylor did. He should have notified his immediate supervisor before moving Shamari out of the area. Next time, he would know better, if he had a second chance.

Captain Phillips dismissed everyone and they all went back to their respective posts. Sean looked at Yadi strangely, as she stood there with an innocent look on her face. He made his way over to her.

"I know you had somethin' to do with this shit, Cruz!" Sean whispered, through clenched teeth.

"I dunno what you talkin' about, Daniels!" she replied. "Why would I do a thing like that?"

"'Cause you don't like Brandi, that's why! 'Cause I don't wanna be with you, that's why!" he announced.

"Sean, please! You wanna be with me, you're just frontin' 'cause you tryin' to impress your girlfriend, Brandi. It's all right, boo, you'll come around."

Yadi walked over to Sean and threw her arms around him. Her embrace was so tight, he had to practically force her arms from around his neck. Yadi had a hollow expression on her face, looking like she was supposed to be in a rubber room with a straitjacket. He began backing up from her. Sean was determined to stay away from Yadi before he had to kill her ass, or even worse, she kill him.

***

A few moments after the disturbance in the visit area, Shamari sat in a pen in the intake area after coming from the clinic. Trying not to dwell on what had just occurred in the visit pen, he was anticipating returning to his cell in the Bing, hoping to get a glimpse of Miss Jones before her shift was over. He put his finger on his busted lip and rubbed his blackened eye while he watched the supervisors and tour commander discuss what happened. He could hear the other inmates who were involved in the melee talking junk about him and complaining about their canceled visits.

Shamari shrugged his shoulders after realizing that he probably had no visit. It just felt good to get out of that lonely cell. Shamari overheard the other inmates call out his name and he felt compelled to scream back. Before he could open up his mouth to do that, he looked up and was surprised to see Sean Daniels standing in front of his pen.

"Yo!" Sean yelled over to the other inmates in the cell. "Y'all wanna know what a real ass whippin' feel like? Lemme grab this key and show y'all!"

The inmates grew silent, with one replying, "Yo, Daniels, man, we ain't got nothin' with you, son! It's just that nigga over there. . . ."

"Just shut the fuck up! The fight is over now so on the noise!" Sean looked at Shamari's swollen face through the bars of the holding pen. "What's up, Wallace?" Sean asked. "You okay, shorty?"

Shamari shook his head. He was somewhat relieved to see Sean. "Yeah, I'm good. What are you doin' in here?" he asked.

"Just checkin' on you, man. Makin' sure you was all right. I'm sorry about that, man. Sounds like somebody pulled a fast one on that rookie officer and you got caught up!"

"Oh, that's what happened? At first, I thought my moms was here to see me then I realized that it was probably a mix-up. I woulda been extra tight if my moms was here and I couldn't see her, man!"

"Nah, son. You didn't have a visit. Somebody pulled a prank, that's all. Just checkin' on you and I'm gonna make sure I check on you all the time from now on."

Shamari was silent but he was happy on the inside. He had been through a lot since he got to the jail and now he was tired of it. Sean only meant well by wanting to look out for him before and he had chased him away. Shamari wasn't about to let that happen again considering the chain of bad events that had come into play since then.

"Thanks, D. I appreciate that. Yo, how's my moms, anyway?" he asked.

Sean hesitated. "She's fine, I guess. Why you ask me that?"

Shamari smirked. "C'mon, man. I know you feelin' my moms! I mean, she's the baddest . . . well, you know what I mean!" Shamari held his head down and paused. "Man, D, do me one solid. Just look out for Mom Dukes, man. I love her to death and I know that you're feelin' her too. That's my bad for actin' like a jackass toward you, son. I guess 'cause I lost my father when I was little, I don't wanna lose my moms too. She's all I really got."

Sean shook his head and gave Shamari a pound. "No doubt, shorty. I'll look out for your moms. She's a class act, for real."

Sean walked away but not before Shamari called him back. "Yo, Daniels!" Sean walked back to Shamari's pen. "Yo, man, do me a favor and call me Shaki. Only my family calls me Shaki, man. And you're officially my family now."

Sean shook his head and walked way from Shamari before the young man could see a tear fall from his eye.

Chapter 33

The next day, after the brief exchange with Sean, Shamari looked at the calendar on the wall of his cell and thought about his father. He wondered what really happened to him because he never could get the full story from his mother. It was all a mystery to him and it was something that haunted him most of his life.

Brandi was a very secretive person and he always imagined her not being the saint she always proclaimed to be. There was no point in asking his grandmother and uncles because they wouldn't bother to tell him, but what was the real truth?

Shamari came to the cell window and saw that it was business as usual in Four South. He witnessed select inmates being escorted to the shower in handcuffs by random officers and the recreation crew walking in to take random inmates out to the yard area.

The bing yard consisted of several "cages" where inmates would be escorted in handcuffs by correction officers and locked inside. Once the bing inmate was locked inside, the officer would open the slot and uncuff the inmate. Although they would be outside, these inmates were still locked in the pens. Shamari felt like a caged animal in those pens and the whole Bing yard experience made him feel like he was in a zoo, but that day, he needed some fresh air to try to clear his head, so he stood at his cell window with his jumpsuit on, waiting for a recreation officer to walk by and put his name on the yard list.

"Yo, shorty, are you ready for the yard?" a big, burly CO asked him. Shamari looked at his nametag and saw that his name was Oldman. He listened as the other inmates screamed the officer's name.

"Yo, Old Man, come get me, son, I'm ready!" an inmate in cell number forty-eight yelled out.

"Nigga, calm your nerves, I got you! Stop callin' my fuckin' name! Damn!" screamed Oldman. He opened the slot on Shamari's cell. Shamari turned around, with his back facing the cell and put his hands out the slot to be cuffed.

"So what up, Shorty?" Oldman announced. "You good?" Shamari shook his head. "Yeah, I see that you mad quiet, not like all these other iggas in here. They always fuckin' screamin' like little bitches about the yard. They ain't goin' anyway! Open cell twenty-eight!" Oldman yelled at one of the officers at the desk.

When the door slid open, Shamari stepped out of the cell backward and Oldman firmly grabbed his arm, guiding him toward the search area. Shamari looked up at Oldman, who was no less than six feet five inches and 250-pounds. Shamari looked like a shrimp next to him.

While Shamari was in the search area, he observed the other inmates in his housing area who were going out to the yard. They were in the dayroom already on the daisy chain. After he was searched, Shamari was added to the daisy chain, and he and the other inmates were led outside to the pens.

"Yo, nigga, it's about time we saw outside, shit!'" one inmate everybody called Dollar exclaimed, once everyone was secured in the pens. Dollar was one of the few old heads in Four South. He had a full beard and looked like he had been through some things in life. For some strange reason, Shamari felt a connection with the man even though he had never seen him before. He couldn't explain it.

"I was tired of bein' in that fuckin' sweat box!" Dollar looked at Shamari, who was in the pen next to him. "What's up, young blood? Don't I know you?"

Shamari looked at Dollar, who looked like he was old enough to be his father. "Nah, not that I know of."

"Nah, I know you or maybe I know some of your family. What's your name?" he asked. Dollar rubbed his beard and continued to stare at Shamari.

"Wallace. What's yours?"

"Dollar. Where your family hail from, young man?"

"We from the 'Stuy. My pops was from East New York."

"Hmm. Your face look mad familiar. What's your pop's name?" Shamari seemed hesitant to tell.

Dollar looked around and understood Shamari's reluctance to tell his business.

"Listen, young blood, I don't associate with these young niggas in here. I'm about one of the realest niggas you gonna meet. I been through it all and I done seen niggas come and go. Word up, I'm thirty-seven years old and I still got enough fuckin' Bing time to last me for the rest of my life. Anytime I get a parole violation and I come back to the Island, they bring my ass right to this Bing and I make it do what it do. I seen your face before in passin' and I was buggin' 'cause you look like somebody I know or knew, if they already dead. That's why I asked to come to the yard. Maybe I'm the person you needed to see."

Shamari shook his head, in agreement. He had been feeling lonely inside of the Bing and the only person he could talk to was Miss Jones.

"Well, my pop's name was Maleek. He got murdered in Virginia when I was five years old. My mom's name is Brandi. She's from the 'Stuy."

Dollar put his hand over his mouth. "Yo! That's where I know you from! You look like your father, too." Dollar stared at Shamari. "Damn, you look just like him! Your name is Shamari, right?"

Shamari was taken aback. "Oh shit, yeah, how you know?"

"Yeah, I remember when your moms first met your pops. She was goin' to the High and she was about to cut some broad over your father first day she met him!" Dollar laughed, as he recollected the memories. "Yeah, we was some fly-ass young cats. Your pops was my nigga, too. Had swag for days. Him and Brandi made a good couple and the way he did her in the end was fucked up. I didn't agree with that shit at all but I stayed out the business and kept my thoughts and opinions to myself. Damn, I had mad love for your moms! That was my girl right there!"

Shamari shook his head as if he knew what Dollar was talking about. Dollar continued to run his mouth.

"Your mother was off the fuckin' hook, too! She used to get money like a fuckin' nigga, if not better. I think your father was kinda jealous and he couldn't compete after awhile 'cause motherfuckers used to request Brandi's product all the time. Imagine your baby mother blowin' you out the water when it comes to gettin' money? That was unheard of back in them days, 'cause if anything, your chick is supposed to be your underdog, your bottom bitch. Brandi was nobody's bottom bitch; she was on top of her game and she pushed her cars and got her money with the best of 'em. She lay some cats down, too. She was nice with the gun, always had a biscuit on her and would use it if she had to. Yeah, Brandi was the truth."

"I know she was," was all that Shamari could muster up to say.

"Man, but the bitter end was how Maleek died, son. Maleek had broke up with your moms to fuck with some triflin'-ass gold-diggin' ho from Virginia and he moved down there for good, leavin' Brandi behind in New York with you. That nigga was actin' like he ain't never had pussy before and refused to come back to

New York to see you, at least. I was the nigga in his ear, tellin' him that how he was treatin' y'all wasn't right and he wasn't tryin' to hear me."

Dollar continued to run his mouth. It was as if he forgot who he was talking to. By the way that Dollar was yapping, Shamari realized that he wasn't the only person that was suffering from loneliness in that Bing.

"I'll never forget when they found him on I-64 and we was down there with him at the time, hustlin'. Some real black-ass, country bumpkin nigga named Smokey set him up. It was a rumor that Brandi had your pops put down but I don't believe that shit. And niggas tried to say she was fuckin' with that nigga Smokey 'cause they saw her in Virginia with the nigga a few weeks before your pops got killed. She was supposedly tryin' to convince the dude to get it done, too, I dunno. Motherfuckers lie so much, I didn't believe that shit, not one bit. Smokey had to disappear, but hey, that's how the game goes when you out in this world hustlin', it's only a few ways out. I think you know about one of them ways, 'cause we livin' the shit right now. This shit is for the birds!"

Shamari did everything in his power to fight back his tears. He knew that Dollar's story had some truth to it because the man knew the inti-

mate details about his mother and father. Shamari
had never met anyone that was directly associated
with his father, so this encounter was bittersweet.
Brandi had never mentioned Dollar's name and
now he understood why. He couldn't help but
think that there was a reason why he needed to
come out to the yard that day.

Dollar sighed. "Shamari, I'm gonna tell you,
son. Stay the fuck outta jail, man. I been comin'
back and forth for most of my life and it's no
joke. It's bugged 'cause I can't even trust myself
enough to stay outta here. You got kids, man?"

"Yeah, I got a son. He's almost a month old."

"Damn, Shorty Wop! You need to be home
with your baby. Don't get caught up. How's your
moms doin'?"

Shamari attempted a smile. "She's good. She's
got her master's degree and shit, a good career.
She's straight."

Dollar sighed. "Good for her. I knew she was
better than that hustlin' murder one shit. As
smart as she was, I'm glad she applied her brain
to somethin' else besides the streets. Now you
have to do the same."

Dollar paused and looked at Shamari as if he
was reminiscing about someone from his past.
He looked like he was about to choke up himself.
He just shook his head instead.

"Tell your moms that I wish the best for her and good luck to you, Shamari. Remember what I said and don't your forget your pops. He lives through you."

Shamari watched as they cuffed Dollar to take him out the pen and back to the housing area. Shamari turned around and stared at the Bronx, which was located across the water from Rikers Island. He took in the cool breeze that was coming off the murky waters surrounding the facility. The water was supposed to be calming but he still felt wound up. He assumed it was all the things that Dollar told him but he couldn't get mad at the man for letting him know the truth. He had nothing but respect for his mother for keeping him from knowing about her past. If his father left him and Brandi the way he did, then Shamari figured that he was better off dead anyway.

Chapter 34

Sean and Unique stood by the bar in their usual hangout spot, Brown Sugar. They played a few games of pool as they waited at the bar for the comedy routine to come on. Sean needed a few drinks and was happy that Unique had called him out to the lounge to treat him to a round or two.

"Yeah, man, it's still on. This woman is certified crazy!" Sean stated. "I feel like Michael Douglas, man! I'm just waitin' to walk in my house and see a fuckin' rabbit boilin' on my stove!"

Unique choked on his beer from laughter. "Yo, man, you stupid! Shit, Glenn Close was a sexy bitch, though! Giving up that pussy on the kitchen sink! Mike couldn't resist that ass, neither!" Unique stated.

"Yeah, but I can resist. Yadi is gorgeous, man. That's what makes it so bad. She could have any nigga she wants, so why does she keep botherin' me?"

"Man, she don't want any nigga! She wants you. She don't care about lookin' like a fool chasin' you 'cause in her mind she's doin' what she feels she's gotta do. In her mind, you and her are already in a relationship!"

"Damn, it's like that? Well, she's not my woman and I wish she would leave me the hell alone. I'm feelin' Brandi and I gotta get rid of this chick so that we can do what we gotta do. It's got so bad that she even started fuckin' with Brandi's son, who's locked up in the jail!" Sean looked at Unique. "Why don't you fuck with her?"

Unique looked around to make sure nobody was listening. "Hell no! I don't want no stalker chick followin' me around and shit. You can have that."

Sean laughed. "I just gotta get her off me. Like give her a one way ticket to Africa or somethin'. And you know what's sad? She got a beautiful little daughter and it's a shame how she's carryin' on over a nigga that don't want her ass. She probably did the same thing to her daughter's father."

Unique shrugged his shoulders and looked toward the entrance. "Damn! Who the fuck is that? She's fine as fuck!"

Sean looked and his jaw dropped. It was Yadi and she was bouncing her way over to them at the bar. He put his head in his hands.

"That's her, Unique. That's the female I was tellin' you about! I don't believe this shit!"

Unique looked like his eyes were bulging out his head and began cheesing. "Shit. She a bad mother . . . shut my mouth!" he joked.

Yadi approached the two men. "What's up, Sean? I knew I would see you here. What you drinkin' on?" Yadi asked. She was wearing her wavy hair wild, looking pretty with her flawless makeup and her Bobbi Brown lip gloss on. Her smooth skin glowed in the dim light as Unique stared at her along with the other male patrons at the bar.

"How you doin', miss?" Unique stated, introducing himself and holding her hand up to kiss it. "I'm Unique and your name is?"

Yadi giggled. "Yadi. How you doin', Unique?"

"Girl, I'm fine but not as fine as you. You are gorgeous, baby!"

"Thank you, Unique. You are so sweet. Too bad your friend, Sean, here don't appreciate it."

Sean arose from the bar seat. "I'm goin' over here by the pool tables, Unique. Good-bye, Yadi."

Yadi smiled. "Oooh, I love playin' pool. You wanna play a game, Unique?"

Unique jumped up to grab a table. "Sure, baby doll. I'll play with you!" He looked at the short skirt and knee boots Yadi had on. He couldn't wait for her to bend over the pool table so he could see her goods.

Sean watched Unique walk away. "What the fuck are you doin' here, Yadi? I told you to leave me alone!"

Yadi pointed her finger in Sean's face. "No, you told me to stay off your property and I did. We are in a public place and you don't own this bar so I could be here anytime I fuckin' want to and I wanted to be here tonight! So get over it." She began to walk away and turned around, blowing a kiss at Sean. "Oh, and by the way, I love you, too, Sean."

Sean simmered as he watched Yadi play pool with Unique. He would have fucked him up, too, had he not been his best friend. Everyone thought that because Yadi was so beautiful that there was no way she could be what he described. If it were the other way around, he surely would have been arrested by now.

Sean walked over to Unique and gave him a pound. "Look, U, I'm out. I feel a little woozy from them drinks," Sean exclaimed.

Unique looked disappointed, until he looked at Yadi. "A'ight, Shiz, go on home. I'll be okay with Miss Yadi over here, right, mama?"

Yadi smirked. "Yeah, you will be just fine, Unique. Your name is Unique, right?" she asked, glancing at Sean. "Yeah, that's right, go on home, Mr. Daniels."

Unique grinned from ear to ear. "Yeah, baby girl, I'm Unique, pun intended!" Unique looked at Sean. "Okay, man, see ya."

Sean looked at Unique and shook his head. He was going to give him a tongue-lashing when he called him the next day.

Sean walked out to his truck and drove home. He was a little skeptical about being in the house with Yadi so close by but he shrugged it off and laughed. He wasn't about to let Yadi run him out of his neighborhood. Once at home, he ran the water for his shower and turned on the music nice and loud.

While lathering up in the shower, Sean let the Calgon take him away, as he sang along with Trey Songz. He was feeling refreshed when suddenly he heard a sound. Sean turned down the radio in his shower and stood still for a brief second. He heard the noise again. It sounded like someone was on the stairs. Sean laughed at himself, thinking about how paranoid he was. All the Yadi drama had him scared of his own shadow.

Suddenly, the lights went out in the bathroom. Sean called out to the shadowy figure in his bathroom. Sean tried to grab the intruder but his hands got tangled up in the shower curtain. He lost his balance and the intruder managed to hit him in the head with a blunt object. Sean fell backward in the tub, with blood gushing from an open wound in his head. The intruder scurried down the stairs, with the blunt object still in their hand. They ran out of the house into the silent night.

Meanwhile back at Brown Sugar, Unique leered at Yadi and imagined her sweet pussy on his tongue, but she was into his boy, Sean. It was highly unlikely that she would want to get with him after all the things he had heard about her. Unique was going to try to convince Yadi to have revenge sex with him. He hoped she went for it. After all, Sean wouldn't mind. Through earlier conversation about her, Sean did suggest that Unique get with Yadi.

"So you just came out tonight on your own, huh?" he said, as he shot the ball in the side pocket.

Yadi stared at Unique, while chalking up her stick. "Yeah, I did. Why did you ask that?" she asked suspiciously. "What has your boy told you about me?"

Unique frowned and moved back so that Yadi could get her turn. "My boy ain't told me shit about you. Is there somethin' that I need to know?"

Yadi smiled. "Nah, it's not anything that you need to know. It's what you wanna know."

Unique shot another ball into the side pocket. He was winning the game and hopefully Yadi.

"I wanna know how does a beautiful woman like yourself decide to up and be a correction officer? You supposed to be on the cover of a magazine or somethin'!"

Yadi laughed. "Well, I never thought about bein' a model. I just wanted to work like a so-called regular person. At the end of the day, I'm just a regular chick with an ordinary job. I don't like all that glitz and glamour shit."

Unique looked at Yadi up and down. He admired her thick legs and clear complexion. He had to have some of that tonight, especially after finding out Sean didn't give a fuck one way or the other. He didn't believe Sean's story about her being all obsessed with him was true anyway. *Sometimes niggas be feelin' themselves,* he had thought while Sean was talking about Yadi. He just knew his boy was overexaggerating.

"Well, sweetheart, I'm here to tell you that you look like Hollywood! You need a manager?"

Yadi attempted to get another ball in the pocket and missed. Unique was the winner tonight.

"Well, Unique. Why don't we go back to your apartment for some drinks?" Yadi winked at him.

"I would love to, baby girl, but I'm a out-of-towner. What about your place?" "Well, I live in Queens, a long, long way from here. What kind of car you got?"

Unique smirked. "I drive a Tahoe. Why?"

"Good. We can hook up there."

As Yadi followed Unique to his truck, she didn't have to think once about why she was about to have sex with Sean's friend. In Yadi's twisted mind, she had concluded that her having sex with Sean's friend would anger him enough to come after her. Unique, who had known Sean all his life, knew that his friend wasn't thinking about Yadi.

Unique and Yadi climbed in the back of his truck and she slipped off the thong panties she wore under her miniskirt. Unique got an instant hard-on, even though he hadn't seen any parts of her box yet. Yadi climbed on top of Unique and began kissing him. As Yadi took charge, Unique was in awe her. He almost began to feel violated by the way she was acting.

"Take out your dick," Yadi instructed. Unique complied. Yadi pulled her shirt over her head to reveal her ripe breasts. Unique instantly grabbed for one and tried to put it in his mouth. Yadi slapped his hand away.

"I got this," she exclaimed. "You wanted some pussy, right?" Unique nodded his head like a puppy. "Okay, so let me handle this."

She lay him back on the leather seats and began performing fellatio on Unique's rod. He closed his eyes as he submitted to her and she loved every moment of it. She thought about what Sean's face would look like when he found out that his best friend had some of her goodies. She wriggled her tongue on the head of his dick. He moaned loudly.

"Shut up!" she whispered. Unique put his hand over his mouth. He didn't want to screw up a good moment. She kept going up and down the shaft and watched as the moonlight beamed on Unique's handsome face. Even then, she had to admit that Unique was sexy as hell, but he wasn't Sean Daniels.

Yadi pulled out her own condom from her bag and put it on Unique's dick with her mouth. She then pulled up her skirt, climbed on Unique, and began slowly riding him. She made sure that he hit every crack and crevice of her pussy.

She wanted to make it good; maybe he and Sean could compare notes. She tightened her pussy muscles and Unique began pumping back. After some minutes had passed, Yadi didn't know what felt better—Unique's good dick or her getting back at Sean by fucking his homeboy. *Maybe it's both,* she thought.

Unique began to get into Yadi's sex. He enjoyed watching her as she twirled her ass on top of him. Lucky for them, the streets were desolate that night. Anyone walking by would have observed his Jeep, rocking back and forth. Yadi swung her long hair in his face and Unique pulled her hair, as he grinded deeper and deeper into her sopping wet twat.

"Uuuhhhh, Unique. I didn't know it was this good. I didn't know," she moaned.

"Yeah, it's that good!" he confirmed.

Yadi ended up having an orgasm first with Unique cumming right behind her. Her body was still shaking for a few seconds afterward.

When they finally parted and got themselves together, Unique looked at Yadi with a mischievous look on his face.

"So you're straight?" he asked. He was hoping that he could at least get a phone number.

Yadi buttoned her short leather jacket and looked at Unique. "Yeah, I'm good. Why are you askin' me if I'm straight?"

Unique sighed. "Why are you women always askin' a question with a question? It's either yes or no. Damn!" he replied in annoyance.

"'Cause y'all niggas always askin' shit that got two meanings. I mean, damn, we fucked, I came, and you came. I can't be no straighter than that, now can I? And don't think about gettin' with me 'cause I'm in love with your boy and he loves me!"

Unique looked at Yadi with a frown on his face. He wanted her out of his truck and fast. He didn't believe his boy at first but now he was convinced that maybe the beautiful woman sitting before him was a little off. Otherwise, where did that last statement come from after she had just had sex with him in the back of his truck?

"Look, it was fun, that's it. You're in love and you think my boy is in love with you. You got your shit off so now you can go tell my boy you fucked me. Won't that make you happy by tryin' to make him jealous? That's what you wanted, right?"

Yadi laughed aloud. "Wow. You are not as stupid as I thought you were, you know that?"

Unique unlocked the doors to his Tahoe. "And you are dismissed. Get the fuck out my truck!" Yadi climbed out the truck and slammed Unique's passenger door. Unique rolled down the window.

. "And yo, shorty, I ain't no fuckin' police so I can slap the shit outta you for slammin' my fuckin' door, too! Remember that!"

Yadi began to get belligerent. "Fuck you, you stupid motherfucker! You and your friend ain't shit!"

"And you ain't shit, neither, because we both got the pussy! My boy gave me permission to fuck you! Ha, ha!" Unique yelled out the window, as he pulled off.

Yadi walked down the dark streets to her car. She sat in the driver's seat and cussed herself for having sex with Unique. Sean and Unique had set her up, with Sean thinking that he could use Unique to get Yadi out of his hair. They were both wrong.

As she wiped tears of frustration from her eyes, she realized that she had to pull out the big guns when it came to Mr. Daniels. Yadi did not like anyone playing with her feelings and she was going make sure Sean paid for putting her through all of this.

Yadi got into her car preparing for her drive back home to Queens. Her phone rang and she picked up the phone. The phone call was what had brought her to Bed-Stuy that night in the first place.

"Yo, it's done. That nigga will probably be comatose before it's all over. That's your man or somethin'?" the male voice on the other end of the phone asked.

"Somethin' like that," she responded. "Nigga ain't shit like the rest of the fuckin' men out here!"

"Wait, hold up, baby! Talk about that one dude, not the rest of us! Anyway, you got my bread?" he asked.

"Yeah, I got that. It ain't life threatenin', is it?" she asked.

The caller sucked his teeth. "What the fuck do you care? Ain't that nigga cheatin' on you?" There was a slight pause. "Meet me on Greene Avenue with the money. I'll be waitin'!"

"Yeah, okay," Yadi meekly replied and turned her car around. A few minutes later, Yadi pulled up alongside a black van and got out to give the culprit the $2,500 she had promised him for the deed.

Later on that night, Unique called Sean's cell phone and house phone repeatedly. Although he didn't get an answer, he didn't think anything of it. He knew that Sean was a little pissed at him for entertaining Yadi, but he had given him the go-ahead to get the pussy, and whether he was serious or not, Unique took the one-way ticket, never looking back. After hearing Sean's voice mail again, he finally left a message, not realizing that his friend was in danger.

Chapter 35

Yadi came into work the next day as if nothing ever happened the night before. Her alibi was airtight and she was relieved, knowing that Sean was not going to be at work for a while. She had covered all the bases so that no one could point the finger at her. *Teach his ass a thing or two about playin' with my feelings,* Yadi thought.

"Excuse me, Cruz," Captain Phillips stopped her in the waiting area. "Did you hear from Daniels this morning? He didn't come in to work today and that's not like him to not call," she asked.

Yadi shook her head. "Nah, Captain Phillips. I dunno what's up with Daniels. Did he take a day off, or call in sick, maybe?"

Captain Phillips frowned. She was worried. "I checked everything. No personal day, no time due, no sick day, no nothing. He's about to be marked AWOL in . . ." Captain Phillips looked at her watch. "In about twenty minutes. Maybe I can get him on the phone. Better yet, somebody needs to go over to his house to find out what's goin' on."

Yadi sighed. She didn't want to go anywhere near his house, although she thought that wouldn't have been a good look for her if she didn't. Everyone knew how she felt about Sean so it would only be right for her to play the part of the worried "friend."

"You know what, Cap? I'll go. I know where Sean keeps his spare key because I stayed with him for a little while, you know, when I had some baby daddy drama!"

Captain Phillips looked at Yadi skeptically. There was something about the woman that didn't sit right with her. She could smell a deceptive person a mile away, because after all, she used to be one.

"Well, okay, Cruz. I don't want any bullshit. I just want to know if my officer is okay. An officer who also happens to be a very good friend of mine!"

Yadi smiled. She knew that Captain Phillips was no fan of hers but she was so far from caring about what the woman thought about her.

"I know, I know, Cap. I got you. Just get the crew together and we can go over there."

After an hour went by, Yadi and two other male officers, COs White and Hall, rode together in a department-issued vehicle on their way to Sean's house in silence. Because Captain Phillips didn't trust Yadi, she sent an extra officer with them.

Hall started up a conversation with Yadira. "So, um, Cruz, what's up with you and Daniels anyway?" he asked. "Are y'all, you know, together?"

Yadi sucked her teeth. "Who wants to know?" she shot back. "Y'all officers are always in the business so maybe you can tell me what's goin' on with us. Since y'all know about everything else that's goin' on up in the jail!"

White laughed. "Aw, please, woman! You are on his shit. He don't want your ass and you're mad about it!" White and Hall gave each other a pound. "That's why you agreed to come on this trip, so you could go see if your baby is up in the crib with the next chick!"

Yadi rolled her eyes at White, with his unkempt uniform and scruffy beard. "You're just mad 'cause I'm not on your dick! Oh, yeah and I heard about your little erectile dysfunction, White!" Yadi exclaimed, holding her fingers up to describe the size of White's genitalia. Hall began laughing hysterically. "Yeah, mmhmm. Think I don't know. We talk in the ladies' locker room all the time and the word on the street is you got a teensy weensy little problem down there in your pants!"

White scowled. "Man, fuck all y'all hoes! Always talkin' shit about a nigga when he cut one of y'all off! Ain't nothin' wrong with my dick! You want me to prove it? Why don't you come over here and let me put it in your mouth!"

Yadi waved them off as they continued to make rude and offensive jokes. She was so caught up in her thoughts, nothing fazed her. Her plan was to act as if she was concerned about Sean. That way it could seem as if she was his savior, hopefully making things good between the both of them once again.

The departmental vehicle pulled up in front of Sean's house. The flashing lights were no mistake as Yadi jumped out of the back seat of the car. Hall and White got out of the car too. They watched as the paramedics brought a semi-conscious Sean out of his house on a gurney. Sean had bloody bandages wrapped around his head. His body was still glistening from the water in the shower, which had been running on him for the last few hours.

Sean's relatives, including his uncle, Deputy Warden Miller, were gathered around and were naturally upset, wondering who could have done such a thing to their loved one. Yadi watched in dread, never anticipating that she would be overwhelmed with emotion. The reality of what she'd done hit her all at one time, as she fainted into the arms of White and Hall, who were standing nearby.

Police officers walked up to White, who had gladly allotted Hall the responsibility of getting Yadira Cruz back in order.

"Umm, is this guy your fellow officer?" the short, stocky, Italian officer asked. "Youse know what happened to him?"

"Nah," White replied. "That's why we're here. He was AWOL from work today."

"Well, looks like somebody came into his house while he was takin' a shower. It seems like the suspect had a key because there are no signs of forced entry, then the asshole cracked him over the head with a blunt object! That's fucked up!" The cop looked at Yadi and Hall. "Hey, she okay? His girlfriend or somethin', huh?"

White looked at Yadi. "Hell no! She's one of his fans, she's not his girl!" They both laughed.

"Wow, youse guys have problems like that in your department, too, huh? Wowee!" The cop looked at the ambulance. "Well, your fellow officer is in route to Kings County. I ain't no doctor but umm, he seemed as if he suffered blunt trauma to his head, and you know the County got one of the best trauma units in the city. Sorry about your coworker, fellas. I gotta be on my way! Take care!" The cops walked away and got back into their patrol car.

Yadi finally came to and leaned on the departmental vehicle, as she watched White and Hall ask the EMTs questions. They had detectives on the scene as well, which made Yadi realize that she may have taken it too far. It was too late to think about what she had done because the damage was done and the money was paid. She now wondered if it was all worth it.

An hour later at Kings County hospital, Sean finally opened his eyes. His head felt as if it were going to explode. He tried to remember what happened the night before but everything seemed blurry. His mother and sister stood by his bed with concern written all over their faces.

"Hey, Ma," Sean began. "What, what happened to me? Why am I in here? Why is my head hurtin'?" he asked, while holding his bandaged head.

"Somebody came into your house and hit you in the head while you was in the shower last night, Sean," his mother replied. "The police said that there was no signs of forced entry, so the person might have had a key. Do you remember anything?"

Sean sighed. The sunlight coming into the hospital room was killing him. His sister closed the curtain and held his hand.

"Who had your key, Sean? Somebody walked in your house with the key and hit you upside the head while you was in the shower," his sister, Ameena, repeated.

"I, I dunno," Sean stammered. "I don't know what's goin' on. Did someone pick up my shield? Did they take my firearm? I can't even tell you what . . ." His voice trailed off.

"They sent someone to pick up your things, sweetheart. Your shield and firearm are safe," his mother responded.

Sean's mother, Tika Miller, sighed out of frustration. It was too bad he couldn't recall what happened. She was concerned about her youngest child, living in that big old house all by himself. She knew that Sean was flashy with the expensive truck and the expensive clothing—it could have been anyone who tried to hurt him. She was just glad that things didn't turn out for the worst.

"C'mon, Meena," Tika stated, making sure Sean dozed off. She placed a loving kiss on his cheek. "Let's go home and come back tomorrow when the detectives come to question him. Hopefully, he can give us some answers then." The women left as Sean drifted into a drug-induced slumber.

News of Sean's "incident" spread like wildfire throughout the Department of Correction. The tongues wagged, as expected, and Yadi stood by in silence, unwilling to answer anyone's questions about her and Sean's relationship. Vanita watched Yadi closely and was worried that she seemed quieter than usual.

"Yadi, you all right?" Vanita asked. "You seem a little quiet these days."

Yadi continued to work. "I'm good, Nita. Why do you ask?" she replied. She couldn't bear to look anyone in the face. The guilt was eating her up.

"Nah, you just seem distant. Is it about Sean?"

Yadi looked at Vanita. "Nah, it ain't about no Sean. He's alive, right?"

Vanita frowned. "Yeah, he's alive." She paused. "Yadi, umm, I ain't sayin' that you had any dealings with that whole situation, but did you, you know, 'cause you had the keys to his house."

Yadi swung around. "What the hell, Vanita? How the fuck could you stand here and accuse me of some shit like that?"

Vanita got annoyed. "The same damn way you accused me of wantin' Devin a few weeks ago! So I guess now you know how it feels!"

Yadi turned around and leaned on the desk. "Vanita, I would never hurt Sean, you know that.

I love that man with all my heart and I, I feel so bad for him. It's a shame you can't even feel safe in your own house!"

Vanita looked at Yadi and continued to work in silence. It was sad because she had gotten to the point that she couldn't believe anything Yadi said. Vanita decided she was going to keep her mouth shut because she had no evidence. She would be extremely disappointed, though, if it came out that Yadi did cause Sean some bodily harm . . . or had someone else do it. Vanita sighed and got back to her duties.

Chapter 36

For the next two days, Brandi was worried that she hadn't heard from Sean or her son. She wasn't allowed to visit Shamari on Riker's for a while and it was hard to get anyone on the telephone to find out what was going on. Sean had always been the liaison between her and Shamari but she hadn't heard from him in days. She had a gut feeling about something, though, and she felt that something was very wrong. Who could she call to ask?

Brandi looked through her cell phone and decided to call the facility's visit area. She remembered Sean had given her the phone number to call him while he was at work. Ever since all the drama went down with Yadi Cruz, she didn't have the tolerance to call there and risk Cruz giving her some bullshit. That would be all she needed. Today, though, she was going to take a chance and call. She hoped that someone else would answer the telephone instead of Yadi.

Brandi dialed the number and waited patiently for someone to pick up.

"Visit area, Officer Garrett speaking," the female officer answered the phone. She sounded very pleasant.

"Hello, Officer Garrett, how are you? I am so sorry to bother you but I just needed to ask you some questions," Brandi stated.

"Who's this?" Vanita Garrett asked. She didn't want to give out any sensitive information to anyone over the phone. It wasn't allowed.

"Um, I'm sorry. This is Brandi Wallace, inmate Shamari Wallace's mother. I came up there before and, and I wanted to find out what was goin' on with him."

Vanita took the phone to her side of the desk. Yadi was too busy opening and closing gates to pay her any attention.

"Hey, Miss Wallace," Vanita greeted with a whisper. "I'm sorry but I have to be careful about this phone stuff. Anyway, how did you get this number?"

"Well, well . . ." Brandi hesitated.

"Look," Vanita whispered. "Before you even say anything, I know all about you from a former friend of mine. Can I call you back from my phone? I'm goin' to meal."

Brandi gave Vanita her phone number. She wasn't sure if she could really trust her but she was taking a chance. She needed to know what was going on in there.

"Please, Officer Garrett, don't let me down. I'm banned from the Island and I haven't seen my son—"

Vanita cut her off. "Listen, I got you. Don't say anymore. I'm gonna call you back in ten minutes, okay?"

Brandi hung up the phone. She paced around her house until Vanita called her back ten minutes later. She breathed a sigh of relief when she heard the officer's voice.

"Hey, Miss Wallace?" Vanita asked.

"Just call me Brandi. What's your name?"

"Oh, I'm Vanita. Vanita Garrett. I wish there was somewhere I could talk to you in person, because I'm in the locker room at work. These walls have ears."

"I feel you, Vanita, and I don't mean to put you through any unnecessary trouble. I was worried about my son. I haven't heard from him in a day or so and that's unlike him. What's going on?"

Vanita sighed. "Well, it's a lot goin' on in here. I swear I wish I could kick somebody's ass, but I need my job. Anyway, Shamari was involved in an altercation in the visit area. Apparently, someone tricked a rookie officer into bringin' him down to the general population visit area and he was put in a holding pen with some inmates he had a previous beef with and they jumped him."

"Oh, my God!" Brandi shouted. "My baby! What is going on in there?"

"Brandi, he's okay!" Vanita appeased. "He held his own. He came out wih a few scrapes and bumps. He went to the clinic and they sent him back to his housing area. He's still in Four South, the Bing. The officer is in a lot of trouble, though, and everyone is tryin' to figure out who called up there for him to bring Wallace for a visit in the first place."

Brandi felt as if she was going to hyperventilate and her voice was quivering. "Vanita, he's okay, right?"

Vanita smiled. She felt a lump in her throat, imagining what Brandi must be going through as a mother.

"He's fine, Brandi. Trust me. Even though I'm a CO, I have compassion for some of these guys in here. He is back upstairs in his cell and he is fine."

"Can I ask you another question? Between me and you, how is Daniels? He's been on my mind and I haven't heard from him in a few days. I was just wondering if everything was all right with him."

Vanita sighed. "Brandi, it's some shit goin' on with Sean. I know that you and him are dealin' with each other, which I'm gonna keep it real, is against the rules. On the other hand, I don't get caught up with jail politics." Vanita paused. "Wait. You don't know?"

"Know what?" Brandi asked.

"Sean is in the hospital." There was silence on the other end. Vanita waited for Brandi to let the news to sink in.

"Hospital? For what?" Brandi inquired.

"Well, someone came into his house two nights ago with a key and bashed him upside the head, while he was in the shower. He was semi-unconscious when they took him to the hospital, but I heard that he's been up since then. They don't have any suspects, yet."

"Oh, my goodness! Do you know what hospital?"

"He's in Kings County Hospital. Brandi, do you think that I could meet with you in person? There's a few things I have to talk about with you, and no, I'm not like the woman you are thinkin' about!"

Vanita must have been reading Brandi's mind. She was skeptical about the meeting but from

Vanita's tone, she knew that it was something
very important that she couldn't discuss at work.
In addition, Brandi was sure Vanita was curious
to meet the woman Sean was seeing and the
woman Yadi was hating on.

"Um, okay. Where did you want to meet?"
Brandi asked.

"Can we meet in front of Kings County? We
can go see Sean together. Say, like around five-
thirty?"   \

Brandi really wanted to see Sean by herself
but she reluctantly agreed to the arrangement.
"Okay, Vanita, that's cool. But how will you know
it's me?"

"Trust me, Brandi, I'll know you when I see
you!"

Brandi hung up the phone and wondered
what Vanita meant by that statement.

At 5:30 p.m., on the dot, Brandi was waiting
in front of Kings County. She looked around,
searching for Vanita in the crowds of people entering and exiting the hospital. She smiled as she
saw Vanita approach her. Vanita was a pretty,
petite woman with a chocolate complexion and
a chin-length bob. Vanita walked up to Brandi
with a smile on her face, as well.

"Hey, Brandi. I told you I would know who
you were!"

Brandi smiled. "Yeah, now that I see you, I remember you from the visit area. You're always in the control room."

They walked into the hospital and Vanita looked around, like she was afraid of running into someone she knew. "Yeah, I kinda play it cool at work. I don't really socialize with too many people there. Me and Yadira Cruz were real good friends until recently."

Brandi frowned. "What do you mean?"

"I know you know Yadi and I know all about the run-in y'all had. Well, she was a good person. Over the years, she had a lot of issues in her relationship with her daughter's father and so on. She had never been much of a social person; she keeps to herself a lot. After things went sour with her daughter's father, she kind of leaned on Sean. They both were crushin' on each other for a minute but after she decided to finally get with Sean, he met you and he was open."

"Open? On me?" Brandi asked with a confident smirk on her face.

"Yeah, open on you. Yadi lived with me for a little while and we used to talk about it. After she found out that Sean was dealin' with you, she just became obsessed with you and Sean, period. Yadi always suffered from low self-esteem and she looked at you as competition."

"I don't see why. She's a beautiful woman, a little nutty, but she's gorgeous. I have to give her that."

Vanita shrugged. "Brandi, you know as well as I do bein' beautiful on the outside, sometimes it's not enough. To look at Yadira, someone would think that she had it all together but she doesn't. She's all messed up inside."

"But, Vanita, I'm confused. Why are you telling me all of this?" Brandi asked.

"Because after hearin' about what happened to Sean and how she approached you about him, I think that she had somethin' to do with Sean's incident. Now that I think about it, she may have had somethin' to do with your son's incident, too."

Brandi frowned as she tried to piece everything together. Vanita might have had a point.

"I love Yadi but right is right and wrong is wrong. And you know, Brandi, I'm not tryin' ta be foul and talk about this woman behind her back. I've been nothin' but a friend to Yadi and she had the nerve to accuse me of sleepin' with her daughter's father. I invited this woman into my home and it just wasn't enough for her. I been her counselor for all of these years and I'm tired now. Now she went off the deep end with this Sean shit."

Brandi got very quiet. She knew that Vanita had a point. "Didn't she have a key to his house before?" Brandi asked.

"Yeah, as I recall. I think she made a copy of the key. Either she came in there herself and did something or someone else came in and did it. Either way, I think that she was involved."

"Vanita, I'm gonna ask your honest opinion. Do you really believe that she would set my son up to get back at me?"

Vanita held her head down. "Well, to be honest, I do. It was too much of a coincidence that your son was called down to general population visits then got into a physical altercation there. It was no mistake. But it's just an opinion."

Brandi put her hand on her head. "This bitch, Yadira, is giving me a headache. I know that's your friend and all . . ."

"We're done, Brandi. I can't be friends with Yadi anymore. She's outta control. Nothin' good is gonna come from her behavior and I don't want to be associated with none of it when the shit hits the fan!"

"Good for you, Vanita. It seems as if you're a sensible-minded person. Sometimes, misery loves company and you have to separate yourself from it."

"I know. I'm gonna miss her but I realize that she's drained me all these years. Now I can get a new lease on life, new friends, new things to do. I'm gonna miss my goddaughter, though."

"Can't you see her? Is she with Yadi?"

"Brandi, I don't know where she is. She could be with her father, which I already know I ain't seein' her if she with him or she could be with Yadi's parents. It's sad but I have to do what I have to do and move on."

Brandi smiled. "Look, you keep my number in your phone and we can talk sometimes. I appreciate you going out of your way to tell me all of this. You didn't have to do what you did."

Vanita smiled back. "I try, Brandi. I try to be a good person. I would have wanted someone to do those things for me," she said.

Both women stood in the lobby, hesitant about going to see Sean in the condition he was in. Vanita finally broke the silence.

"Okay, Brandi. Let's go upstairs and see Sean. You ready?" Brandi shook her head and they walked toward the visitor's information desk.

Chapter 37

After getting Sean's room number, Vanita walked in first. She was surprised to see that Sean was alert and eating his dinner while watching *The Bernie Mac Show* on the small twenty-inch TV mounted above his bed.

"Hi, Sean!" Vanita announced.

Sean held out his arms to hug her. He had IV tubes in his arms. "Hey, Nita!" he replied. "What's up, homegirl?"

"What's up, Sean? How are you feelin'?" Sean touched his bandaged head.

"I get these bad headaches but after they give me some drugs, I'm good. I should be comin' home at the end of next week. They still gotta run some tests, to make sure there's no extensive damage."

Vanita fixed his sheets. "Good. Take your time comin' back to work okay?"

Sean agreed. "I know. You know I gotta ride this shit out for a little while. I needed a break. Unfortunately, it had to be like this."

Vanita looked at the door. "Look, someone is here to see you. I wasn't sure if you was up to it so I told them to wait outside. Do you mind if they come in?"

Sean swallowed. "It ain't Yadi, is it?"

Vanita laughed. "Hell no, Sean! I ain't even fuckin' with her no more. That bitch is a wrap but I'll tell you about that when you feel better."

Sean tried to look past Vanita. "So who's outside?" he asked.

Vanita walked to the door and opened it. Brandi walked in and Sean's face lit up. He tried to sit up in the hospital bed and Vanita made him relax.

"Hey, Sean," Brandi said with a smile. She leaned over and kissed him on the lips. "Are you okay?"

Sean rubbed his head. "Yeah, baby. Thank God I'm alive! I just wanna find out who did this shit to me!" Sean quickly changed the subject before his mood soured. "Did you hear from Shaki?"

Brandi frowned. "Shaki? Did you just call him Shaki?" she asked.

Sean laughed. "Yeah. He told me to call him that."

"When?" Brandi asked.

Vanita looked at Sean. "Oh, yeah, I told Brandi what happened with her son in visits."

"The day he had the fight, I went to the intake area to check on him. He was good. We had a nice talk and that's when he told me to call him by his nickname. He said only his family and close friends call him that."

Brandi's eyes lit up and she hugged Sean. She could relax now that Sean had told her that he had seen Shamari and that he was fine. Brandi hugged Sean and he kissed her on the cheek.

"Thank you, Sean. It sounds like you finally made an impression on him. This jail mess is getting to him now. He finally gets that it's no joke in there."

"You're right. He does get it now." Sean was silent for a moment as he held Brandi's hand and looked into her eyes. "You know I'm real glad that you're here, baby. How did you and Vanita hook up?"

"She called the jail lookin' for you, Sean," Vanita volunteered. "She hadn't heard from you or her son and she was worried, of course."

Sean smiled and put his arm around Brandi's slim waist. "Aww, you was worried about me? That's so sweet!" They all laughed.

"Yeah, I was worried about you. Even though that whole Yadira thing had me a little hot under the collar, I just needed to know if you were okay," Brandi replied.

"I'm just tryin' to understand what happened to me. One minute, I'm in the shower washin' my ass, then in the damn hospital the next."

Brandi and Vanita looked at each other. "I decided to hook up with Brandi so that we could come visit you together. This woman right here is crazy cool. I hope that y'all really get with each other."

Brandi rolled her eyes. "What about Yadi?"

Sean cut her off. "Brandi, don't worry about her anymore. Her days are over," he said.

They continued to talk about Yadira and Sean getting out of the hospital. His spirits were up now that he had the woman he really cared about by his side. Eventually, Vanita left so that they could spend the last moments of the visit alone.

"Vanita is so cool," Brandi stated.

Sean agreed. "She always has been, I just wanted to tell you somethin'."

Brandi glared at Sean. "Oh, my goodness! What do you have to tell me now? Is it bad news?"

Sean cut her off and looked Brandi straight in the eyes. "I wanted to tell you that I'm really feelin' you."

Brandi froze, not knowing what to say. "Sean, we just really start kicking it and you have a head injury."

"But I'm not buggin', I know what I'm sayin', okay?"

Brandi looked at Sean, who looked so helpless lying there with his bandaged head and IV tubes in his arm. Her heart began to soften and she forgot all about Yadi and her past.

"Sean, I'm feeling for you, too. Let's just finally make it happen for us," Brandi said.

Chapter 38

The day after Vanita and Brandi visited Sean, Yadi headed to Kings County. She parked her car a few blocks away and walked down Clarkson Avenue. As she got closer, Yadi felt her heart palpitate. She felt as if she was going to pass out, she was so nervous. She hoped that she would have a positive reception from Sean, considering all of the things they had been through. Yadi felt bad about what she did, but maybe this is what it took to get what she wanted and that was Sean Daniels.

Yadira knew that he was in Kings County Hospital but she was hesitant about going to see him, unable to face his family and friends. She also did not know if her presence would be welcomed, unsure of what negativity Sean had fed his people about her. In order to maintain her appearance of innocence, she would have to suck it up and visit him.

Yadi entered the hospital and walked toward the desk. She asked for Sean's room and got a visiting pass. She took the elevator upstairs and had to stop to catch her breath. *I hope no one is in this room with him* she thought as she looked for Sean's room number.

She walked in the room and, thankfully, Sean was by himself. He looked so peaceful, lying in the bed with the bandages wrapped around his head. His hair was cut on the side where the injury was. Yadi put her hand on his face and Sean opened his eyes. When he did, he jumped as if he had seen a ghost.

"What are you doin' in here?" Sean asked, with his voice hoarse from sleep.

Yadi smiled and continued to rub his face. "I'm here to see you, baby. How are you feelin'?" she asked.

Sean removed her hand from his face and he grimaced as he attempted to sit up in the bed. Yadi tried to help him and he resisted.

"Look, I don't need your help!" Sean exclaimed. "I'm good. Why did you come here, Yadi?"

Yadi sighed loudly and pulled up a chair. "I felt bad about all the things that I put you through and I came here to offer my sincere apology to you. It's just that, I, I love you, Sean and when you started rejectin' me . . . I dunno, I guess I just bugged out."

Sean rubbed his head. He didn't feel like talking to Yadi right now, especially about their imaginary relationship.

"Look, Yadira, I don't feel like talkin' about this shit right now. I'm in the fuckin' hospital, in pain, after some motherfucker walked in my house and clocked me upside the fuckin' head in the shower. I got bigger shit on my plate than to talk about you and me. As far as I'm concerned, you and me never was and I personally regret the day we had sex. No, I regret the day I let you into my house, 'cause it's been nothin' but downhill for me ever since!"

Yadi held back tears. "I didn't come here for this shit, Sean! I just came to pay a visit to a friend and this is how you treat me?"

Sean sat up. "Bitch, you . . ." he began, grimacing from the pain in his head. He looked up at the ceiling. "God, forgive me because I don't like callin' women bitches but—" Sean looked at Yadi. "But bitch, are you fuckin' crazy? What am I sayin'? You are fuckin' crazy! You think I dunno what's goin' on?"

Yadi stopped crying. "What's goin' on? What do you mean?"

"I been livin' in Bed-Stuy all my life and nobody has ever ran up in my house like that! Now all of a sudden, as soon as I start goin' through the bullshit with you, I end up in the hospital. I remembered you havin' keys to my house, Yadi! I know you made a copy and somebody came in my house with a key!"

Yadi tried to look surprised. "What the fuck are you talkin' about, Sean?" She stood up. "Are you sayin' that I had somethin' to do with this shit?"

Sean looked in Yadi's eyes. "I'm not tryin' to say it, I done said it." There was an eerie silence in the hospital room. The only noise that could be heard was the TV.

Yadi began to get on the defensive. "Who's feedin' you these lies, Sean? Is it that ho, Brandi? I shoulda fucked the bitch up when I had a chance!"

Sean frowned. "You see, Yadi, you underestimate people, walkin' around here playin' with people's lives and shit. After what you did to her son, I think Brandi is the last person you wanna see! Stay the fuck away from her! "

Yadi paced around the room. Sean watched as Yadi began to unfold right before his eyes. He knew then that Yadi was more than just a woman in love with him; she was a bonafide mental patient obsessed with him. At this point, Yadi's eyes were bulging out of her head and she began to wave her hands over her head.

Yadi couldn't believe that Sean would accuse of her of all these things. Everything that she did was for her and Sean's benefit. She wanted him to see that they should be together. Why was Sean making her out to be the bad guy?

"Sean, I didn't do anything to her son! Why would you say that about me? You know that I am not that type of person—"

Sean cut her off. "Damn! You're a compulsive liar, too, huh? What else is wrong with you, Yadira? You walk around lookin' like you just hopped off the cover of somebody's magazine and in reality, you ain't nothin' but a fuckin' head case! I see why Devin didn't want to be with you anymore!"

Yadi threw something at Sean, barely missing his injured head. She began screaming obscenities at him and medical staff ran into Sean's hospital room. Security was called immediately and Yadi had to be forcibly removed from the area. The nurses ran over to Sean to see if he had suffered any additional injuries. Fortunately, she left Sean unscathed. Relieved that their patient was okay, the nurses walked out of the room to watch the drama unfold with the crazy visitor.

"We have to get police protection for Mr. Daniels!" the head nurse stated to one of her colleagues, as they left his room. "There's no telling who did this to him and they got these crazy people coming to see him! He doesn't need this type of drama because he's a recovering patient!" She picked up the phone to contact the head of security at Kings County.

Yadi was escorted downstairs to the lobby. She had the wild-eyed look of a deranged woman and her hair was all over the place. Yadi looked around at the small group of people that had gathered around to look at her.

"Miss, your things were retrieved from the room, and either you leave the premises, or you run the risk of being arrested," the hospital police officer said, while handing Yadi her belongings and pointing to the door. Her breathing became more rapid. She had to try to calm down because she couldn't afford to get arrested. She had almost forgotten that she was an officer too.

"I'm fine, I'm fine, just leave me alone, please!" she exclaimed, wriggling herself from their grasps.

The officers looked at each other. "Well, so that you know, you are not allowed back up to Mr. Daniels's room for the rest of his stay here. If you decide to visit on your own accord, you will be arrested for trespassing!"

Yadi sucked her teeth and walked away, leaving the officers wondering about her behavior.

"We should have taken her ass to to the G building!" one officer exclaimed, referring to the mental ward at Kings County Hospital. Yadi walked outside and the night air hit her face like a ton of bricks. She walked back to her car with a defeated attitude, not realizing that she may have sealed her own fate.

Chapter 39

The knock on his cell door startled Shamari. He jumped in his sleep but he did not wake up from the beautiful dream he was having. He was physically and mentally exhausted because, after all, being in the Bing took a toll on an inmate's mental state. He had not been able to get a good night's rest because he had to be subjected to catcalling and yelling throughout the day, and of course, someone banging on their cell door all night.

So far, he had seen a few officers being drenched with urine by a disgruntled inmate or two, or maybe having a tray of hot grits thrown at them since he'd been there. He looked at the savages who were once men, who smeared feces all over the wall of their cells and who masturbated to female correction officers through their opened cell slots.

He also couldn't believe some of the idio-syncracies that were entertained by the officers and supervisors that worked there. They stayed entertaining outrageous requests from inmates by giving them extra sugar or multiple boxes of Kellog's Frosted Flakes cereal, just to have order in the housing area. Shamari was upset because he hadn't been able to make a phone call. One of the inmates would either break the phone or refuse to give it up. Therefore, he just chose to remain humble and pray that he would be sent upstate to begin his bid.

Shamari stood against his cell window after hearing Jones's high-pitched voice. He thought about her all the time, being that she was the closest thing to feminine that he probably would see for a while. She had an occasional conversation with him every now and again, which he appreciated. Shamari kept to himself and did not get involved in jail politics, choosing to listen to Jones instead of running his mouth with the various ingrates locked up inside their funky cells. Suddenly, Jones appeared in front of Shamari's cell. He smiled when he saw her face.

"Hey, Mr. Wallace! How are you?" she asked.

Shamari rubbed his chin. "I'm fine, Miss Jones. How are you?" he replied.

She smiled back. "Now that's how you talk to a lady. Ask us how we're doin', show that you care, even if you really don't!"

Shamari laughed. "Nah, that ain't true. I care." Shamari changed the subject. "I got my things ready. Are you goin' to escort me to the shower?"

CO Jones put on her Nike baseball gloves and removed the department-issued handcuffs tucked in the waistline of her uniform pants so that she could escort Shamari to the shower.

"Yeah, Wallace, I got you." Jones opened the slot to Shamari's cell and cuffed him. On the walkie-talkie, she instructed the officer to open Shamari's cell. Carrying his toiletries in a pillowcase, Shamari walked alongside Jones, with his hands cuffed to the back. He felt himself getting aroused from the touch of Jones's gloved hand and, as usual, enjoyed her Gucci perfume as she escorted him to the shower area.

Once Shamari was locked in the shower, he put his hands through the slot to be uncuffed. Jones stood there for a few seconds in silence, as Shamari turned on the water.

"You know, Wallace, you look like Ray J, Brandi's brother," she said.

Shamari laughed. "Yeah, people say that all the time. It's all good, though."

Jones continued to stand there and Shamari was confused. "Miss Jones, you a'ight?"

"Put your dick through the slot, Wallace," she whispered as she looked around to see if anyone was looking. A look of confusion came over Shamari's face.

"Huh? Put what?" he asked, not sure if he had heard her correctly.

Jones came closer to Shamari's face. "Pull your dick out your jumper. Hurry up!" she whispered.

Shamari pulled his erect penis out of his jumper and put it through the waist-high slot. Jones took off her gloves and began massaging his erect penis. She looked at his love muscle and smiled.

"You are a cutie, Wallace," she stated in a husky voice. "Do you know what I would do to you?"

Shamari was unable to answer. He was in a daze, enjoying the softness of Jones's hand, jerking his dick back and forth. He imagined himself having sex with the pretty officer, cursing her for allowing him to be disrespectful. He was having a selfish moment, thinking that he should have been in the Bing since he arrived in the jail. Maybe then, he wouldn't have been cut and he would have been enjoying Miss Jones' hand jobs.

"How does that feel, baby?" she asked in a sensual tone.

"Good, Miss Jones, real good," Shamari replied, while staring in her eyes through the gated shower pen. "Oh, man, you're gonna make me cum," he uttered as he prepared himself for a much-needed release.

Shamari watched in disbelief, as his semen was washed away in the shower drain. He fell back against the wall as Jones stood there with a self-righteous look on her face.

"You liked that, huh?" she asked.

Shamari looked at Jones. "Hell, yeah," he replied. "But why did you do that?"

CO Jones paused for a moment. "You looked like you needed a stress reliever. There's plenty more where that came from. Plus, you look like Ray J and I love me some Ray J," Jones replied, fluttering her eyes flirtatiously. Jones backed out the shower area and walked away, leaving Shamari speechless and satisfied.

Shamari was awakened from his wet dream by another loud knock on the door. The dream about Miss Jones jerking him off in the shower seemed real as shit.

"Yo, Wallace, you want a shower?" the male CO asked.

"For what?" replied Shamari.

"You headed for Downstate this mornin'. You're outta here, shorty," the officer replied.

Shamari pumped his fist in the air. "Yesss!" he said aloud. He looked at the CO who was still standing at the door. "Yeah, I'm gonna take a shower. I'll be ready in a few."

The CO walked away and Shamari jumped around in his cell. He was headed for Downstate, which was like the admissions facility for inmates headed to an upstate prison. He wanted to get off Rikers and do his time. He had a son who needed him and his mother wanted better for him. After going through this ordeal, Shamari knew that he was not coming back to jail again. It was for the birds!

The same CO had notified him earlier escorted Shamari to the shower. He went in the shower for about fifteen minutes. After he was finished, the officer locked him out of the shower and immediately escorted him to his cell.

He packed up everything, giving away magazines and other impermissibles to a few of his fellow inmates. No more did he have to be fed through a slot or be handcuffed every time he exited his cell. Although he wasn't exactly free, when he got upstate, he could be a lot more mobile than he was in the Bing.

Shamari anxiously waited to be escorted to the receiving area, where he would wait for the Downstate bus. Sometimes inmates going upstate would be in the intake area all day, depending on how many state-ready inmates had to be picked up throughout Rikers Island. He hoped that that would not be the case with him.

Shamari had gotten cool with the DOC staff, thanks to CO Jones, who went beyond the scope of her duties to make sure he was comfortable during his stay in Four South. He finally grasped that the COs were human beings too, and that they had jobs to do. They had to support their families, like he would have to help support his son when he came home. CO Jones, the steady three to eleven officer, was a little extra at times but even he reminded himself that she had a job to do and dignity to maintain, as well. They had developed a mutual respect for each other, making Shamari's transition into manhood and maturity less complicated.

He struggled emotionally after the death of Amber, realizing that life was too short to be worried about trying to make fast money and living the life of a gangster. It wasn't until his baby mother passed away that he learned to appreciate the life that he had. He had a mother who loved him and extended family, as well, who looked out for his best interests.

Even his uncles, who ran the streets and did their dirt, never meant for their sister's son to be caught up in the streets like they were. He thought about everything these people had been trying to tell him for years, although his father's death had said it loud and clear. It took him to go to jail to see that it was only the next step before death, and obviously, he loved being alive. Life had too much to offer.

It was six-fifteen in the morning and Shamari was told that he would not be leaving the housing area until eight a.m. He asked to use the telephone and the COs obliged.

A CO came to Shamari's cell and slipped the slimline phone under his cell door. He called his mother's cell phone and she picked up immediately.

"Oh, Shaki!" she screamed. "Oh, my baby! Are you all right? Did you get the money I sent you last week?"

Shamari laughed. "I'm straight, Ma. I was callin' you to tell you that they're about to send me upstate."

Brandi got quiet and the tears began to fall. "Upstate? Already?"

"Yeah, Ma, upstate." Shamari felt a lump in his throat. "Ma, it's okay. Just look at it like I'm gettin' closer to comin' home. I'm gonna do this time and get back on New York City soil. And you can come see me up there. It's six-hour visits up there."

Brandi cried silently. She didn't want to upset Shamari before he left. "So what time are you leaving?"

Shamari sighed. "It depends on the time the bus comes to get me. It'll be other people on the bus from other jails, too, but I may not be stayin' at Downstate that long. They just admit us then they'll move us to another state facility, which will most likely be where I'm gonna stay for the duration of my time."

Brandi wiped her face. "My friend told me about your incident," said Brandi. She was careful not to mention Sean's name over the phone. "And he called you Shaki."

Shamari chuckled. "Yeah, I told him to call me that. I didn't want to admit it but he is a good dude. He's good for you, Ma."

"You think so, baby?"

"No doubt. Heard he was in the hospital, at least that's the rumor. What happened?"

"Somebody came in his house and knocked him upside the head while he was in the shower."

"Whaaat?" Shamari replied. "How did they get in?"

"They think somebody had a key. They're doing an investigation now."

"Dag, that's effed up! Man. Tell him that I hope he gets better soon."

"I will, baby, I will. You just take care of yourself. We are gonna be fine out here, and as soon as you can get to a phone, you call me, okay?"

"No doubt, Ma. I will most definitely do that. Oh, yeah, Ma, how's the baby?"

Brandi beamed. "Oh my goodness, Shaki! He is so adorable! He looks just like you when you were a baby! He's getting so thick and he's a good baby. I'm going to get him this weekend."

"So when I get myself settled in, could you please bring him to see me, Ma. I haven't seen my son since he came into this world."

"Of course. I don't really like that idea, but we don't have a choice. Hopefully, this would be the first and the last time. It's not good to bring a baby up there around all those germs."

"I know, Ma, but I wanna see him. I need to bond with him, because when I get home, I wanna raise him. I'm gonna work on tryin' to get me an apartment and a job." Shamari paused. "I wish that Amber was here, Ma."

"I know you do, Shaki. In her honor, you do the right thing by your son and yourself. You deserve more than being locked up in somebody's jail."

Shamari sighed when the recording came on the phone.

"Well, Ma, my six minutes is almost up. I love you and tell the baby I love him, too. Oh, and tell your peeps I said thanks for everything."

Brandi tried desperately to hold back her tears. "I love you too, baby. Love you so much.

And I'll tell him." The phone clicked off and Brandi pulled off the road and cried. She picked up her phone and called her secretary.

"Hey," Brandi said, when her secretary picked up the phone. "I can't make it in today. I'm coming down with the flu."

Brandi turned her car around and headed home. She needed to regroup.

Chapter 40

Yadi sat in Captain Phillips's office with a disgruntled look on her face and her arms folded across her chest. She listened intensely, as Captain Phillips practically chewed her head off.

"Cruz, I am not happy with your performance in visits. Ever since I've been the area supervisor here, there has been nothin' but chaos and I'm not feelin' it! You need to shape up or I am goin' to request that you are removed from your post," Captain Phillips warned.

"What do you mean, removed from my post? I think I hold my post down better than anybody does in visits! I come to work damn near every day and do exactly what's in the scope of my duties. I read my directives and my rules and regu—"

Captain Phillips cut her off. "Look, Cruz, save it! You think I'm stupid, don't you? I'm not talkin' about your work ethic; you do your job but you can't get along with anyone! I don't know what's goin' on in your personal life but whatever it is you're bringin' it here! I've been where you're at right now, and if you don't get some help, you're goin' to end up goin' crazy." Captain Phillips thought about the time she wanted to kill herself. "You really need some help. I'm about to call C.A.R.E. for you." Captain Phillips picked up the phone on her desk.

Yadi sucked her teeth and stood up. "You about to call who? Look, Captain Phillips, I don't need no fuckin' help! I'm fine!" she yelled. "I just got shit goin' on at home and I'm tired of everybody actin' like I'm the fuckin' bad guy! What about everybody else and their problems?"

Captain Phillips stood up and walked from behind her desk. She didn't take Yadi's reaction personally.

"Cruz, I can look at you and tell that you are about to explode! You need to talk to someone about what's goin' on with you. Don't take offense but I feel like somethin' just isn't right with you."

Yadi opened the door. "Are you finished analyzin' me, Cap? If so, can I go back to my fuckin' post? I don't have no time to be interrogated by no fuckin' reformed ho!" she shouted, looking at Captain Phillips up and down. Yadi walked out the office, slamming the door behind her.

Captain Phillips sighed and plopped down in her chair. She could have written Yadi up for being insubordinate but what for? She knew that Yadi had enough to deal with, starting with herself.

On the way back to her post, Yadi did not have any regrets about the nasty things she said to Captain Phillips. "The bitch should mind her business", Yadi mumbled under her breath. Captain Phillips had a shady history with the Department of Corrections. She was a woman rumored to have fucked inmates, so who was she to tell Yadi some shit about needing help? She chuckled aloud and walked back onto her post with a strange smile on her face.

Due to the chain of events, it was going to be a long, drawn-out day. Visitors were filing in for the evening visits from one p.m. to nine p.m. Yadi conducted her business as usual and tried to avoid Captain Phillips's evil eye. She also distanced herself from Vanita. They walked around the post without as much as one word.

It was a hostile environment due to Yadi's mental instability but she was unconcerned about the growing chatter around her. She was more preoccupied with Sean and his well-being than she was her coworkers who had pooled together to get her removed from her post and possibly the facility.

Yadi left her post later that day to go to meal, and the officers in the corridors gave her looks of disapproval. She began laughing aloud; pretty sure that everyone had lost his or her mind except for her. *They are just hatin',* she thought, not realizing that she had been talking to herself and answering back, too. The tangled web of insanity was about to unravel.

Captain Phillips walked on the post with Vanita. "Garrett, are you okay?" she asked.

Vanita plopped down in a chair. "Yeah, I'm good, Cap. Just kinda exhausted, that's all," she replied.

Captain Phillips leaned on the desk. "I spoke with Cruz like you asked me to. She cussed me out, too."

Vanita shook her head. "Damn. Well, you tried and so did I. She's losin' it, though, slowly but surely."

"I went to see Sean the other day. He seems to be doin' a lot better."

Vanita sighed. "He should be comin' home tomorrow. I'm hopin' they find the people that done this. Even though I personally think that bitch Yadira Cruz had somethin' to do with it."

***

The next day, when Sean arrived home from the hospital, his older brother, Twan, volunteered to stay with him until he felt comfortable enough to stay home alone. Sean insisted that he would be fine. By no means was Sean a punk and he would make sure that next time he would be ready for any motherfucker who tried to violate his home. Sean put his loaded Ruger in the nightstand drawer next to his bed.

Before Sean walked in his house, all the locks had been changed. His family had his burglar alarm system installed, as well. Sean even changed his cell and house numbers immediately. Not wanting to take any chances, he parked his truck on Long Island at his sister's house and opted to drive her Toyota Camry instead. He had to remain low key, at least until everything died down.

As far as Yadira Cruz was concerned, Sean was going to stay on point with her. She had pushed his buttons for far too long and it was time that he fought back. Brandi was the woman he chose to be with and no one was going to stop him from being with her. Nobody.

After looking in the mirror to check out his healing wound and the fresh Caesar haircut that his brother gave him earlier that day, Sean got into his bed after taking the painkillers, which were prescribed for him by the doctor. While he waited for the medication to take effect, he heard his doorbell ring twice.

"I can't fuckin' believe this shit!" Sean shouted to no one in particular. He walked downstairs, but this time with a loaded Ruger in his hand. He looked through the peephole in the downstairs door and saw that it was Brandi. He smiled and swung the door open. The smile was quickly erased from his handsome face when he saw what was going on.

Chapter 41

Meanwhile, across town, Brandi was worried that she still had not heard from Shamari. *He should be in Downstate by now,* she thought as she walked to her apartment building from her car. It would take a while for him to be processed before he would be settled in to make a phone call to her. Because of this, Brandi was not able to function at work, knowing that her only child was in some "man's" prison. Once she talked to him, she would feel much better.

Instead of wallowing in her misery, it was six-thirty in the evening when Brandi decided to get out of her bed to go to Pathmark for some Häagen-Dazs ice cream. She could not wait to get into bed and dig into some butter pecan, her favorite flavor, and watch a few DVDs she had rented from Blockbuster.

She was going to make her days off from work seem like a mini-vacation, considering all the bullshit that was going on around her. She would do all of this and call Sean, who was home from the hospital by now. Brandi wanted to see him but she understood that he needed a few days to himself first.

Coming from Pathmark, Brandi parked her car on the street. She walked toward her building, with her ice cream in her hand. She couldn't wait to get upstairs to call Sean.

Brandi almost made it to her building when suddenly someone pulled her hair from the back and put a gun to her head. She felt the cold steel against her skin and her body froze instantly. Brandi grimaced as she felt hot pee roll down the leg of her dark denims and dropped her ice cream to the ground. *What is going on?* she thought.

"Yeah, bitch, you thought I wasn't comin' for you, huh?" the female voice asked. "You thought I forgot all about your ass, huh?"

Brandi held her hands in the air. "What do you want from me?" she asked.

"I want you to stay away from us. Ever since you came into our life, it's been nothin' but a mess! Turn around and look at me!"

Brandi turned around slowly and faced Yadi. It looked as if the woman had been crying all night, with her reddened eyes and swollen face. She had a crazed look in her eyes.

"What are you doing, Yadi?" Brandi began.

Yadira recklessly waved the gun at Brandi. "Shut the fuck up! Don't ask me shit 'cause you know what it is! You're a grimy bitch that stole my fuckin' man from under my nose! Now you got him disrespectin' me and not wantin' to be with me anymore! You're the one that's a fuckin' disgrace!"

Brandi turned around hoping to see someone walk or drive by but she had no such luck. Starrett City was usually busy around that time of day but for some strange reason, no one was in the area when she needed them the most.

"Yadi, can we please talk about this?" Brandi asked.

"Shut up, bitch!" Yadi yelled. "Let's go to your fuckin' car and go pay Sean a visit. I want you to tell Sean to his face that you're not gonna see him anymore!"

Brandi painstakingly walked to her car and pressed the keyless entry to open the door for Yadi. She could have tried to run away but in the state of mind that Yadi was in, she did not want to take that chance. After all, she was a mother and a grandmother. Brandi was just thankful that she didn't have her grandson when Yadi rolled up on her.

Brandi got into the driver's side and started the car up. Yadi poked the gun in her ribs.

"Drive this car to Sean's house, you stinkin' bitch! You know where he lives, right? You been fucked there enough times, haven't you?" Yadi exclaimed.

Brandi reluctantly pulled off and made her way to Sean's house. The ride to the Bedford-Stuyvesant neighborhood was nerve-wracking. She looked straight ahead, not daring to look at the foul-faced woman sitting in the passenger seat of her expensive car. Brandi took a quick glance at the clock in her car and it was 7:15 p.m. when they arrived in front of Sean's house. Yadi had not uttered one word the entire trip, and by the time they pulled up on Sean's block, Yadi had completely lost it.

"I'm sick of you subpar chicks thinkin' y'all could fuck with a beautiful woman like me!" she stated, as they got out of the double-parked car. "What makes you think that you could compete with me, huh, Brandi?"

Brandi glared at Yadira. She was losing her patience. She just shook her head, amazed at how crazy Yadi sounded.

They walked down the steps to the door that led to Sean's family room. Yadi shoved the gun into Brandi's back. A tear slowly crept down

Brandi's cheek. Brandi rang the bell and Yadi moved to the side so that Sean couldn't see her when he opened the door. Meanwhile, Yadi was lingering in the dark corner with the gun aimed directly at Brandi's head.

Sean opened the door with his Ruger in his right hand and saw that it was Brandi. As he went to hug her, the smile on his face disappeared. He saw Yadi appear from the side of his house with a gun in her hand and was more than surprised.

"What the fuck?" Sean said, with a shocked look on his face.

Yadi laughed and pushed Brandi inside, making her fall at Sean's feet. She pointed the gun at the both of them. Sean gripped the Ruger and hid it behind his back. He didn't expect Yadi to show up on his doorstep.

"I should fuckin' kill the both of y'all motherfuckers!" Yadi screamed, with spit spraying from her mouth. "I can't stand the sight of y'all, standin' here in my face, lyin' to me! Makin' me look like a damn fool!" Yadi rambled on.

Yadi held the gun in her hand so tight, her knuckles were turning white. She slowly placed her finger on the trigger and pointed the silver gun at the both of them.

"Yo!" Yadi screamed, swinging the guns in their faces. "Sit down, you pathetic motherfuckers! Can't stand the sight of y'all right now!"

She made them sit on the couch. Brandi sat next to Sean, shivering from fright. Sean just sat in one place, watching Yadi and careful not to make any sudden movements. He just sat in one place, carefully sliding his gun between the couch pillows.

"See what you're makin' me do, Sean?" Yadi shouted, pointing the gun at him, then at Brandi. Brandi closed her eyes, tightly.

"See what happens when you choose a bitch over me? I'm a good fuckin' woman and you wanna trade me for some punk bitch with a jailbird son!"

Brandi wanted to jump up and beat Yadi senseless but maintained her composure. She had to remain calm or end up a statistic.

"My son don't have anything to do with you and me!" Brandi said, unable to compose herself at the mention of Shamari's name.

Sean interrupted before everything went awry. "Yadira, you don't have no beef with her. It's me. I'm the one that you claimed rejected you. Leave Brandi out of this!"

"Fuck her! Fuck Brandi! Thinkin' she's all that with her nice clothes, thinkin' she better than somebody! You ain't nobody, bitch, 'cause I'm the law!" Yadi screamed and pointed the gun in Brandi's face. "I'm a correction officer! You couldn't do my job in a hundred years!"

Sean cut her off. "Please, Yadi! Nobody gives a fuck about you bein' a correction officer, okay? If you kill us, you are goin' to jail! Do you understand that? To jail! Why would you wanna subject your daughter to that?"

Yadi began nervously pacing around the room. "Sean, my daughter has her father and grandparents to take care of her. She's better off without me. I fucked up 'cause you don't love me, Devin doesn't love me, my family thinks I went bonkers . . . I just don't give a fuck anymore!"

Sean frowned. It sounded as if Yadi might hurt herself, as well. He couldn't allow that to be on his conscience. "Yadi, put the gun down, please. We don't need any more drama. Maybe we could work somethin' out—" he pleaded.

"Sean, baby, you don't seem to understand. I just love you so much. I need you to hold on to." Yadi began crying. "I don't have anyone except my baby and she is too young to understand me. I wanna be with you, Sean! I can make you so happy! Pleeeease!" she cried out, holding the gun in shaky hands. She was sweating profusely.

Sean shook his head. He didn't want to say anything that would set her off so he had to think of something else that would make her put the gun down. Maybe he could try to get Brandi out of the house so that she could call the police.

Sean tried to soothe the tensed Yadi. "Look, Yadi, you need to calm down! You gonna get into a whole lotta trouble if you hurt us! Just put the gun down, please!"

Yadi wailed and let off a warning shot in the air. Sean watched as dust fell from a gaping hole in the ceiling. He shook his head in annoyance and fear for his life.

"Why are you doin' this to us? Brandi don't even know you!" Sean asked.

"Oh, so you takin' up for her now? I thought I was your girl, Sean!" Yadi asked, waving the gun in their faces.

She then raised the gun and pointed it toward Brandi's direction. Sean just sat in one place, carefully sliding his gun between the couch pillows.

Yadi pulled her victim by the hair, dragging Brandi onto the floor. Once she was on the floor, Yadi gave Brandi a swift kick to the ribs. "Now get the fuck out so that I can be alone with my man!"

Brandi slowly got up from the floor and tried to stand up. Her ribs felt as if they were about to crack in half from the impact. Brandi thought back to a time when a female wouldn't dare step to her, let alone put their hands on her. Holding her rib cage, she realized how much she had evolved as a woman. Yadi would have definitely been six feet under if a younger, more volatile Brandi had anything to do with it.

Yadi grabbed Brandi by her shirt and led her to the door. "Get the hell out of here, you fuckin' ho! I better not see your ass around here no more or else I will murder you, bitch!" Then Yadi pushed Brandi out the door and locked it.

Sean frowned and realized that Yadi was not letting that gun go, no matter how crazy she sounded. All he could think about was Brandi getting the cops over there before Yadi killed him.

Outside, Brandi got up from the stained concrete, brushing the dirt off her bloody, scraped knees. She searched her pockets for car keys and limped to her car. Rubbing her bruised ribs, she broke down and began crying. Brandi wondered how she had even got involved with all of the craziness between Sean and Yadi.

On the outside looking in, she was able to relate to Yadi's conflict and pain. At one time, Brandi was madly in love with a man who was not in love with her. Those feelings of rejection drove Brandi to conspire murder. Ironically, almost fourteen years later, Brandi found herself face to face with Yadi; a woman who felt the same way she did when she found out Maleek was leaving her for another woman. Those feelings of rejection forced Brandi to do something that she never thought that she would do, and that was conspiring to kill Maleek.

At that moment, Brandi regained her senses and thought about Sean. If Yadi felt anything like she did back then, Sean was as good as gone. She had to hurry up and get help for him.

Brandi limped to her car. She looked through her bag to retrieve her cell phone. As she attempted to dial 9-1-1, her phone beeped and she realized that her cell phone battery was dying.

"Shit, shit, shit!" Brandi said. Sean was in trouble and there was no time to waste. Brandi didn't want to knock on the door of any of Sean's neighbors and she didn't have time to look for a working pay phone. This meant she would have to drive to the nearest precinct to get help, which was approximately two blocks from Sean's house. Brandi just hoped that it wouldn't be too late for him, because truthfully, Yadi sounded like she was on a murder-suicide mission.

In the meantime, at Sean's house, Yadira had him sit on the couch in the family room, while she walked back and forth with the gun in her hand. She threw her thick mane back and forth across her shoulders as she listened to Sean. He talked about how much he really cared about her, even though at that moment he could have killed her himself.

"Yadi, put the gun, down, baby girl, please," he said sweetly. Sean gave Yadi a million-dollar smile. "We're good. Brandi is gone." Yadi walked back to Sean, who was still sitting on the couch. She tried to kiss him and he pulled away.

Yadi laughed aloud and Sean frowned. "Oh, Sean, you are so stupid! You think I'm gonna let you get away with playin' me? You knew how much I loved you. You knew this but you proceeded to fuck with Brandi, a visitor bitch comin' to Riker's Island to see her jailbird son! You have officially reached an all-time low. We're correction officers. Those visitors are beneath us!"

Yadi continued with her ranting and raving. "Sean, we can be together. I can live here with you and eventually become your wife. Don't you want me to have your baby, Sean? We can make beautiful babies together!"

Sean was growing angrier by the minute. Fortunately, for him, the love-crazed maniac hadn't realized that he had his own gun hiding behind his back the whole time. He would have hated to have to blow Yadi's head off her shoulders in self-defense. All he could think about was her daughter.

"What the hell are you talkin' about, Yadi? How could you think some shit like that? What's the next step, huh? You got a gun in your hand, kidnapped Brandi, I mean, why are you even puttin' yourself and us through this shit?"

"Because," she shouted, waving the gun above her head and crying again. "Because I'm tired of y'all triflin'-ass men puttin' me through shit! I just wanna be happy, you know, is that a crime? I wanna be able to love somebody and they love me back, unconditionally!"

Sean smirked. "You got the nerve to talk about lovin' somebody? What about you loving yourself first? You up here with a gun in my fuckin' face, tryin' to force me to be with you and that's supposed make me love you?" Sean paused. "At one time you had me, Yadi. You had me thinkin' you were the complete package. Instead, a few days with you and you turned into a whinin' basket case, always wantin' a nigga's undivided attention all the time like you can't function unless you got some dick in your life. You're on some real selfish shit! That ain't no love!"

Yadi frowned and pointed the gun at Sean. Sean stood up and pointed his Ruger at her too.

"Play yourself if you want to. I will smoke your ass right in this house, woman or not," Sean warned her.

Yadi held the gun in her hand, staring at Sean. A few more seconds, her hands began shaking. She finally broke down and Sean was able to take the gun out of her hands. She fell to the floor on her knees with her face in her hands. He gripped his Ruger in his right hand, afraid that it might slip from his sweaty grip. Who knew what Yadi had up her sleeve? Sean let her sit on the floor and cry as he absent-mindedly placed her gun behind the bar.

Yadi held her head up and looked Sean in the face. He was scowling at her and shaking his head.

"Sean, I am so sorry! I know I fucked up! It's just that I love you so much! You have always been good to me and I took our friendship for granted! I just thought that after I broke up with Devin, there was a possibility we could be together." As Yadi shook her head, her wild hair framed her face. "I just needed to be with somebody," she whispered, while breaking down in tears.

"Why stress bein' with a man, Yadi?" he replied. "You have a family, a daughter that worships the ground you walk on. You don't need a man to make you feel complete. You can get as many men as you want. Sometimes you just gotta accept certain things as they are and move on with your life. Forcing me to be with you is not going to work!"

Yadi buried her head in hands again. Sean plopped onto the nearby bar stool and took a deep breath. *She's a pathetic bitch,* he thought as she sat there and sobbed loudly. Sean didn't feel sorry for Yadi this time. He had been there for Yadi when she needed him the most and this was how she repaid him.

Suddenly, the bell upstairs rang. Sean glanced at Yadi, who was in a fetal position in front of his fireplace. He hesitated to leave her there alone but he couldn't but help but wonder if it was Brandi with the cops. Sean ran up the stairs to see who was behind the voices on the main level of his brownstone, leaving Yadi sitting on the floor and looking into space.

When he arrived upstairs, two police officers walked in, with Brandi behind them. She'd already filled them in on the story, so they came ready to remove Yadi from Sean's residence, in handcuffs. One of the officers looked down and saw the Ruger in Sean's hand.

"No, officer, I'm a CO and this is my off-duty weapon!" Sean put the gun on the banister. "I got my badge upstairs. The suspect is downstairs," Sean said, holding on to his pounding head.

However, before anyone could reach the steps, they heard a single gunshot coming from downstairs. When they got down there, they discovered

Yadi in a bloody heap on the floor. One of the police officers kneeled down to check her pulse. That was when he saw the gunshot wound by the right side of Yadi's temple and the warm gun in her hand.

Her hair was matted with blood and brain matter was scattered all over Sean's hardwood floors and the wall nearest to her body. On the side that the bullet entered, it looked as if her head had deflated. Brandi screamed loudly and covered her eyes, as the officers walked over to Yadi's limp body with their guns drawn. The partner looked at the second officer, who still had his gun drawn. He motioned for him to put the gun down.

"She's dead," the officer said. Sean stood there in shock, while Brandi put her hand to her mouth. Sean looked behind the bar and noticed that Yadi's gun was missing. Guilt ran through his veins and he felt personally responsible for her death. *Why didn't I hold on to the gun?* , he thought.

"Oh my God! Yadi, why? Why here? Why this?" Sean uttered, as tears fell from his eyes.

As Brandi wailed loudly in the background, she realized that she and Yadi had much more in common with other than Sean Daniels . . . .

Chapter 42

The next morning, Vanita called Captain Phillips several times to find out the whereabouts of Yadi Cruz. She hadn't come to work and she didn't call in sick. Captain Phillips sat in her office and tried to figure out what was going on in the visits. First, Sean Daniels went missing a few weeks ago and now Yadira Cruz. Vanita, who didn't have any idea what was going on, just went along with her normal routine until the phone rang in the visit area. It was Sean on the other line.

"Hey, Sean! How does it feel to be home?" Vanita asked, while conducting her obligatory duties at the same time.

Sean cut her off. "Yo, Nita, I got some real bad news," he whispered.

Vanita sat in a chair and held the receiver tightly. Her heart dropped. Her gut feeling told her that it was about Yadi.

"What, Sean? What is it?"

"Yadi is dead. She killed herself in my house last night." There was silence on both ends of the phone.

"She did what, she did who? I, I don't understand, Sean."

"Yadi killed herself in my house. I, I can't get into the details over the phone." Sean was choking up. "Look, Nita. Just come by my house after work." The phone went dead.

"Captain Phillips!" Vanita screamed out, running out the control room to her supervisor's office.

Devin was asleep on his old bed in his mother's house. His feet were hanging off his old full-sized bed but it felt good nonetheless. At least he had a place to stay after Yadi got him kicked out of her co-op apartment. Suddenly, his mother burst into the bedroom, scaring him so badly he almost had a heart attack.

"Oh my God, Devin! Wake up, baby, wake up!" she screamed. Devin hopped up and looked at his mother.

"What happened, Ma? What's wrong?" he asked, his heart beating a mile a minute. He watched his mother break down in tears.

"I . . . I was just on the phone with Yadi's mother and, and—" she stammered.

Devin was growing impatient. "Is it Jada? What is it, Ma?"

"Yadira killed herself last night. She shot herself in the head."

Devin fell off his bed onto his knees. "Noooo!" he yelled.

Meanwhile, in an upstate prison, Shamari hadn't been able to call his mother because they had moved him from Downstate, a maximum security prison to Greene Correctional Facility, a medium security, located in Coxsackie, New York. He sat around trying to keep himself busy until he was able to call his mother; he knew that she was probably worried sick about him.

Shamari seemed to be handling the situation pretty well, although he longed to be home. Unlike some of his cellmates, he knew that freedom was nine months away. Shamari was careful to keep his time a secret from the other inmates, afraid that someone would be jealous and try to pull him into negativity. He knew that he had someone who relied on him being there and that was his son, who had not asked to come into this world.

Shamari picked up the Sunday newspaper and began reading the articles. Naturally, his favorite ones were the crime articles, reminding him of things that he didn't want to do to ever end up in jail again. As Shamari read on he came to page five of the *Daily News* and a small article caught his attention. Reading it, he frowned and looked around at the other inmates, who were lazily scattered throughout the housing area. He leaned back in the chair and shook his head.

"Miss Cruz is dead? Killed herself in fellow officer's home?" Shamari blinked at the name. "Correction Officer Sean Daniels?" Shamari hopped up and to try to see if he can use the phone.

As the days went on, it was uproar in Yadira's facility, due to her suicide. Although it wasn't far-fetched because of her behavior, no one saw that day coming. Yadira had all the signs of a person with a mental condition, but not suicidal. This was a result of her refusal to acknowledge her problem and get help, combined with her love addiction and the stress of trying to have some normalcy in her life. This led Yadi came to her breaking point. Unfortunately, it was a tragic end for her and for everyone involved.

Chapter 43

As Sean patched up the hole that Yadi had shot in his ceiling, he thought about all the things that he had been through with her. *Damn,* he thought as he climbed down the ladder, a touch of white paste on his face.

He felt sad about her death, but he got pissed thinking about her selfishness. Her funeral was in another day or so and he didn't want to go. Out of respect, he was going to force himself to put on his dress uniform, the uniform law enforcement personnel usually wore for the funerals of their fellow officers. He was a certified wreck, but unfortunately, his troubles were not over. He would now have to answer to the Department of Corrections, and of course, Yadi's concerned parents. They deserved to know the truth.

Sean went to his ringing house phone and answered it. He was in no mood to be bothered with anyone and he expressed that when he picked up his phone abruptly.

"Hello?" he shouted into the phone.

"Mr. Daniels?" the female voice stated on the phone.

Sean frowned. "Who's this?" he asked, suspiciously.

"This is Yadira's mother. How are you holdin' up, sweetie?

Sean wondered how she got his phone number. Now he felt trapped. He didn't know what to say to Yadi's mother and he felt his face flush from embarrassment. What do you say to a mother whose child committed suicide in your presence? Was she going to blame him for what happened?

"Oh, um, hello, Mrs. Cruz. I apologize for the way I answered the telephone. It's just that I had been gettin' so many phone calls the past couple of days."

There was an uncomfortable silence. "I understand, young man, I do." Mrs. Cruz sighed. "I wanted to speak with you because I can only imagine what you are goin' through with everything that's transpired over the last couple of days. And I wanted to let you know that I don't blame you for the death of my daughter.

"I know you were wonderin' how I got your number. I spoke to her friend, Vanita, and she gave me your information. I hope you don't mind."

"No, I don't mind. I knew that I would have to speak to you eventually and I knew that you would probably want answers. I just thought that this was another sympathy call. I don't deserve the sympathy, Yadira and your family does."

Mrs. Cruz sighed. "Well, Sean, it's always hard for mothers to lose a child. I would think that my daughter would be buryin' me, if anything. Yadira was a lovely woman with a good heart and good intentions, but unfortunately she spent the majority of her life searchin' for somethin', somethin' that she had more than her share of, and that was love. Besides, this was not her first suicide attempt. She attempted suicide a few times before, but we were always able to talk her out of it. When Yadira was sixteen, I had her committed for a few months, you know, tryin' to make sure she had the proper treatment. She was on medication for a while and then she just stopped takin' it."

"I didn't know that. But what I don't understand is how did she become a correction officer? You have to pass a psychogical exam before you can become a CO."

"An old friend of the family is a psychologist for the NYPD. He helped push her paperwork through. I didn't want her to take the job because

I felt that it was too stressful of an environment for her to work in, considerin' her mental state. Of course, Yadira always butted heads with me about everything and she took the job anyway." Mrs. Cruz sighed. "Sean, Yadi sent me a letter. I just received it today."

"What does the letter say, Mrs. Cruz?" Sean asked, wanting to hang up the phone. He didn't want to be rude to Yadi's mother but he also did not want to relive what occurred that night.

Sean listened as Mrs. Cruz quietly shuffled through paper. "Sean, I can't read everything on this paper but I will say that my daughter loved you. She thanked you for takin' her and Jada into your home. Also, she wrote something very disturbin'. I want to tell you because it is only fair that you have some type of closure." Mrs. Cruz sighed. "She said here that she paid someone to assault you in your home."

There was complete silence on the phone, as they both took in the contents of the letter. Sean was mortified when Yadi's mother confirmed his worst fear. He always felt that Yadi had something to do with his incident.

"Sean, I am so sorry. We didn't raise Yadi like this, and me and her father gave her the best of everything," Mrs. Cruz paused. "Look, Sean, I just want you to stay home and get well," instructed Mrs. Cruz, interrupting the silence. "I didn't raise her like this and I can't tell you how I feel right now. I can only imagine how you feel about all of this."

Sean sighed. "Mrs. Cruz, why did Yadira do this? I never did anything to her but treat her with the utmost respect, and now I'm findin'out that she had set me up?"

Sean shook his head, thinking about all the things he went through with Yadi over the course of a few months.

"I know, sweetheart, I know but you know what? It's all over now. We have to move on. Yadira forced our hand. Don't let this confession make you bitter."

"You're right. I don't wanna be bitter and I'm pretty sure you don't wanna be, neither. But how can someone that claims to love all of us be so selfish? How did Yadi just pick up a gun and end her life without even thinkin' about how it would affect her loved ones, especially her daughter?"

Mrs. Cruz smiled. "That's true. I can't argue with you not one bit. I just wanted you to know that it wasn't your fault. You can move on with a clear conscience. Oh, I also wanted to thank you for takin' Yadi and my granddaughter in. I appreciate that."

"It was no problem, Mrs. Cruz. You take care and my deepest sympathy to you and Mr. Cruz."

"Good-bye, sweetheart."

"Good-bye, Mrs. Cruz."

Sean hung the phone up and leaned against the wall for support. It was terrible the way that everything ended between him and Yadira. Never in a million years would he have thought she would have killed herself, let alone in his home. He knew then that it was time for him to settle down; no more playing the field. Sean never wanted to experience anything remotely close to what transpired between him and Yadira Cruz.

As Sean attempted to get his house back in order, his bell rang. He looked out the door and saw a man standing outside. He went to grab his Ruger and walked toward the door.

"Who is it?" Sean screamed from behind the secured glass door.

"What's up, Daniels? It's me, Devin. Jada's father," the stranger responded.

Sean frowned and opened the door. Devin stood on his stairs and held his hand out for a handshake. Sean relented but didn't invite Devin inside. He wasn't sure why Yadi's daughter's father was there in the first place.

"I'm sorry to bother you, man. I just needed to talk to you. Is it okay if I come in?"

Sean sighed and reluctantly let Devin inside. They both stood in the foyer area, looking at each other for a brief moment.

"I know you heard a lot of negative shit about me, man, and I just wanna clear the air. My daughter, Jada, always talks about you, and if she likes you, then I know you must be a pretty cool dude."

Sean smiled when he thought about Jada. She was definitely a beautiful little girl. Now her mother was gone forever.

"Yeah, Jada is my little buddy," Sean said, with a smile on his face.

Devin paused. "Well, I'm sorry about what happened here, man. I knew that it wouldn't be long before Yadi broke down."

"Damn," Sean said.

"We all knew, but she refused to take her meds," said Devin, with a spaced-out look on his face. He sighed. "Look, Daniels, I'm here to tell you that I loved Yadira for many years and I guess she loved me, but she used to drive me crazy with all the accusations and the constant abuse. Just put it like this; our relationship was one big roller coaster! She caused property damage to my cars, emptied my bank accounts, made allegations against me, got me arrested, and the list goes on. I stayed with her crazy-ass on the strength of my daughter."

Devin continued to vent. "When Jada was born, it only got worst. I have other children, too, but I refused to allow my other children to witness her outbursts. All that shit just made me resent her ass even more, but I was stuck because of the child support; I'm already paying for my two other kids. I couldn't afford to leave."

Sean looked at Devin in amazement, and while he talked, everything finally made sense. He thought about all the times Yadi came to work and complained to him and Vanita about Devin. How he didn't want to touch her, how he was so cold toward her. If she behaved anything like the way that Devin described, Sean understood why Devin didn't want to be bothered.

"All this time I thought it was you, man. That is, until she start fuckin' with me! Beautiful woman but very insecure—" Sean began.

"Nah, Daniels. Yadira wasn't well. That woman brought out the worst in me, somethin' that I hope will never resurface again. Like I said, I stayed because I was fearful for my daughter."

Sean shook Devin's hand. "Well, thank you for comin' through, man. I needed to hear that from your mouth. I didn't wanna keep blamin' myself for what happened here."

Devin took a deep breath. "I just feel sorry for my daughter and Yadi's parents. I have to admit, she went out Yadira style, though." Devin opened the front door and looked back at Sean as he was walking out. "Keep your head up, Daniels."

"You, too, Devin. I'll be seein' you around."

Sean watched as Devin walked down the stairs and pulled off in his truck. It had been a long day. Sean walked up to his bedroom. Once he was comfortable in his bed, he finally trailed off into a deep slumber.

Chapter 44

A few months after Yadi's suicide, Brandi was finally able to gather up enough strength to see Shamari. The drive up to Greene Correctional Facilty, located in Coxackie, New York was scenic but unnerving. Brandi glanced in the rearview mirror at her grandson, who was asleep in his infant car seat as she made her way up the winding road to the prison. She looked at the drab concrete walls and the barbed-wired fence surrounding the prison that had to be at least seven stories high.

Brandi took a deep breath and parked her car in the visitor's parking lot. Prison visits were customary for her, considering her brothers were incarcerated a few times. She would have never thought that her own son would be locked behind those walls too, but unfortunately, it was a bleak reality.

After a tedious search process, Brandi sat at the table, waiting for Shamari to walk out on the visit floor. The baby was asleep in her lap when she spotted Shamari walking toward them from the back of the prison.

Not having seen her son in three months, Brandi began to cry, while inspecting him from head to toe. The cut he received while doing time on Rikers Island had healed and didn't look as bad as it did when she first saw it.

"Oh my God, Shamari!" she announced. "You look so good! You look nice and healthy."

Shamari hugged and kissed her on the cheek before sitting down. He held his arms out and Brandi happily passed him his son.

"Thank you, Ma. So do you." Shamari stared at his son. "Ma, he's so beautiful! Look at my boy, Ma!" Shamari beamed, rubbing his baby's head.

Brandi smiled. "That's your son, baby! He's a good little baby, too."

Shamari kissed his mother again. "I miss you, Ma. You look like you lost a little weight over there."

Brandi held her head down. "It's been crazy these past months, Shaki. Not talking to you, Sean and our problems."

"Miss Cruz's suicide."

Brandi looked at her son. "How did you know about that?"

"Ma, c'mon. We read the paper in here and watch the news. I heard about what happened. The papers said something about her kidnapping somebody but no name was mentioned. They said it was three people involved. Were you there that day?"

"Yeah. She made me drive her to Sean's house with a gun pointed to my head."

Shamari looked up from staring at his sleeping son. "I spoke to you a day or two after that happened. Why you never told me that?"

Brandi held her head down. "I didn't want you to worry, Shaki. You have enough things to worry about."

Shamari shook his head. "She put a gun to your head? Man, you lucky I wasn't home at the time. I woulda killed the bitch myself! Ma, you should have told me that."

Brandi shushed Shamari and looked around nervously. "Be respectful!" she sighed. "Well, it's all over now and we could move on with our lives. I'm glad it's over."

"Are you and Sean still cool? Or are you gonna fall back from him for good now?" he asked.

"I don't know, Shamari, I don't know," Brandi replied.

The baby began to move around and was about to wake up. Brandi gave him one of the three bottles she was authorized to have on the visit. Shamari put the bottle in the baby's mouth and he drifted back to sleep.

As Shamari fed him, he continued to rub the baby's head and kiss his chubby fingers.

"He smells like baby lotion," Shamari said. "Ma, you know what I miss?"

Brandi looked at her son and grandson. It was a beautiful sight; with the exception of Shamari in his state greens and the state correction officers operating the visit floor.

"What do you miss, baby?" she asked.

"I miss my pops, Ma. I miss havin' him around. Even though I was young when he died, I can remember some of the times that we spent together. Damn!" Shamari's eyes suddenly began to water. "Why he had to die, Ma?"

Brandi held her head down. She felt guilty about Maleek's death, now that she actually saw what her son was going through emotionally without him. However, thinking back to Maleek's attitude toward her and Shamari at the end, she selfishly figured that he was better off dead. Her son probably would have suffered more knowing that his father was out in the world, but didn't want to have anything to do with him. That would have killed her.

She understood how Yadira felt about wanting Sean; she felt the same way about Maleek, but she wasn't about to take her own life. She loved her son so much that she was willing to conspire to kill someone to prove that, and that was what she did.

Brandi closed her eyes and held Shamari's hand tightly. "Baby, your father is in a better place now. Just make sure that you are here for your son."

He had been holding the information that Dollar told him for a while. He had to tell his mother what he heard. He figured it was now or never.

"Ma, I know what happened between you and my father," he said softly.

Brandi felt her throat tighten up. She closed her eyes as if she had to adjust her eyesight. Everything was a blur and she felt herself hyperventilating. "What do you mean, you know what happened with me and your father? We parted ways."

"I know that you got him done, Ma. I know the full story."

"Who, how would you know this?"

"While I was in the Bing, I ran into one of my father's old homies."

Brandi frowned and her heart began to palpitate. "Who might that be?"

"Dollar. Do you remember, Dollar?"

Brandi looked around the visiting room and swallowed. "Yeah, he was one of Maleek's boys."

"All I have to ask is, why? What made you do what you did?"

A part of Brandi wanted to deny it, but she was tired of the charade that she had put on with Shamari. She was going to be honest with him.

"I . . . I am so sorry, Shamari," Brandi stuttered. "I'm trying to understand why Dollar would speak on me and Maleek's relationship with you, but that's neither here nor there, I guess." She cleared her throat. "Your father hurt me. He left you and me for another life with someone else. I was pissed about it, of course, because I had given everything to this man. My world revolved him, right down to the hustling and a killing that I committed trying to protect him. I know that we all have choices, but I aimed to please Maleek, who was my first everything. But it wasn't until he left when I realized that you were one of the most important people in my life. I wanted to protect you from the hurt. The hurt when you realized that your father left you and was not coming back. I would much rather tell you that your father was dead than to tell you that your father didn't love you enough to stay with us and be a father to you. So I recruited an old connect of mine and convinced him that Maleek needed to go. If he couldn't be with you and me, then he wasn't going to be with anybody. That's how I felt at the time."

Shamari kissed his son. "I don't know what to say and I don't know how to feel about that, Ma. You took something away from me and now I would never know how it would have been. He might have come around later on in my life."

Brandi's shoulders tensed up. "You're right but it wasn't only about you, Shamari. When Maleek died, that fucked-up side of me died with him. I was released from his clutches and I was able to rebuild my life. He had to go. If he had been alive, we wouldn't have made it this far in life. We would have all been dead, the three of us. That was the type of life that we were living at the time."

"You're a strong woman. You did a good job raisin' me alone. A lot of young men and women have been raised just by one parent and they turned out to be okay. Why couldn't it have been like that for me?"

"You're right, baby, you're right," Brandi replied.

Shamari took Brandi's hand. "Ma, I love you. You are the best mother a nig—I mean, a dude could have. I know there was no easy way to tell me what happened to Maleek. One side of me does appreciate you keepin' that a secret for as long as you did. I guess when you livin' that type of life, death is one of the two ways out. And according to Dollar, jail is the other way out."

"But do you know what the end result of all that was, Shaki? Regret. Guilt. Those are some of the things that I had to live with all this time. Do you forgive me?"

Brandi reached over and embraced Shamari. She gently placed soft kisses on her grandson's forehead.

"Yes, Ma, I forgive you." Shamari paused. "When Amber died, I thought I was going crazy. I even asked God why didn't he take me. I'm the one that committed the crimes. I'm the one that was doin' time in jail, and he passed over me and took Amber. Being in that jail cell didn't help much, neither. But now I see that He has a purpose for me. Dollar told me that my father lives in me, and with that, I'm gonna be a better man and father to my son. I'm gonna do some of the things that he probably should have done or maybe he wanted to do before he died."

Little did Brandi and Shamari know there was a method to Dollar's madness.

"Yo, man, you can't keep dissin' your baby mama this way," a young Dollar said, while riding with Maleek in his truck. Maleek had just ignored yet another phone call from Brandi.

"Man, go 'head with that! If you so concerned, why don't you be my son's daddy? I got too much shit goin' on right now to be bothered with Brandi and Shamari! Do you see all the money we gettin' down here?"

Dollar sighed. "Nigga, you just don't get it, do you? Nothin' good is gonna come from you dissin' your kids the way you do! You got other kids in Brooklyn, too—"

Maleek cut him off. "Well, I ain't claimin' them other ones! Them bitches was nothin' but hoes to me. Brandi was my wifey!"

"But now you treatin' her like a ho! I may be a street dude and a hustler, but my kids . . . I don't play that with my kids and I got three myself! They get as much of their daddy as I can give them when I ain't gettin' that paper."

Maleek sighed. His $10,000 Gucci link chain with a diamond encrusted piece glistened in the Virginia sunlight. He pulled off the highway to get out and take a leak. Dollar looked at Maleek and rolled his eyes. Maleek went behind a tree, relieved himself, and walked back toward the truck. When Maleek got back into the driver's seat, Dollar had his gun out. By this time, another vehicle had pulled up behind them. It was the wee hours of the morning and traffic was very light. Perfect time for the perfect murder.

Maleek held his hands up in the air. Dollar snatched the chain off his neck and rifled through his pockets for his wallet. Maleek hadn't noticed that Dollar had on black leather gloves, gloves that they wore when they were about to lay somebody down-forever.

"Oooh, shit, Dollar! This is how you gonna do me?" Maleek asked, with a smug look on his face. "You gonna fuck me over like this?"

"Nigga, you fucked yourself! I don't like your fuckin' attitude!"

Maleek attempted to open the driver's side door but Dollar shot him in the chest before he could open the door all the way. Dollar stepped out of the truck after killing Maleek. The driver of the second car was standing near the driver's side door and stepped back, shooting up the Land Rover with Maleek's dead body in it. After the truck and Maleek's body were riddled with bullets, Dollar and Smokey got into the Q45 and took off down I-64 together. Dollar looked out the passenger side window and cried like a baby. He wished he could have been Shamari's daddy because he was secretly in love with Brandi. Why she had picked Maleek instead of him, he could never figure that out.

"What's up, man? You straight?" Smokey asked him, as they headed back to Norfolk.

"Yeah, I'm good," Dollar replied. He tightened his grip around the warm gun in his hand. Smokey had no idea that he was the next fatality on Dollar's list . . . .

Since Yadi's suicide, almost everything was pretty much back to normal in Sean's life. He had been back a work for almost a week and most of his coworkers were extremely sympathetic toward him. Sean was just happy to be finally forgiving himself, realizing that what happened was not his fault. He continued to thank God every day and promised to make sure that he wouldn't take his life or anyone else for granted. Yes, Yadi had taught him a lot.

However, there was someone missing from his life and he grieved more about that then he did Yadi's death. Brandi had not contacted him since the incident. Sean was devastated about that but the space between them gave him chance to put his life into perspective. Now he finally was able to figure out what he really wanted out of life and love.

One night, after a hard's day's work, Sean's cell phone rang. Asleep in his bed, he leaned over and answered the phone. He had enough of the sympathy calls and he looked at the ringing telephone, hoping that it was not one of those calls.

"Hello?" he answered, groggily.

"Hey, Sean. It's me. Brandi." There was silence on his end of the phone.

"So you just now callin' me, huh? Do you realize what's been goin' on for the past few months?" Sean shouted, sitting up in his bed.

Brandi sighed. "Sean, I know, I don't have any excuse for not calling you. I . . . I just needed time to get myself together."

"Get yourself together? Yadi killed herself in my house! What about me?"

Sean's selfish attitude angered Brandi. She could not believe that he would only think about himself at a time like this.

"Well, since you wanna put it like that, Sean, the reason why I was in that predicament in the first place was because of your ass! I think that you know that because you didn't attempt to call me neither. Remember, I am the one that she forced, by gunpoint, to your house that night. I don't believe that you could only be thinking about yourself!" she shouted back.

Sean paused. He calmed down and realized that she was right. Brandi should be even more traumatized than him because she could have lost her life.

"You know what, Brandi? I apologize. It's not your fault. I just thought you had forgotten about me, that's all."

Brandi calmed down, as well. Her voice sounded shaky, like she was about to cry. "I said, I need a moment to get myself together. What I went through that night was traumatizing. I have a lot going on over here, too, you know. I'm helping to raise my grandchild who has no mother and an incarcerated father. I've been devoting a lot of my time to family these days. And plus, I've been taking little Shamari to his father on a regular basis."

"You are? That's what's up. How is he holdin' up in there?" Sean asked.

"He's okay. He looks good, been working out and getting his mind right. He has matured a lot."

"Well, he's a grown man, Brandi. He's in a place with some grown-ass men. From what he went through on Rikers, Shamari seems like he knows how to handle himself. Trust me, I know."

Brandi smiled. "I'm relieved to know that but I just want him to come home. We need him here."

"He's gonna be okay. It's a learnin' experience." There was a slight pause.

"Did you go to Yadi's funeral?" she asked.

"No, I didn't but I spoke to her mother and her daughter's father. They told me about her mental health and about how she was bipolar or some shit like that. Her daughter's father told me how she refused to take her medication."

"Medication? She was on medication? Wow. She was such a beautiful woman! Who would have ever known?"

"I know, right? That's why they say not to judge a book by its cover."

Brandi chuckled. "Yeah, I know." She sighed. "Sean, you know, I really care about you, right?"

"I care about you, too, Brandi. I know I may be pushin' it right now because we haven't spoken to each other in a minute. Would you like to come over? I really wanted to see you."

Brandi smiled. "I really wanted to see you, too, Sean. I'll be there in fifteen minutes."

When Brandi arrived at Sean's house, it was as if all the bad events that had transpired there flooded her memory again. Sean was looking good, having lost a few pounds from all the stress that he had to endure the last couple of months. She walked in and there was an uncomfortable silence between them. Sean was the first one to speak, after inviting her into the living room. They took a seat on the couch and just stared at each other for a couple of moments without speaking.

"You look good, Sean," Brandi said. "You lost some weight."

Sean looked down at his flat stomach. "Yeah, I been workin' out. I started trainin' again, you know, with the boxin' and um, yeah, you look real good, too."

"Thanks." She cleared her throat. "Sean, I know that a lot is going on in your life right now. You're trying to put the pieces together and I understand that totally. But what I came here to say is—" she began.

Sean cut her off. "I think I know, Brandi. We can't be together."

Her eyes widened with confusion. That was not what she was thinking. "What do you mean, we can't be together?"

Sean sighed. "'Cause it was just too much shit that went on between us. Bein' together will remind us too much of all the Yadi bullshit. Yadi reminds you too much of you."

Brandi looked away with a guilty look on her face. "What made you say that, Sean?"

"Brandi, I knew about your past before you even told me about it. I knew about your hustlin' days, how you killed people and caused havoc in the streets. I even knew about Maleek and how you set him up to be killed when he left you for another woman. You didn't want to let him go so that's why you did it. You didn't want the other woman to have him if you couldn't have him.

Sean continued. "I'm sorry, baby. I care about you, you know I do, but after all this shit that happened with Yadi, I can't take a chance and be with another woman that's like her. Yadi took her own life and she might have wanted to take mine, too. I can't chance that happenin' with you or any other woman. I, I just need some time to myself."

Brandi was stunned. It didn't matter how Sean found out about her history because he was right. She looked down. "Um, Sean, I don't know what to say. I could tell you and prove to you that I'm a changed woman, but at this point, considering everything that happened, you're not trying to hear that and I don't blame you." She stood up. "Well, I guess that I'm gonna be leaving and I hope that one day, you change your mind and look me up. I know it's hard to trust a woman right now but I'm telling you that I really care about you, Sean."

"And that's the shit that scares me the most, baby, is you caring about me too much." Sean stood up and kissed Brandi on the lips. "I care about you, too. That's why I'm lettin' you go. This shit has scarred me, Brandi, and you don't deserve this. Neither of us do."

Brandi hugged Sean and he followed her to the door. She turned around and waved at him, half-hoping that he was only joking and would call her to come back inside, to make love to her and tell her that everything was okay. However, that never happened. Sean watched her walk to her car and when she turned around, he was gone.

Brandi climbed into the driver's seat of her Lexus and cried her heart out. As she pulled off, she cussed the day that Yadira Cruz was born, not realizing that she, too was also guilty of being "crazy in love."

ORDER FORM
URBAN BOOKS, LLC
97 N18th Street
Wyandanch, NY 11798

Name (please print):_____

Address:_____

City/State:_____

Zip:_____

QTY	TITLES	PRICE
	16 On The Block	$14.95
	A Girl From Flint	$14.95
	A Pimp's Life	$14.95
	Baltimore Chronicles	$14.95
	Baltimore Chronicles 2	$14.95
	Betrayal	$14.95
	Black Diamond	$14.95

Shipping and handling-add $3.50 for 1st book, then $1.75 for each additional book.
Please send a check payable to:
Urban Books, LLC
Please allow 4-6 weeks for delivery